When Love Isn't Enough

Stephanie Casher

THE PANTHEON COLLECTIVE (TPC)

www.pantheoncollective.com

This is a work of fiction. Names, characters, organizations, and events portrayed in this novel are either products of the author's imagination or used fictitiously.

For Alysha, Stephanie, Devin, Marcus, Nico,
Jaelah, Isabel, Sophia, Pono, Ola, Benjamin, Vincent, Ava, Wyatt
and my children yet to come...

May you always find the courage to chase your wildest dreams.

Acknowledgements

Well this certainly has been an adventure. ☺ There are so many people who've supported me along this long and windy road, and I'm so excited to finally get the opportunity to thank them in print. In no particular order...

Robert Max... You read my words, saw my destiny, and single handedly placed me on this path. Your love and unwavering faith started me on this whole crazy journey, and for that I will be eternally grateful.

Megan... You've always been my biggest fan, suffering through those early drafts and telling me I was wonderful anyway. Words cannot express how much I love you and cherish our friendship.

Chris, Gail, and Carla... Thank you for seven years in a day job that provided ample room for me to travel, write, and pursue my writing aspirations. Your support on this mission has been truly priceless.

Lisa Rose and Kim Ferrell... Thank you for helping to bring my cover to life! I am so blessed to be surrounded by such talented and creative people.

Omar, my Kindred... We did it! You have been an incredible critique partner, sounding board, and all around cheerleader. I feel so blessed to have you in my corner. Manhattan penthouse timeshare, here we come!

The OG authorpreneurs, Edwardo Jackson and Thomas Brooks. I learned so much from both of you about the hustle and pushing the product. Thanks for the advice, guidance, and kinship.

Deatri King-Bey... What can I say—you're the best. Your feedback was priceless, and I've learned so much from working with you.

To all the authors I read, love, and admire… Your work and words not only entertained me, but inspired my craft, making me a better writer. To the unknowing mentors on my quest—Wayne Jordan, Donna Hill, Lolita Files—thank you for taking the time to reach out with timely guidance and words of encouragement for an up and coming author…

To my advance readers—Ahna-Kristen, Dara, JohnJohn, Jordana, Kelly, Big Eric, Kim, Auntie Herdesene, and Cousin Imani… Thanks for all the helpful feedback and for loving my book!

To Christina, Faby, and Gabe, three of my oldest and dearest. Who knew lifelong friendships could be born on the 2nd floor of Casa Huerta? ;-) Thank you for being such a central part of my most formative years. I appreciate all the love, counsel, and incredible memories we've made together. SLUG LIFE!

To the awesomest network of friends a girl could ask for—FC/Matio peeps, Slug homies, writer friends, McGrawGirls, play cousins —thank you for believing in me, cheering me on, reading my blogs, and providing a continuous source of inspiration and companionship. I cherish each and every one of you.

To my family (Casher-Sabaot-Garrett-Pabrua-Damasen-Williams), for their love and support. I feel so blessed to be a part of this incredible gene pool.

Much love also goes out to my in-laws, the Garrard-Register descendents, and of course Mama Phyllis… Thank you for welcoming me with open arms.

And finally, to James, for helping me find my happy ending… Having you on my team makes everything easier, and having you to share life with makes everything sweeter. You're the best partner this writer could ask for, and I love you more than words…

Chapter One

Samantha Merrick had spent her whole life playing by the rules and doing what was expected of her. But even good girls are susceptible to making bad decisions, or a series of bad decisions, as they try to figure out who they are.

She woke up that fateful morning with a hangover and a strange boy in bed next to her. Where was she? Squinting in the darkness, her lover's form came into focus—chin-length blond hair, muscular arms, a perfectly sculpted chest. A thin sheet covered the lower half of his body, and like her, he was completely nude. Her eyes darted around the unfamiliar surroundings until they landed on a surfboard propped in the corner of the room. *Ah yes, the surfer dude.* It all trickled back to her.

She felt around in the dark for her clothes. Regret, combined with the aftertaste of tequila and stale cigarettes, triggered a mild nausea. Determined to sneak away before he woke, she crept out of his bedroom, not bothering to leave a note. She had no desire to see him ever again.

Samantha jumped behind the wheel of her trusty Toyota,

the pounding in her head merciless. As if on autopilot, she maneuvered her car toward the beach. She always ended up at the water's edge whenever she felt the urge to run. The ocean was her sanctuary, and she could sit for hours on the edge of the cliff, releasing her problems into the sea, the waves eroding layers of regret as they crashed against the shore.

As rough as her second year of college was starting out, she was glad she had decided to come to school at UCSC. The sleepy, coastal town of Santa Cruz was everything Samantha hoped it would be, and she often marveled at how blessed she was to attend college in such a beautiful place, amongst such progressive, liberal-minded people. She'd been having the time of her life.

But the events of last summer changed all that. Her awestruck wonder and sense of adventure had been replaced by a searing cynicism, the quest for knowledge taking a backseat to the more pressing pursuit of finding something, *anything*, to numb the pain. Samantha was no longer concerned with freeing her mind. All she wanted to do was forget.

She pulled into the deserted parking lot as the sun crept upward in the morning sky, erasing the last traces of night with its ascent. Sunrise was a particularly magical time, the pre-dawn air curiously still, as if the day were holding its breath, waiting to be born. The dew-speckled ground glistened in the morning sun and cast an aura of shiny newness across the landscape. Samantha grabbed a blanket and took a deep breath, drawing in the crisp, salty air. The promise of a new day was one of the few things that still inspired her.

The Santa Cruz coastline had no shortage of scenic vistas, but Samantha was partial to a secluded ledge off West Cliff Drive. As she made her way down the narrow footpath, she was surprised to find a guy sitting in her spot. He was staring across the ocean, legs hanging over the side, motionless like a statue. Samantha was tempted to look for somewhere less populated, but decided against it. If she relocated now, she'd miss the sunrise, so she selected a spot on the western side of the cliff. Together, yet apart, they watched the sky slowly change from red, to orange, then gold, before finally fading into blue.

Half an hour passed before he moved. When he finally looked her way, a startled expression marred his serene features. He blinked and shook his head, as if she were a mere apparition he expected to disappear. Samantha smiled at him and waved. A simple, casual gesture to assure him she was indeed real.

"Sorry I'm in your spot," he called out. Samantha's heart stopped. How could he have possibly known that?

He pulled a pack of Marlboro Lights from his breast pocket and held one out. "Smoke?"

Samantha joined him at the edge and took the cigarette

from his outstretched hand. Their eyes met, and she was struck by this odd sense of familiarity.

"Forgive me if the answer is yes," she began, "but do we know each other?"

A sly smile played on his lips. He lit her cigarette, then his own, saying nothing.

"Did I say something funny?" she asked, irritated by his non-response.

He took a long drag from his cigarette and chuckled. "Do you often meet people and forget you've met them?"

"No," she snapped. Her thoughts flashed back to the nameless boy whose bed she had just fled. "Well, sometimes..." She cocked her head and looked at him curiously. "You didn't answer my question."

He smiled at her again. "No, we've never met."

"Then how did you know you were in my spot?"

"Let's just say that I love sunrise as much as you love sunset."

Samantha was intrigued. How did he know she loved sunset? How did he know this was her spot? Who was this presumptuous stranger?

She examined him more closely. He was very attractive, with an aura of cool that suggested he was much older than the college boys she was used to seeing around campus. His caramel skin tone matched her own, and he had a head full of curls where an afro should have been, betraying his mixed-race heritage. Samantha couldn't shake the feeling that she knew him from somewhere, and wondered if maybe she'd seen him at one of the multicultural functions on campus.

As if reading her mind, he confessed, "I've seen you here before."

She let out a nervous giggle. "What, are you stalking me or something?"

"Not exactly."

Another long pause. Samantha grew more confused by the second.

"Relax," he said finally, sensing her discomfort. He gestured to a large Victorian off the main road. "I live up there. The window on the second floor, with the wind chimes outside of it, is mine." He smiled again. "Watching you talk to yourself is one of my favorite ways to spend the afternoon."

A wave of vulnerability washed over her—this man *had* been watching her! "Oh, I see, you're like a peeping Tom or something."

He laughed and put out his cigarette. "No, I'm a people watcher. You happen to be a very interesting person to watch."

He captured her eyes in a penetrating gaze, as if he was looking *in* her, rather than at her. Samantha felt herself being drawn to him psychically, hypnotically, a level of intimacy present that hadn't been earned. She turned away to break the spell.

"So why do you come out here and sit on the cliff by yourself?" she asked. "I mean, you can obviously see the sunrise fine from your window."

He reached into his pocket and pulled out his cigarettes again, offering her another. She declined.

"Don't get me wrong, the view is great from up there. But there's something special about this spot. When you sit right here and look out across the water, all you see is ocean for miles in three directions. All evidence of life and the city is behind you." He took a drag from his cigarette, exhaling slowly. "When I'm feeling overwhelmed, all that water makes my problems seem so small and insignificant. It's quite humbling really, a great way to start the day, with a fresh perspective."

Samantha's curiosity was piqued. "Do you come out here every morning?"

"Nope. Only when I'm feeling a little lost."

The word echoed in her head. *Lost.* One simple syllable that perfectly described the past four months of her life. Minutes passed as they sat together in shared solitude, looking across the sea.

"So what's got you up and out on the cliff so early?" he asked, breaking the silence.

She smiled at him knowingly. "I guess I was feeling a little lost this morning, too."

Concern filled his dark-brown eyes. "You want to talk

about it?"

Samantha drew in a deep breath. It had been so long since she'd confided in someone. She had tried talking to her friends, but they were too busy partying their lives away to be of much help. If she was told to move on and get over it one more time…

"I don't want to bore you with my problems," she said.

"I can think of many adjectives to describe you, my dear, and boring would not be one of them. Talk to me."

Strangely enough, something in his eyes made Samantha feel like she could trust him. "Have you ever had something happen that made you doubt every instinct you've ever had, every decision you've ever made?"

"Of course, that's what the coming of age process is all about. Life throws you challenging situations to toughen you up. Like a rite of passage."

Samantha picked up a stick and drew designs in the sand. "Maybe so, but some days I wonder if I'm going to make it through to the other side."

"You will," he assured her. "Heartbreak and disappointment build character."

"But that's just it—how can any experience build character when I don't even know who I am anymore? Getting up every day and going through my normal routine… It's like trying to squeeze into clothes two sizes too small."

She threw the stick over the edge of the cliff in frustration. "My old life just doesn't fit me anymore."

He took a moment to search her face, as if seeing her for the first time. "I know exactly what you mean."

"You do?"

"More than you know. But isn't that what going away to college is all about? We're supposed to be finding ourselves, right?"

"Supposedly, but I only feel more and more alienated from my surroundings as the days go on. Sometimes I don't know *why* I do some of the things I do." Her thoughts returned to the anonymous boy she'd spent the night with, and a fresh wave of shame washed over her. For the first time she felt slightly self-conscious. She had literally just rolled out of bed and hadn't looked in a mirror since sometime last night. She probably looked tore up!

"Don't worry," he said. "You look fine."

Was he reading her mind? She lifted her head and found him looking at her. This time she didn't retreat from his gaze, choosing instead to look deep into his eyes. They were beautiful. *He* was beautiful. She could have spent the entire day sitting out there looking at him. A few moments ago, he was just some random guy she'd met on a cliff. Until she felt it. *Click.* It was quiet, and it was subtle, but it was there. *Click.* And she had no words...

She was lost in his eyes when he became distracted by the

appearance of an older couple making their way down the path, hand in hand.

"Looks like we have company." He collected their discarded cigarette butts and put them in his half-empty pack.

Samantha glanced at the older couple and smiled, though she was secretly disappointed they were no longer alone. She wasn't ready to part ways with the mysterious stranger.

Once again, as if reading her mind, he asked, "You wanna get some coffee or something? I'm just about due for a caffeine fix."

Samantha's heart skipped a beat as she tried to hide her relief and excitement. "Sure," she answered, as casually as she could manage. "That sounds great."

He rose to his feet and extended a hand to help her up. She felt a shock of electricity when they touched, and much to her surprise, he continued to hold her hand as they started toward the path.

"Wait," she said, pulling away reflexively. "I don't even know your name."

He smiled at her again and she melted. "Tony," he responded. "Well actually, it's Anthony, but no one ever calls me that. You?"

"Samantha," she replied softly. "Most people call me Sam."

"It's nice to meet you, Samantha." He extended his hand again and she took it.

Yeah, she thought. *Nice to meet you, too...*

Chapter Two

*T*hey exchanged life stories over coffee. Samantha couldn't get over the instant connection she felt to this stranger. They had both grown up in a predominantly white, middle class suburb, where they had been one of the few brown kids in their schools. Straight-A students throughout high school, they were both majoring in Sociology at UC Santa Cruz. Children of divorce, neither of them was very close to their fathers. To discover that he shared the same rare ethnic mix—Black and Filipino—was icing on the cake. The similarities were numerous and startling—he could have been her twin, the male version of herself. He was new and familiar at the same time.

Conversation flowed easily, and Samantha found herself revealing more to him about her life, fears, and dreams than she ever had with anyone. It had been so long since she'd had a sympathetic ear that the sentiments poured out of her like water rushing through a broken dam. Tony listened attentively when she spoke, eyes full of empathy, asking thoughtful, probing questions that pushed her to look deeper into each issue. He appeared to have an intuitive understanding of exactly what she was feeling, and on those few occasions when Samantha had to pause to search for the perfect word to complete her thought, he would often jump in and finish her sentence. It was eerie, like he truly had the ability to read her mind.

Coffee turned into lunch, and as the hours passed, Samantha discovered she was able to read his mind, too. Tony was one of those long-winded individuals prone to rambling, as if his tongue could hardly keep up with the speed at which his mind churned out ideas. Sometimes his thoughts would break off into a seemingly meaningless tangent, only to wrap back around and come full circle four tangents later to make a very insightful and profound point. To a normal person, he may have been hard to follow, but Samantha was able to keep up with him through every random turn and subtle iteration. A couple of times, Tony paused dramatically mid-sentence, as if testing their newfound connectedness by challenging her to complete his thought. His face would register amazement, then amusement, as Samantha confidently finished his interrupted sentences, assuring him they were indeed on the same page so he could continue with his profundicizing.

Samantha was captivated. Tony was by far the most interesting person she had ever met—definitely an intellectual, very spiritual, yet refreshingly grounded. She was spellbound by his elaborate narratives and soapbox diatribes, delightfully entertained by his wit and humor, and impressed by his unique perspective on the world. This man had a truly global consciousness! His words resonated so deeply at the core of her being that at times she resisted the urge to pinch him, pinch herself, just to confirm that he was real. She couldn't remember the last time she'd enjoyed someone this much, and as the day wore on, she felt the blossoming of a powerful physical attraction. It made sense—he was stimulating in every possible way. As a matter of fact, Samantha was on the verge of being *over*stimulated.

After lunch they decided to drive up the coast to one of the more secluded beaches. No topic was off limits—they delved into subjects such as politics, social problems, religion and spirituality, women's rights, and institutionalized racism. With very few exceptions, they agreed on virtually everything. They even shared the same secret fantasy of abandoning Capitalist society altogether in favor of a simple little life on a remote island somewhere in the sea of their choosing. The only difference in their fantasies was that Samantha preferred the Mediterranean, while Tony dreamed of the Caribbean.

They strolled down the beach side by side, marking a path just above the water's edge, footsteps in sync. Samantha marveled at how easy it was to share silence with him as well.

After an entire day of nonstop conversation, they had lapsed into a contemplative silence, both lost in their own thoughts. Talking out her anxieties had cleared her head, and the heavy weight she had been carrying around had temporarily lifted. She felt steadier and lighter, experiencing peace and contentment for the first time in months.

As they made their way back to the car, Samantha started to tense—she didn't want the day to end. She unlocked the passenger side door, but Tony made no effort to get in the car. Instead, he folded his arms across his chest and studied her thoughtfully. "This is crazy."

"Which part?" she asked, relieved that he didn't seem to be in a rush to leave.

"Do you realize we've been together for almost twelve straight hours?" A slight tremble in his voice betrayed a flicker of insecurity. "I can't believe you're not sick of me yet."

"Are you kidding? I can't believe you're not sick of *me* yet," she confessed, mirroring his quiet vulnerability back at him.

Tony reached up to brush an eyelash off her cheek. "To tell you the truth, I can't imagine ever being sick of you Samantha."

Samantha caught her breath. No one had ever said something like that to her before. He turned her head toward him and their eyes met. There it was again… *Click*. Time stood still. Looking into his eyes, she felt a renewed sense of hope, like maybe it was possible for her broken heart to heal. She had resolved herself to a lifetime of loneliness, vowing never again to let someone get close enough to hurt her, but the strength of their connection was undeniable. This man made her want to believe in love again.

"What's crazy to me," she started, struggling to regain her composure, "is that even though we just met this morning—"

"It feels like we've known each other forever," he finished simply.

Samantha looked up to find sad and troubled eyes staring back at her. A dark cloud colored Tony's disposition, and she had no idea what had brought it on. She scanned his face for a clue to what was going on in his head, but the mind-reading thing didn't work this time. "What is it?"

He said nothing. Instead, he took her hand and led her to a bench a few feet away. After they were both seated, he started speaking again. "I have never wanted to kiss anyone more than I want to kiss you right now."

Samantha's heart caught in her throat. "Okay... But why do you look so tortured about it? Kissing is supposed to be fun."

"I have a girlfriend."

The words hung in the air—all her buoyant hopes and blissful feelings instantly deflated. Now she understood why he looked so sad and troubled. She had no doubt that a similar expression had settled on her own face. Of course she would meet the man of her dreams, only to find out he was unavailable. Of course. Her self-protective walls snapped back into place as she scolded herself for being so foolish and trusting. The disappointment stung and burned much more than it should have, and though she tried to hide it, she doubted she was successful. It was hard to appear unaffected when all she wanted to do was scream, curse, and throw things. But not yet, not in front of the man. That tantrum would have to wait until she was in the privacy of her own home.

"I can't believe that after twelve hours you're just now getting around to mentioning that," Samantha muttered. She grabbed the pack of cigarettes from his front breast pocket.

"I know, I'm sorry. I don't want you to think I was intentionally misleading you—I swear that wasn't it. Honestly, I didn't think about her at all for most of the day, as terrible as that sounds. It wasn't until the chemistry kicked in and I realized you and I were bonding at this ridiculously rapid rate that it occurred to me 'Shit, I have a girlfriend.' But by that time we were having such a great time, I didn't want it to end. I still don't want it to end. I figured as soon as you found out I had a girlfriend something would change." He searched her face. "I can see in your eyes something already has."

It was her turn to say nothing. She was in a state of shock, speech wasn't even possible at this point.

"Samantha, I have never met anyone like you before. It

sounds crazy, but I have this feeling we were supposed to meet, you know, that our paths were supposed to cross. This is some crazy Fate shit, right? I knew the second I turned my head on the cliff this morning and saw you sitting there that it was Fate. All things happen for a reason, right? This had to have happened for a reason, right?"

Samantha lit her cigarette, saying nothing.

"You totally think I'm a jerk; it's written all over your face. See, I was afraid this was going to happen." He stood up and began to pace. "That's the only reason I didn't say anything earlier. Not to make excuses or anything, I just... well... I just didn't know what to do. I mean, this has never happened to me before, you know what I mean? Samantha? Damnit woman, will you say something?"

She ignored him. He lit a cigarette in frustration.

"How long have you guys been together?" Samantha managed finally. Of all the questions racing through her mind, that was the one that came tumbling out first.

He stared at the ocean, unable to look at her. "Four and a half years."

"God Tony." How could this be? They had hit it off so well. "Do you love her?"

Tony paused for a long while before answering. "It's complicated but... Yes, I love her."

Samantha's heart sank—that wasn't the answer she'd

wanted to hear. "Then what exactly is it you want from me?" she snapped, not bothering to mask her bitterness.

Tony sat down beside her, eyes pleading, but she continued to avoid his gaze and fixate on the ocean, refusing to get sucked back into what she had been starting to feel for him.

"I know this is incredibly selfish of me," he began softly, his expression pained and miserable. "But I can't just walk away from this." He hesitated for a few seconds, and then continued. "I was hoping, for now at least, that we could be friends."

Samantha shuddered. "Friends," she repeated. "Do you know how many traumatic childhood memories you conjured up with that sentence?" A dry laugh escaped her lips. She had way too much pride to let him see how devastated she really was.

He relaxed at the sound of her laugh, the playful twinkle returning to his eyes. "Give me your car keys."

"Whoa." She pulled her purse out of reach. "You drop that bomb on me, ruin my lovely afternoon, and now you want my car keys? You may be cute, but you're not that cute."

His playful tone evaporated. "Look, I know you feel I've misrepresented myself, and if you decide you want nothing to do with me, I'll have to accept that. But girlfriend or no, I haven't felt like this in a long time, and that's the truth. Please, just give me a few more hours, a chance to end this day the way it should have ended. One perfect day, from sunrise to sunset. That's all I ask."

She should have run screaming in the other direction, far away from this man named Tony and the tidal wave of emotions she was feeling. Her rational mind flashed warning signals, cautioning her to get out while she still could, but her heart wouldn't cooperate. Why was he so irresistible?

"Where are you going to take me?" she asked suspiciously. She didn't have any intention of turning him down, but refused to come off as too eager.

"Will you just give me the keys and trust me?"

Trust. Now there was a concept foreign to Samantha. Her ability to trust had been crippled by her last relationship, but for some reason where Tony was concerned, trust was disturbingly automatic. Even with this new revelation about the girlfriend, every instinct she had was telling her to give in and go with him, consequences be damned. She'd finally found someone she could open up to, who understood her, and she didn't want to give that up.

Handing him her car keys, Samantha couldn't help but smile at the way his face lit up when he realized she wasn't going to deny his last request. Yup, she was about to board a runaway train. The only thing left to do was hang on and try to enjoy the ride...

Chapter Three

They were cruising back toward town on Highway One, with Tony behind the wheel, and Samantha staring vacantly out the window at the passing scenery. The afternoon sun was beginning its descent into the West, having traced a perfect arc in the sky since its first appearance over the mountains earlier that morning. Time flew by when they were together, the euphoria of true companionship transporting them to another world where they were the only occupants. But as much as they might have wished it so, that wasn't reality. They weren't the only two people on the planet, not by a long shot.

Tony was conflicted about how to proceed with his new friend. While he felt confident that he could keep things platonic, spending any amount of time with a woman that was not your girlfriend was like asking for a soap opera to unfold in the middle of your life. No matter how innocent things were, someone could still get hurt. But despite the potential complications, he couldn't bring himself to walk away. The feeling appeared to be mutual.

Tony took his eyes off the road for a moment to steal a glance in Samantha's direction. Knees drawn against her chest, she absentmindedly twisted and untwisted a strand of long, curly hair around her index finger. She did that unconsciously when she was nervous, one of the many things he'd discovered about her during the course of the day. He couldn't deny that he was attracted to her—she was by far the most beautiful, intelligent, and insightful girl he'd ever met. But the timing was all wrong.

"Where are you taking me again?" she asked impatiently, breaking into his thoughts.

"It's a surprise."

"I don't like surprises. You can't prepare for a surprise."

She was starting to close off toward him. Her eyes had been cold and expressionless ever since they left the beach, and she was becoming increasingly irritated by his refusal to tell her where they were going. "You're a control-freak, aren't you?"

"You say that like it's a bad thing."

Tony laughed, unable to hide his amusement at having pushed one of her buttons. The slight flare of her nostrils and flush in her cheeks was such a turn-on—she was gorgeous when she was angry. "You need to learn how to be more spontaneous. For example, this thing with the car keys. You couldn't just trust me and give me the keys when I asked for them. Oh no, you had to fight me. Now, thanks to your stubborn resistance, we might be late for our next adventure."

Samantha turned to face him, fire flashing in her eyes. "First of all, I've been plenty spontaneous today, thank you. I've been running around town with a complete stranger, blowing off all kinds of homework. We just met twelve hours ago. It would have been a little naïve of me to hand over my keys to some stranger without—"

"I really wish you'd quit referring to me as a stranger," Tony interrupted. "I'm no stranger, Samantha."

His statement completely disarmed her. She softened her tone and continued in a less hostile manner. "Well, regardless, I think I'm entitled to know where we're going. Don't you think I've had enough surprises for one day, Mr. 'I have a girlfriend.' "

Tony flinched. "Touché Ms. Merrick, touché." He turned onto West Cliff Drive. "But I'm still not spoiling the surprise."

Samantha leaned back and resumed her hair-twisting. "Fine, have it your way."

Tony followed the winding road alongside the ocean until he got to his house. He still couldn't believe his luck in finding a sublet in one of Santa Cruz's prime coast side locations—the luxurious estates in the upscale neighborhood started in the million-dollar range. The Victorian he lived in used to be a frat house until the University shut the fraternity down after a tragic hazing incident. Now the eight bedrooms were rented out to UCSC upperclassmen and graduate students. He pulled Samantha's car into the crowded lot toward the rear of the property.

"What are we doing back at your place?"

"I need to grab a few things for the next mission. You promise you won't take off while I'm gone?"

"How can I? You still have my car keys."

Tony put the key back in the ignition and clicked on the radio. "I trust you," he said with a smile. He hopped out of the car and jogged toward the house.

Samantha looked at the keys dangling from the ignition. She could easily slide into the driver's seat, start the car, and drive away. That's what she *should* have done anyway. Glancing up at the three-story house looming in front of her, she wondered if the girlfriend lived there, too. What would she think about Samantha spending so much time with her boyfriend? Yeah, if Samantha was smart she'd get the hell out of there. But before rational thought could be converted into rational action, Tony reappeared clutching a brown paper bag and a burgundy sweatshirt.

"That was fast."

He tossed the sweatshirt into her lap. "In case you get cold later."

Samantha was floored by his ability to anticipate her every

need. It was starting to get a little chilly, and she still had on the thin silk blouse she'd worn the night before. The sweatshirt was perfect. "Thanks," she mumbled as she slipped it over her head.

Tony backed out of the driveway and headed for the hills. They passed the University and continued up the mountain toward Bonny Doon, which struck Samantha as odd because the farther up the road you went, the more remote it got. She'd been up there a few times on hiking expeditions, and it was nothing but rock and forest past a certain point. "Where are we going again?" she asked nervously.

"I told you it's a surprise. But we're almost there."

They continued to follow the windy road up the hill. Samantha shook her head, scolding herself. She used to be so cautious, but her behavior lately had been so reckless and self-destructive. What was she thinking, handing over her keys to some strange man and allowing him to take her to some secluded location just before nightfall? He could have been a serial killer for all she knew, though in her heart she was certain she was safe. Safer than she'd ever been. She was more afraid of the uncharted emotional territory she was wandering into, yet here she was, against her better judgment, throwing caution to the wind, thrilled and excited to have finally found a kindred spirit. True, she had no idea where they were going, and maybe she should have been more concerned about that.

But they were having so much fun, it was a detail that was easy to overlook.

Tony pulled over in front of a barbed wire fence and killed the engine. "We're almost there."

"You've been saying that for the past half hour."

"Well, this time I really mean it." He grabbed the paper bag out of the backseat and popped the trunk. "Do you mind if we bring your blanket along for the mission?"

"Not at all." Samantha grabbed the blanket and folded it neatly. "I take it we're going on a hike?"

"If you're still up for it."

"I've come this far. It would be pretty silly to turn back now."

Tony led them onto a slightly overgrown trail that wound up and around the mountain. The trail was level for the most part, and whenever they came upon a section that was steep or tricky to navigate, Tony would reach back to help her up, his strong hands holding her steady as she struggled with her footing. They climbed for about fifteen minutes until they reached the top of the hill they were traversing.

Mesmerized by the scene that lay before her, Samantha stopped and caught her breath. They were standing atop the highest point in the area, high above the trees. She could see clear to the ocean from where they stood, and the sun was starting to sink down toward the horizon line. The entire sky was changing from orange to a deep pink before her eyes, a gentle breeze rustling the tips of the treetops below, filling the air around them with a gentle, soothing hum.

She gasped. "This is the most beautiful thing I've ever seen."

Tony laid the blanket on the ground in front of them and gestured for her to sit. "I'm glad you like it."

"It's the most beautiful thing I've ever seen," she repeated.

He pulled a joint from his pocket, lit it, and passed it to her. "This is my absolute favorite spot in town. I don't think many people know about it—I've never seen anyone else up here."

Samantha took a hit off the joint and passed it back. "How did you find it?"

"Luck pretty much. I hike up here all the time. Then one day I noticed this barbed-wire fence, and it piqued my curiosity. It's the only fence in this area—I had to see what was on the other side."

"You rebel," she teased.

"This is my sacred, secret place," Tony said. "I've never brought anyone up here with me before."

Surprise registered on Samantha's face. "Really? Wow, I'm honored. This spot is incredible. You know that song that goes 'I'm on top of the world, looking down on Creation?'"

"The Carpenters, right? My mom loved that song."

"Mine, too. That's how I feel right now. The colors alone—the greens of the trees, the blue of the ocean, the red of the sky turning into violet—it's totally surreal."

"I knew you'd be able to appreciate it. Being a connoisseur of sunsets and all."

Samantha tore her eyes away from the setting sun to look at him. He wasn't watching the sky at all, his eyes fixed intently on her face. She resisted being drawn in by his hypnotic gaze. "What's in the bag?"

"Oh, I almost forgot." He reached into the paper bag and pulled out a bottle of red wine and corkscrew.

"You've certainly thought of everything, haven't you?"

"Well, that was the plan."

"Right, the perfect day..."

"From sunrise to sunset."

Tony uncorked the wine and passed the bottle to her. She took a healthy swig. The sun was melting into the ocean now, as the sky slowly darkened. They sipped wine in silence for a few minutes, passing the bottle back and forth, quietly watching the sun disappear. With the sun's exit, the air around them cooled and Samantha fought back a slight chill. But after a few more sips of wine, she felt the emergence of an inner warmth radiating outward, balancing out the change in air temperature perfectly. Samantha laid back and focused on the night sky stretching out above her, marveling at the field of stars that appeared cluster after cluster, growing brighter with each passing minute.

"I can't believe how bright the stars look up here."

"I know. There's barely any light pollution, so the stars really sparkle. It's like a whole other world."

"I really gotta hand it to you, Tony—this day has been absolutely perfect. Well, with the exception of the whole 'I have a girlfriend' moment," she said with a good-natured chuckle.

"Yeah, talk about a mood killer, huh?"

Samantha rolled onto her side. He was reclined as well, leaning back on his elbows, face turned skyward. Samantha didn't know if it was the weed or the wine, the clean air or the cool breeze, but she was feeling calmer, steadier, and ready to migrate into choppy emotional waters. Besides, avoiding the subject wasn't going to make the girlfriend go away.

"So tell me about her."

Tony drew in a breath. "What do you want to know?"

"Whatever's relevant. I don't know. We've talked about everything else and it just flowed. You said you wanted to be friends, right? Well, friends talk about their significant others."

Tony sat up and turned to face her. "Okay, let's see. Her name is Angela. We've known each other since we were kids, and she was one of my best friends in high school."

"Wow, you two go way back."

"Yeah, we do. After graduation, most of our friends left to attend four-year universities, but neither of us could afford to go away to school, so we stayed behind and went to a local junior college to save money. Somewhere along the way, the friendship turned into something more, and before I knew it, a year had passed and we were moving in together. After that we were pretty much inseparable, until I decided to come up here."

"She's still in L.A?"

"Yeah. She wanted to move with me, but I told her no."

"How come?"

"This was my one chance to get out in the world and be on my own. You know, figure out who Anthony Carteris really is, without having Angela or my family to lean on. I desperately needed for something to be about me, and *only* me, for a change."

Samantha smiled. "So have you found yourself yet?"

And so much more, he thought, looking at her fondly. "I'm getting there. With each new experience, the more I am changed. I've discovered that I have a burning desire to travel the globe—India, Africa, all over. The more I learn, the more I need to know! And that's where me and Angela's paths seem to diverge." He sighed. "She's content with her life exactly the way it is. She's not an explorer. Instead of yearning for change, she wants everything to stay exactly the same. She has her reasons for feeling that way—an unstable childhood, loads of abuse, an absentee father, the works. But that's not me. I need different things, things I know she can't give me."

"I see."

"She hasn't changed at all since high school, and I feel like I've changed so much in the two years that I've been in Santa Cruz. Sometimes I wonder if she's even noticed."

"I know what you mean. There's nothing worse than feeling like the people who are supposed to know you best, don't know you at all."

"Tell me about it. To be honest, I've thought a lot about ending the relationship. But it's hard because we've been through so much together. Angela has supported me, emotionally and financially, when I was really struggling. Stood by me through some really hard times. I don't know if I would have made it back to school without her in my corner, pushing me. She's my best friend, and it's hard to imagine life without her, even though I do feel we've been drifting apart."

Samantha let silence fill the air between them as she absorbed all this new information. She hadn't realized Tony had entertained thoughts of ending his relationship. But even so, Tony was not yet a free man, and it was clear that he was deeply bonded to this woman. As much as she was drawn to him, mentally and physically, Samantha had no desire to be the third party in a love triangle.

"So what are you going to do?"

"About what?"

"About Angela."

"Well, I graduate in June, and then I'm moving back to L.A. I was going to deal with it when I got home. How can I break up with her while I'm up here and she's down there? After five years, she deserves better than that."

Night had fallen, and the moon hovered huge and full above them. He looked so beautiful sitting there bathed in moonlight, and she couldn't help but yearn for things she knew were wrong. Could they really make a friendship work without acting on their attraction, or was she kidding herself? "What are we doing here, Tony?"

"What do you mean?"

Samantha looked him directly in the eye. "You know exactly what I mean."

Tony took her hand, and she shivered at his touch. "I think you are an incredible woman, Samantha. I've only known you a day, but it's long enough for me to know that there is something very special about you. I'm convinced you have come into my life for a reason. I just need some time to sort out my situation. I'm not asking you to sit around and wait for me, or be the other woman, or anything scandalous like that, but I do need you in my life." He lifted her chin so their eyes met. "We need each other. I'd really like to give this friendship thing a try."

Samantha knew how complicated and painful this situation could turn out for everyone involved, but he was right—she needed him. She had finally found someone who actually understood her, someone she could really talk to. She'd just have to find a way to keep her hormones in check. For everyone's sake.

"Let's just take it one day at a time and see how it goes, okay?" she offered.

Tony's face lit up with a smile that rivaled the glow emanating from the moon. He squeezed her hand. "Thank you."

Chapter Four

*I*t was almost midnight when Samantha finally returned home from her day with Tony. She was a mess. After being numb for so long, the sudden surge of emotions had kicked her into sensory overload. She had completely lost the ability to separate right from wrong, appropriate from *a really bad idea*. All she knew was that she felt alive again, for the first time in months, and wanted that feeling to last. Samantha was so preoccupied trying to process the day's events that she didn't even notice the disapproving look on her housemate's face when she walked into the room.

"Hey," she mumbled, crossing in front of the TV on the way to her bedroom.

Gabe paused his video game. "Is that all you have to say for yourself?"

The harshness in his tone caught Samantha off guard. Gabe didn't do angry. In fact, he was one of the mellowest guys she'd ever met. "Excuse me?"

"Look, Sam, I'm all in favor of sexual independence and

a woman's right to get hers, but if you're going to go home with some dude you met at a party, then disappear for a day and a half, call somebody. Faby was freaking out when you didn't come home this morning—she was ready to file a missing persons report."

"Gee, sorry, Dad. I didn't realize I had a curfew."

A paternal frown creased Gabe's brow. "Don't cop attitude with me. We were worried about you. Where the hell have you been all day?"

Samantha filled Gabe in on her day with Tony. He listened patiently as she went on and on about how wonderful Tony was and what a great time they had. Gabe was actually relieved to hear that Samantha had finally found someone she didn't consider disposable. Until she got to the part about Tony having a girlfriend.

"I don't know, Sam," he said, shaking his head. "I think you're better off leaving this one alone."

"I know," she agreed, not too convincingly.

"But you're going to see him again anyway."

"If I do, it'll be strictly on the friendship tip, I swear."

"Uh huh."

Samantha hit him with a pillow. "Hey, give me a little credit, will you? I—"

"Where the *hell* have you been?" Faby demanded, slamming the front door. "I thought you had been raped and murdered and were lying in a ditch somewhere!"

Samantha looked up at her best friend, a petite Latina with the ability to strike fear in even the largest opponent. Fearless, outspoken, and never one to back down from a challenge, Faby had taught Samantha a lot about embracing her inner bitch. Samantha loved Faby to death, but she could live without the drama queen theatrics. "I'm fine, Fabs."

"Next time freaking call someone, my God." Faby threw her keys on the dining room table and plopped down on the couch next to Samantha. "You're still wearing the same clothes you had on yesterday—are you just now getting home? Where have you been? With that guy? The surfer dude?"

"No, not that guy," Samantha corrected, flinching at the memory of the stranger she'd spent the night with. "I met someone else."

"What? When? Where?"

Faby could hardly contain her excitement as Samantha described her day. Six months ago, Samantha had gone through a painful and devastating break-up with her high school sweetheart. The sweet, fun-loving girl they'd all come to know and love seemed to have vanished overnight as Samantha became increasingly distant and withdrawn, choosing to push people away instead of opening up about what was bothering her. With the exception of the random guys she picked up at parties when Faby dragged her out,

Samantha hardly socialized at all anymore. But even those occasional hook-ups were short-lived. Like Gabe, Faby was a tad overprotective, and did not approve of Samantha's slutty, self-destructive streak. It just wasn't her. But listening to her talk about this Tony fella was like having the old Samantha back. Maybe this would be the guy to break the spell.

Faby bounced up and down on the edge of the couch, eager to hear more. "He sounds great. When do we get to meet him?"

Samantha avoided Faby's eyes. "Um..."

"Don't get too excited, Fab," Gabe interjected. "Sammy here is leaving out the best part of the story."

Samantha shot him a nasty look. "I was getting there."

"Getting where?" Faby asked.

"He has a girlfriend."

Faby's eyes widened. The old Samantha would have never messed around with a guy with a girlfriend. "Oh, uh uh... After everything you went through with Eric, how could you even think of—"

"It's not even remotely the same thing," Samantha insisted. "I'm not planning to start a torrid affair with him." Gabe raised an eyebrow in disbelief, which she ignored. "Seriously, it's not about sex. He actually *gets* me. We understand each other. It's been so long since I..." Her voice trailed off. She was wasting her breath—they weren't going to get it. There was only one person who could understand what she was feeling right now, and unfortunately, he was in a house across town. "You know what, forget it. If you're done scolding me, I'm going to bed."

Samantha didn't wait for either of them to respond before retreating to her room. She had been floating so high when she got home, but between the two of them, they had managed to totally kill her buzz. Samantha changed into boxers and a tank top and climbed into bed. Staring at the ceiling, she realized she actually missed him. She had been so content in her loneliness before, but right now she'd give anything just to hear his voice. In less than twenty-four hours Tony had managed to completely get under her skin. How had he gotten in when no one else even got close?

Pulling out the piece of paper he had scribbled his phone number on, she studied the digits. Underneath his number he had written "Call ANYTIME." She was tempted. Scared out of her mind, but tempted. But after careful consideration, reason prevailed. She reached for the lamp instead of the phone and tried to get some much-needed rest.

Chapter Five

Samantha emerged from her Sociology of Learning class the following afternoon still dazed and disoriented from the events of the previous day. She was being haunted. Tony had not only visited her dreams the night before, but was also the first thing on her mind when she opened her eyes in the morning. The images persisted with annoying clarity throughout both of her midday classes, to the point where she could hardly remember a thing Professor Roby had said about Freud's theory of Child Development.

When Samantha looked up and saw Tony on a bench outside her classroom, she had to do a double-take to make sure he wasn't a figment of her overactive imagination. Tony's face lit up as they made eye contact, and in two seconds he was standing in front of her, flashing that disarming smile, way too close for comfort.

"Hey," he said, pulling her into a hug.

Samantha was almost offended by the way he inserted himself into her protected personal space. She wanted to push him away, but that impulse only lasted about half a second. As soon as his arms closed around her, Samantha realized what a calming effect he had. She allowed herself to relax into his embrace, once again feeling her grip on reality start to slip, as if being in his arms was the only thing that could put her world back on its axis. But they weren't in some romance novel—they were in the middle of the Social Sciences quad and people were starting to stare. After a minute, she withdrew from his embrace.

"Hey yourself," she volleyed back, as casually as she could manage. "Fancy meeting you here."

"I was in the neighborhood." He winked. "Learn anything interesting today?"

"If I did, I honestly couldn't tell you what it was." Samantha glanced back toward the classroom. The past two hours were a blur. "My focus was kinda off today."

"That's interesting. I had the opposite problem. My focus was fine, razor sharp. I just wasn't focusing on the teach."

"Oh yeah? What were you thinking about?"

"What a great time I had yesterday," Tony said with a smile. "What about you?"

A blush crept into Samantha's cheeks, her body temperature rising in response to their combustible chemistry. "I guess we can add that to the list of things we have in common."

Once again, Tony fixed her with a soul-searing stare.

"Did you put a spell on me, woman? I can't seem to get you out of my head."

Samantha backed up a few paces. "I can assure you, I did no such thing."

Tony took a step forward. "Are you sure? I feel downright possessed."

She held up a hand to halt his advances. "I appreciate the compliment, but spells aren't really my thing. Besides, if I had that kind of power at my disposal, I would have made your girlfriend disappear, too, while I was at it." Samantha knew it was a low blow, but pretending Angela didn't exist wasn't going to do either of them any good. As much fun as it was to flirt, she couldn't allow herself to lose touch with the reality of the situation.

Tony sensed her bitterness and his spirit sagged. "If you want me to stay away..."

"I don't want you to stay away," Samantha said quickly, betraying the true feelings she was trying so hard to hide. "I just wasn't expecting to see you again so soon, that's all."

"Well, as you shall soon learn, I am the king of unexpected. I was about to head down the coast for sunset. Wanna come?"

Samantha didn't know what came as more of a surprise —his invitation, or how badly she wanted to go. She conveniently forgot about the midterm review she had later that evening. "Sure."

Tony smiled and gestured for her to follow him to the parking lot. He stopped beside a sky blue Volkswagen bus and opened the passenger side door.

"Nice ride," Samantha commented as she climbed in. "Very Santa Cruz."

"This is my baby," Tony explained, firing up the engine. A gentle rumble rolled through the van, causing the seat below them to vibrate. "I've had her for six years now, long before I came to Santa Cruz."

Samantha glanced over her shoulder at the interior of the bus, which indeed had a very lived-in feel. "I've never met a Black man who rolled in a VW bus before."

"Yeah, neither have I," he said laughing. "What can I say, I cherish my individuality."

Tony pulled out of the parking lot and headed toward the highway. "So where to?" she asked.

"South."

"South? Can you be a little more specific?"

"I could, but that would ruin the surprise."

They ended up just south of Monterey in the ocean side town of Carmel. Parking on one of the quiet, tree-lined streets, they explored the town on foot, soaking up the neighborhood's quaint, old-world charm. Even though they were the youngest and brownest people around, Samantha couldn't help but fall in love with the place. Strolling down shady cobblestone lanes past storybook cottages, arm and arm with her prince, it was like being dropped into the middle of a fairytale. Every wood trim siding and faux-thatch roof played a part. She was so enthralled by the magic of her surroundings that she half-expected to see Hansel and Gretel skipping down the street.

Downtown was a bit on the bougie side, peppered with expensive boutiques and galleries catering to an upscale clientele. But even though shop windows boasted excess and opulence, the area still retained a peaceful rustic ambience. Carmel's famed art scene was thriving, with galleries on every block showcasing sculptures, paintings, and jewelry by local artists. They chatted easily as they gallery-hopped, Tony's off-the-wall interpretations of some of the more abstract pieces providing all the entertainment she needed. The man had an opinion about everything, and his sarcastic commentary had her in stitches. Samantha had never laughed so much in her life.

"Clam chowder," he blurted out as they stood in front of a large canvas streaked with golds and greens.

Samantha turned her head to the side and squinted at the mesmerizing swirl of colors. "You know, I'm just not seeing it. This doesn't look anything like clam chowder to me."

Tony laughed. "Not the painting—I'm hungry. We need

to find some chowder." Samantha had learned that when Tony was struck by a craving, he needed to attend to it immediately. He took her hand, attempting to pull her away from the gallery window.

"But what do you think this is?" Samantha asked, refusing to be budged. Tony had a mild case of ADD, always anxious to move on to the next thing. Samantha preferred to move a bit slower and savor things.

Tony turned back to the painting, giving the piece five seconds of his full attention. "It's clearly a painting of a man, on acid, running through the forest toward the sunrise."

Samantha erupted in a fit of giggles—that was exactly what it looked like! Shaking her head, she allowed Tony to lead her down the street as he set off on his next mission. They browsed the multitude of sidewalk cafes and fine dining establishments, several of which served chowder, until Tony found exactly what he was looking for. Ordering their food to go, they headed down to the beach for a sunset picnic.

With the exception of a handful of people walking their dogs, the beach was deserted. They chose a spot on the north end, hidden from view in a little cove. Once again, it was as if they were the only two people on the planet.

Samantha took a bite of the warm chowder, her face contorting into an expression of pre-orgasmic bliss. "This is so good!"

Tony nodded. "Agreed. I can't believe you've been in Santa Cruz for over a year and have never sampled one of the area's signature dishes."

"I've had chowder before, but never in one of these." Samantha gestured to the hollowed-out loaf of sourdough bread that held her soup. "This is genius."

Tony smiled at Samantha's youthful exuberance. She approached new experiences with the wonder of a child, her excitement infectious. Tony, several years her senior, seldom experienced that kind of awestruck wonder anymore. But as he showed Samantha the world, it was like seeing everything for the first time through her eyes. She made him feel young again. "Good food, gorgeous sunset, great company," he mused. "Looks like we've got another perfect day on our hands."

"Sure does." The sky had exploded in color, as if God himself were casting an invisible paintbrush across the heavens, blending blue with purple and pink, a touch of orange on the edges, a magnificent watercolor masterpiece. Samantha stared at the blue-green water, the surface clear as glass, waves rhythmically caressing the shoreline. "I can't get over the color of the water. It doesn't look like this in L.A. at all."

Tony followed her eyes. She was right—the ocean in Northern California was nothing like the murky-green waters of his native Santa Monica. The more time he spent away from L.A., the less desire he had to return. "Do you think you'll move back after graduation?"

Samantha laughed. "I can't even imagine what I'm going to be doing next Wednesday, much less what I'll be doing two years from now." She tore off a piece of bread. "My family is there, and we're incredibly close, but I have to admit it's nice to finally be out from under the shadow of my obnoxiously gifted siblings. Between my valedictorian sister and basketball star brothers, the bar is set so high that everything I do feels totally mediocre. Life is so different without that constant pressure to live up to the Merrick legacy of excellence." She set her bread bowl aside. "Gosh, that sounds so jealous and petty, doesn't it?"

"Not at all. My baby sister graduated from Yale while I was suffering through night classes at Santa Monica City College, trying to earn enough credits to transfer here. Now she's working on her Ph.D. Trust me, I feel you."

"Yeah, I guess I'm still trying to figure out what I'm good at. Maybe when I do, it won't feel like such a competition."

"So if you could do anything, what would it be?"

Samantha drew a circle in the sand. "I have no idea. I take all these classes, trying to find some sort of calling, and all I learn is what I *don't* want to do. Turns out, I don't want to be a psychologist or college professor—my top two career choices when I started school. I hate science, so that rules out anything in the medical profession. No desire whatsoever to go to Law School. I'm running out of options, and I have to declare a major soon."

"Don't be so hard on yourself—nobody knows what they're doing in their twenties. You'll find the answers you're looking for, just give it time."

"What about you? You're only a few months away from graduating. Have you figured out what you want to be when you grow up?"

"Not exactly, though like you, I'm pretty clear on what I don't want to be. Stagnation equals death as far as I'm concerned, so I'm pretty much anti- anything that would require me to be tied down. Being stuck in some tedious 9-5 corporate grind is my worst nightmare. That doesn't leave many options. I'm not sure I want to be in L.A. either."

"But your girlfriend is in L.A."

"I know. But that's not home for me anymore. I think my future may lie along another path."

Samantha fell silent. He made everything much harder when he said things like that. It was too easy to twist his words into exactly what she wanted to hear. "This is my first time in Carmel," she said, changing the subject. "I didn't know it could get any prettier than Santa Cruz."

"You ain't seen nothing yet. Have you been to Big Sur?"

"No. Where's Big Sur?"

"About an hour south of here. Don't tell me this is your

first time venturing out beyond the county line."

Samantha blushed, feeling hopelessly sheltered. Growing up in the suburbs hadn't exactly instilled her with an innate sense of adventurousness. "Aside from the occasional trip to the mall in Capitola, I can't say I've explored much outside the city limits."

"And why is that?"

"I don't know—I just spend a lot of time at home." She paused. "I've been in a mood the past few months."

Tony laughed. "You're hilarious."

"Why do you say that?"

"Because you remind me so much of me. I was exactly the same way until Damion convinced me to come up here for school—closed off and content. But Santa Cruz opened up a whole new world for me. I think it could do the same for you if you let it." The wheels in his head were turning. "Do you have your books with you?"

"Most of them."

"Good. We're going to Big Sur."

"Are you serious?"

"This is one of the most beautiful places in the country. The scenery deserves to be seen and appreciated. It's time for you to get out there and experience the world instead of just reading about it."

"But I have a midterm I need to study for."

"I know of this waterfall," Tony rambled on, barely registering her protest. "It's the most tranquil spot. We can study there."

"But where will we sleep?" she asked, panicked. Her heart pounded at the thought of running off with him.

"We can camp in the van." Sensing her trepidation, he quickly added, "I'll keep my hands to myself, I promise."

Geez, he has an answer for everything. "Well, if you can promise that we're really going to study..."

Tony nodded enthusiastically. "I can. Is that a yes?"

Once again, her defenses melted like butter, all sense and reason completely out the window. With Tony, she just didn't know how to say no. "Sure, why not?"

Chapter Six

*I*t was late when they finally reached Big Sur. Tony parked alongside the river, a quarter-mile from the main road. Darkness closed in as he shut off the headlights, the moon hidden from view by the dense forest that surrounded them. The soothing sounds of the river provided instrumental backing for the chorus of crickets, and the air around them danced to the tune of nature's song.

Tony climbed into the back and converted the two rows of seats into a long bed. Since he spent a fair amount of time on the road traveling, the van was stocked with all the comforts of home—warm blankets and pillows, several jugs of water, candles, an assortment of camping supplies, and of course, his guitar. He never went anywhere without his guitar.

Samantha lit a few candles while he set everything up. "You're quite the nature boy," she commented, impressed by the transformation. "Where'd you learn to camp?"

"When I was growing up, we had a neighbor who'd go on these fishing trips once or twice a month," he explained, shaking out a fleece blanket. "After my dad left, I think he felt sorry for me, you know, not having a dad around. He used to take me fishing every once in awhile."

"You know how to fish, too?"

"Yup. And for the record, this is hardly camping." The bed was made, so he gestured for her to climb in and join him. "When we're sleeping on the side of a mountain, with nothing but stars above us, *then* we'll be camping."

"Without a tent?" Samantha looked at him like he'd lost his mind. "That's insane."

"I'm telling you, there is nothing like it. It's not quite warm enough for backpacking, but this summer we'll definitely have to take a trip to the Sierras. Imagine hiking up into the mountains with nothing but a backpack. You'd be amazed how little you need to actually survive. It will totally humble you."

"I don't know, that sounds a little intense. I'm the suburban princess, remember? I'm still getting used to all this outdoorsy stuff."

"You gotta try it at least once," he insisted. "If you don't like it, we don't have to do it again." He smiled at her knowingly. "But you'll love it."

Samantha noticed the ease with which Tony threw around the words "we" and "us." He was constantly making plans for the future, as if a future for them was an absolute certainty. While she was starting to long for the same thing, she wished she had a fraction of his confidence. All she saw was a road littered with obstacles.

Tony picked up his guitar and strummed the opening chords to Bob Marley's "Redemption Song." "Do you sing?" he asked.

"In the car. In the shower. But never in front of other people."

"Sing for me. I bet you have a beautiful voice."

Samantha leaned back and drew her knees to her chest. "Nope, not gonna happen."

Tony started the verse himself. *"Emancipate yourself from mental slavery, none but ourselves can free our minds. Have no fear for atomic energy, cause none of them can stop the time."* He turned his eyes on her. *"Won't you help me sing? These songs of freedom. Cause all I ever have. Redemption song."*

"Your turn," he said, continuing to strum the familiar chords.

Samantha shook her head, stunned into speechlessness by the raw talent she witnessed. She knew Tony was musically inclined, but had no idea he could sing as well. There was nothing more romantic than a candlelight serenade by a beautiful man. There was also nothing sexier.

"Stop," she said.

Tony stopped playing, eyes lifting to meet hers. "What's the matter?"

"You just have to stop." She shifted uncomfortably. The

walls of the van started to close in on her, a tiny metal box filled with smoldering embers about to spontaneously combust.

Silence filled the air between them as Samantha tried to regulate her blood pressure. Her heart was racing, desire coursing through her veins. Tony didn't help matters by fixing her with an intense stare, his eyes filled with longing and lust.

He laid the guitar across his lap. "Did I do something wrong?"

Samantha released an exasperated sigh. "We're supposed to be doing platonic."

"This is platonic."

"Is it?"

Tony rested his head against one of the fogged-up windows. He knew what she was talking about. The connection between them was ballooning to epic proportions with each passing minute. But instead of quenching the fire, he was fanning the flames of forbidden love. He couldn't help it — everything was so much better when she was around. "I'm not trying to seduce you," he responded.

"I know you're not. But we agreed to be friends first, and all this…" she made a sweeping gesture with her hand, "makes it kinda hard."

"Yeah, it's definitely kinda hard," Tony joked, unable to resist the double entendre.

She threw a pillow at him. "You're impossible. I'm trying

to be serious here. We need to bring it down a notch before we do something we regret."

Tony set his guitar aside. "Alright, maybe we should call it a night then."

Samantha glanced nervously at their sleeping surface, barely larger than a twin bed. What had she gotten herself into?

Reading her mind, he said, "Don't worry, I promise I'll behave."

Samantha settled in beside him as he blew out the candles. They plunged into darkness once again. "Goodnight Samantha."

"Goodnight."

They lay shoulder to shoulder under the large blanket, barely touching. After a while, Tony's breathing slowed, and she assumed he had fallen asleep. Samantha opened her eyes in the darkness. She couldn't sleep. Painfully aware of his presence, the distance between them—though necessary—felt unnatural. She couldn't deny how at peace she felt when she was with him, and the strong feeling of destiny at work. But connection notwithstanding, she was still lying in bed with someone else's man, and that was wrong. Why was it so easy for them to forget Angela existed?

Samantha tossed and turned for almost an hour, agonizing about things over which she had no control. Restless and tormented, she didn't know if she'd ever be able to fall asleep when she felt Tony reach for her. Without saying a word, he pulled her into spooning position, the curves of her body fitting perfectly against his, as if poured into a mold made especially for her. It was going to take every ounce of willpower she had to make it through this night.

Chapter Seven

Samantha felt the warmth of the morning sun on her cheek, and before she could open her eyes, the soothing hum of the river reminded her she was not at home. As she began to stir, the arm around her waist tightened and drew her closer. Tony's arm. Awash in a fresh wave of guilt, she forced herself to sit up, tearing away from his embrace.

Samantha's sudden withdrawal wrenched Tony from the dream he was having. He opened his eyes and found Samantha peering out the window at the thick blanket of trees, a long strand of hair wrapped tightly around her index finger. "Good morning," he said.

"Morning."

"How'd you sleep?"

"Good. You?"

"Great. I had a pretty intense dream though."

"About what?"

Tony smiled. "I'll tell you over breakfast."

They packed up and headed back toward Highway One

in search of food. In the light of day, Samantha was able to fully appreciate the beauty of the area. Dense, towering redwoods surrounded them, the sun just barely peeking through. The road marked a crooked path through the trees, with towering mountain peaks on the left, and the Big Sur River to the right. Tony knew the area well, and within minutes they were pulling into a parking spot in front of the Big Sur River Inn.

They were quickly seated near the massive stone fireplace in the lodge's crowded restaurant. After ordering breakfast and two cups of coffee, Tony proceeded to describe his dream.

"I was being held hostage in a German prison…" he began, his voice dropping to a low conspiratorial whisper. Any time he told a story, he performed it like he was on stage at a spoken word open mic. Sometimes she wondered if he'd missed his calling.

"Sayid from *Lost* was there," he continued. "He was the leader of the *Gestapo*. They were trying to get information out of me, information I didn't have. After being tortured and knocked around a bit, I was sure they were going to kill me. Sayid had a knife to my throat, and I could feel the blade cutting into my flesh. But before he could finish the job, there was a massive earthquake, and the roof collapsed. I was buried alive."

Samantha added a generous amount of cream and sugar to her coffee. "You call that a dream? More like a nightmare."

"There's more. I was buried under all this concrete and rubble, completely unable to move, when I hear a rumbling in the distance, getting closer and closer, louder and louder. Suddenly, there's another cave-in, then a blinding white light. I figure I've died and gone to heaven, when I see this hand reaching for me. I grab the hand, and am pulled toward the light, which turns out to be the headlight of a large spaceship."

And she thought *she* had an overactive imagination. "Okay."

"Once I get settled in the cockpit of the ship, I look to my left and discover that you're the pilot. You saved me, Samantha."

Shivers ran up her spine. "I saved you, huh?"

"Yes. And then we flew off to a galaxy far, far away."

Samantha blushed. "Sounds lovely." How was she supposed to process this unsolicited glimpse into his psyche? He was playing with fire and asking her to provide the gasoline.

Thankfully the waitress arrived with their orders, and since they were both starving, they attacked their food in silence. The large portions disappeared quickly, Samantha finishing first. She sat back satisfied, rubbing her belly. "That was delicious."

Tony surveyed the empty plate in front of her. "I can't even tell you how sexy that is."

Samantha felt the heat in her face again. "What?"

"That you cleaned your plate like that. Angela barely eats.

She just picks at her food and freaks out about calories. It's pretty bad."

"Like eating disorder bad?"

"Sometimes I wonder. She doesn't make herself throw up or anything, but she is definitely preoccupied with her weight. Her mom, before she up and left, did a real number on her self-esteem."

Samantha took a sip of her coffee. "I don't get it. You seem so anti-drama. How'd you end up with someone with so much baggage?"

Tony signaled for the check. "She wasn't always like this. Or maybe she was and I just didn't notice. It's gotten a lot worse since I came up here for school though. Me leaving really brought out her clingy, insecure side." He paused. "We've been having problems."

"I'm sorry to hear that."

Tony glanced down at the bill the waitress had brought. "No you're not."

Samantha opened her mouth to defend herself, then sat back and closed it. Why bother with denials—he could obviously see right through her. She fumbled with the clasp on her wallet. "What's the damage?"

"Don't worry about it, this is my treat."

Samantha went for the bill, and he snatched it out of her reach. "But you got dinner yesterday," she argued.

"Yes I did, and I'll probably get dinner tonight as well. It's your reward for being such wonderful company. You just focus on enjoying yourself."

And enjoy herself she did. The next stop was Limekiln State Park, about twenty miles south of Big Sur. After loading up their backpacks with the necessary provisions, they set off into the forest, hiking alongside Limekiln creek as it meandered through the canyon. The water was waist deep in some parts, tumbling over large boulders to form mini-waterfalls in others. They crossed the creek several times during the hike, treading gingerly on makeshift bridges made from rocks and fallen tree limbs. Samantha felt like Indiana Jones as she hopped from log to boulder as whitewater rushed beneath her. One misstep and she would be very, very wet.

The deeper into the woods they went, the farther they got from their problems, until once again they were transported to that magical place where they were the only two people who existed. The natural beauty was breathtaking, and Samantha was mesmerized by the sights and sounds of Mother Nature at her finest and most pristine. She didn't think the scenery could get any more picturesque, until they came upon the silver cascade of Limekiln Falls stretching above them.

Samantha stood at the foot of the waterfall and looked up at over 100 feet of water pouring down the side of the mountain. She'd never seen a waterfall up close before, and was transfixed.

"You keep doing this," she yelled over the roar of rushing water.

"Doing what?"

She tore her gaze away from the falls long enough to capture his eyes. "Showing me things I've never seen before."

And this is just the beginning, he thought. He set his bag down on some flat boulders alongside the river. "I was thinking we could hang out here for awhile and study. We've got a few more hours of daylight left before we have to head back."

"You're serious about doing homework out here?"

"Of course. The last thing I want is to be branded as a bad influence. Then you won't want to hang with me anymore."

"I don't think you need to worry about that," Samantha mumbled under her breath.

Tony pulled out his Nonverbal Communication reader and she followed suit, reaching for her Sociology of Emotions textbook and trusty pink highlighter. They read quietly for almost an hour as the sun rose high into the afternoon sky. As the air around them grew warmer, Tony was unable to resist the temptation of the cool water that beckoned. He set his reading aside. "Break time."

Samantha looked up, wiping beads of sweat from her forehead. She was surprised to find he'd removed his shirt and was slipping out of his pants. "What are you doing?" she asked, averting her eyes.

"Going for a swim."

"Really?" She surveyed the surrounding area. With the exception of an occasional hiker, they were completely alone. The thought of taking a dip in the clear, cool river sounded heavenly. "I don't have a swimsuit."

"So?"

She folded her arms across her chest. "Sorry, buddy, there is no way you're talking me into going skinny-dipping."

"Of course not," he said, holding back a naughty smile. The thought had definitely crossed his mind somewhere between the parking lot and the falls. "You're wearing a bra and underwear, right?"

"Yeah, but…"

"What are you waiting for then?" He slipped off the rock into the river. Dunking his head underwater, he shook his head of curls as he resurfaced. "Feels good!"

Samantha didn't need much more convincing. Stripping down to her bra and panties, which were thankfully black and non-transparent, she joined him in the water. Their laughter echoed off the canyon walls as they frolicked like school kids, splashing around in the mountain pool. After they were done with their swim, they laid out on the rocks, drying off in the hot sun. Every muscle relaxed as all remnants of stress and tension left her body. She had truly underestimated the healing powers of nature.

They camped on the beach that night, telling stories by starlight as the waves crashed against the shore, tracing their dreams in the sand. Somewhere along the way, all of her walls came down, her vulnerabilities cast aside as she invited him into previously unexplored corners of her heart. Tony really felt like the missing piece to her soul. She'd never felt so in sync with another human being, and with each passing moment felt herself falling for him more and more. Why did he have to have a girlfriend?

Chapter Eight

"That's it, I'm calling the cops," Faby proclaimed, for the fifth time that morning. She was pacing the floor in the living room, wearing a hole in the rug as Gabe and her boyfriend Carlos faced off in a game of NBA Live.

"I'm sure she's fine," Carlos replied, accustomed to his girlfriend's overreactions. For some reason, Faby seemed happiest when the lives of those around her were in chaos; it gave her the perfect opportunity to swoop in and save the day. She got that from her mother, the original Mrs. Fix It. Carlos cursed as Gabe sank another 3-pointer, putting him up by fifteen.

"It's been *two days*," Faby continued, refusing to be brushed aside. "Gabe and I asked her to call if she wasn't going to come home. What if something happened? We can't just sit here and do nothing."

Gabe looked at the clock again. He wasn't one to jump to conclusions, but for once, Faby's concerns were warranted.

Samantha was the responsible one in the house—you could set your watch by the girl's routine. She wasn't the type to just take off or flake. When she missed a study group meeting the night before, her absence set Gabe's worry-meter on high alert. But he wasn't trying to get the cops involved. He hated cops. "Just give her one more hour."

"You've been saying that since breakfast! Her shift at the coffee shop starts in an hour. Provide me with one logical explanation for why she'd disappear without—"

The front door opened and Samantha walked in. She froze in place as all eyes trained on her like heat-seeking missiles. "What?"

"Where have you been?" Faby demanded. Momentarily relieved to see her friend alive and well, she rushed over to her. "I don't know whether to hug you or hit you."

"I'd think twice before proceeding with the latter," Samantha warned. "I'm sorry I didn't call, but there was zero cell reception where we were at."

"We?" Faby asked. "Were you with that guy with the girlfriend?"

Samantha narrowed her eyes. "His name is Tony."

"Whatever. You didn't…"

"No Faby," Samantha said loudly, so as not to be misunderstood. "We did not have sex." She ignored the disbelieving smirks that passed between Gabe and Carlos. "I told you, it's not about that."

"So what *were* you doing for two days? Two days, Sam! Put yourself in my shoes—how would you feel if I disappeared for two freakin' days."

Samantha hung her head. "I said I was sorry. We were camping in Big Sur, totally off the grid."

"You were camping?" Gabe asked. "In the middle of the week, two days before a midterm?"

"I had my books with me—we studied. You'd be amazed how much easier it is to concentrate out in nature. No phones, no TV, no distractions. I got all my reading done."

Gabe took a moment to examine Samantha more closely. She didn't have a drop of make-up on, but the glow emanating from her sun-kissed cheeks was more alluring than any shade of blush. Her windswept hair—which she usually wore pulled back in a bun—was loose and free, wild curls framing her face. She definitely looked like someone who had just spent two days in the woods. Gabe came from a long line of hunters and outdoorsmen, and could relate to the aura of serenity radiating off his friend. It was amazing what a little fresh air could do. "Where did you go?"

"Limekiln Falls."

"Nice." Gabe turned back to the video game. "Next time, call."

Samantha started toward her room with Faby hot on her

heels. "I'm not done with you yet."

"Of course you're not," Samantha muttered. She needed a hot shower, not a lecture. "But make it quick, cause I gotta clean up and get to work."

As Samantha unpacked her bag, Faby sat down on the edge of the bed and studied her roommate. A dreamy expression softened Samantha's usually stoic features as she hummed a melody Faby had never heard before. A change had definitely come over her, but Faby didn't think it had anything to do with spending quality time with Mother Nature. "You're falling for him, aren't you?"

"I told you, we're just friends."

"You didn't answer the question."

"He has a girlfriend, Fab."

"You're still not answering the question."

"I don't know how to answer your question. It's not a matter of 'falling.' There is this unexplainable connection between us, like I've known him all my life. Yes, I'm attracted to him—he is an incredible human being. But it doesn't go any further than friendship until he's free from his relationship. Until then, we're just kickin' it, I swear."

Faby stared at her, stunned. Samantha actually lit up when she talked about the guy. "Wow, you've got it bad."

Samantha sighed and turned away. "You know what? Forget I said anything."

Faby couldn't say she was in full support of Samantha moving forward with this Tony person, but she had a hard time disapproving of anything that put a smile like that on her friend's face. This was a situation that needed to be monitored very closely. "I want to meet him."

"You do?"

"Yes. That way I'll know whose ass to kick if anything happens to you."

Samantha laughed. "Nothing is going to happen to me." She grabbed a towel and headed for the bathroom.

Faby watched Samantha depart, a noticeable spring in her step. *But something already has…*

Chapter Nine

*T*ony unloaded his bus and sat down on the front porch to smoke. Most of his housemates were out enjoying the picture-perfect Santa Cruz weather, and the three-story Victorian he called home was quiet and deserted. Tony appreciated the time alone with his thoughts, the majority of them focused on Samantha. The girl was like a breath of fresh air—smart, but not pretentious, strong-willed but incredibly sweet. She was also drop-dead gorgeous, with no idea how powerfully her beauty affected others. Simultaneously down to earth and out of this world, Samantha was everything he wanted in a woman, and he wanted her around all the time. They'd been apart less than an hour and he was already going through withdrawal.

His roommate's light blue Honda pulled into the drive. Damion, Tony's best friend since childhood, was a graduate student in the History of Consciousness program, and the primary reason Tony had chosen to continue his education at UCSC. A move that had turned out to be nothing short of life-altering.

Damion came up the front walk, a case of beer under his arm. He stopped short when he saw Tony on the porch. "Where you been man? Your lady's been blowin' up the phones looking for you."

"I headed down to Big Sur." He put out his cigarette. "With Samantha."

The involuntary arch of Damion's eyebrow signified his amusement. "Oh really. You two have fun?"

"Not that much fun," Tony replied, ignoring Damion's smirk. "I'm not trying to cheat on my girlfriend."

Damion took a seat beside him. "Let me tell you a little something about women." He cracked open a beer and passed it to Tony, then opened one for himself. "You ran off and spent two *nights* with another woman. Whether you messed with her or not, Angela is gonna call it cheating, so you might as well be gettin' some." He took a swig. "Trust me, your ass is gonna be lit up regardless."

"This isn't about sex, man. I think I'm falling in love with her."

Damion couldn't conceal his shock and surprise. He had tried several times to expose Tony to a world beyond Angela, but he'd never taken the bait. "Like that, huh?"

"Like nothing I've ever felt before."

The men sipped their beer in silence. Further explanation wasn't necessary—Tony had said it all.

After a few minutes, Damion asked, "So, what's the problem?"

Tony sighed. "I love Angela."

"Obviously not that much if you're fallin' in love with other people." Tony shot him a nasty look. "What? I'm just sayin'."

"I don't want to hurt anyone."

"Yeah, good luck with that, Tone."

The house phone rang. Damion grabbed the case of beer and stood up. "Twenty bucks says that's Angela. You got this, or are you going to continue this distressing pattern of conflict avoidance?"

Tony followed him inside. Damion's Psychology degree really got on his nerves sometimes. "I got it." He reached the phone just before the machine picked up. "Hello."

"Where have you been? Did you get any of my messages?" Angela was furious. She hated that Tony was attending college so far away, amidst swarms of horny, young women. Not being able to get a hold of him for days at a time did nothing to ease her anxiety.

"I went camping for a few days, spur of the moment thing."

"In the middle of the week? Who were you with?"

"My friend Sam. I needed a break."

Naturally, it didn't occur to Angela that Sam might be a woman. "I thought you were too busy to take breaks. Why didn't you just come home? I miss you, baby. I haven't seen you in over a month."

Tony was fresh out of excuses. Even before Samantha

came into the picture, he had been avoiding the emotionally draining trips back home. All they did was fight these days. "The quarter will be over in a few months, then I'll be home for good. It's just really hectic right now."

"That's bullshit," Angela spat, days worth of anger spilling forth. "I'm just not a priority to you. You'd rather spend your free time chasing tail than with the woman you supposedly love."

"My priority is to pass all my classes so I can get this degree," Tony fired back. "The quicker I finish school, the sooner I get to come home. I'd think you'd be on board with that."

Angela felt the tears well up in her eyes. It had been an emotional week, and she needed Tony so bad. All she wanted was to hear his voice and feel his arms around her, but Tony was acting so cold and distant that he was no comfort at all. "It's so hard being down here by myself. I have no one to talk to."

"What about CeCe and Reina?"

"They don't have time for me now that they have kids and boyfriends. Please, babe, I really need to see you. I can call in sick next Friday, take a long weekend…"

The desperation in her voice wasn't falling on deaf ears, but Santa Cruz was Tony's sacred, Angela-free, space. He wanted, needed, for it to stay that way. "I told you, there really isn't room here in the house. Damion and I share a tiny room—we'd have no privacy. Besides, I have midterms next week, and then I'll be tied up with daily rehearsals for this play. I'd hate to have you come all the way up here, then have to neglect you."

"Yeah, I guess it's much easier to neglect me from a distance."

"Angela..."

Angela had a lot of experience with the inattention that preceded abandonment. Her father left before she was born without so much as a forwarding address, and then when she was fourteen, she was dropped on her grandparent's doorstep by a mother who decided to choose crack-cocaine and a drug-dealer boyfriend over her only child. Angela's grandparents, their racism firmly entrenched, never forgot the Black man who corrupted their only daughter with drugs, and promptly disowned Angela when she brought her own Black boyfriend home to meet them. Everyone she'd ever loved had abandoned her—she didn't know why she expected Tony to be any different. "Everyone leaves," she mumbled, her voice thick with self-pity. "I know it's just a matter of time before you leave, too."

"You should call Reina and plan a girl's night out," Tony suggested. "Sitting home alone isn't good for you."

She pretended not to hear him. "Ever since you left I've been so lonely. I don't have *anyone.*"

Guilt stabbed at his heart. Guilt for what he'd already

done, guilt over what he was going to do. This was the precise reason he avoided Angela's phone calls—her depression was fucking contagious. "It'll be alright, Ange, just hang in there."

Tony listened to her sob and complain for another hour before he was able to get off the phone. All she did these days was bring him down—he couldn't live like this anymore. He had to get out. But how?

Chapter Ten

Samantha awoke to a soft knock on her door. "I'm sleeping!" she yelled, pulling the covers over her head. Gabe tossed the cordless onto her bed. "Phone's for you."

"Who is it?"

"I don't know. Some guy." He shut the door behind him.

Samantha picked up the phone. There was only one guy she wanted to talk to right now. "Hello?"

"Miss me yet?"

A smile spread across Samantha's face. She was thankful Tony wasn't in the room to witness his effect on her. "We haven't been apart long enough for me to miss you."

"Says who? I started missing you as soon as I pulled away from your house."

Samantha noticed a change in Tony's voice. "What's the matter?"

Tony was quiet for a moment. "I just got off the phone with Angela."

"Oh." Samantha calmed the butterflies in her stomach

and put on her friend cap. "How'd that go?"

"Terrible. She is so fragile, Sam. I don't know how I'm going to break up with her."

Samantha tried to suppress the inappropriate delight that burst forth upon hearing this news. "You've decided to break up with her?"

"After the past few days we've had, I don't see any other option. I want to be with you, Samantha."

The nervous butterfly feeling returned. "I want to be with you, too."

"I'm glad the feeling is mutual."

Me, too, she thought.

"My current relationship is so unhealthy," he continued. "You helped me see that. You've opened my eyes to a world of possibilities I'd never imagined. If you hadn't come along, who knows how long I would have stayed."

While Tony meant for his words to be comforting, they actually sent up a red flag in Samantha's mind. She didn't like being cast as a homewrecker. "Wait, are you saying that if we hadn't met, you would have stayed with Angela? Even though you're not happy?"

"Hard to say. It's… complicated."

Samantha sat up in bed and crossed her legs. "You keep saying that. Uncomplicate it for me—what kind of hold does this woman have on you?"

Tony pondered her question for a minute. "I'm... I'm afraid of turning into my father."

The pain propelling Tony's statement came across the phone line loud and clear. "How so?"

"Angela is a lot like my mom," he explained. "A wonderful, caring woman, but pretty helpless on her own. Angela relies on me for everything, just like my mom relied on pops for everything. He was her world, and when he left us, my mother was devastated. Completely wrecked. Even though she still had me and my sister, she pretty much lost the will to live.

"I was ten years old when my dad left, and all of a sudden I had to step up and be the man of the house. Two years later, my father remarried, and that really pushed her over the edge. She was on and off antidepressants until she passed away. The doctors were never able to give me a straight answer about what killed her, but in my mind, I always figured she died of a broken heart."

Samantha wiped tears from her cheeks. Tony had never revealed the circumstances surrounding his mother's death, and her heart was breaking for him. "How old were you when she passed?"

"Twenty. It was the worst year of my life. For so long I blamed myself, like maybe if I'd tried harder I could have saved her. I was inconsolable. My sister was away at school on the East Coast when this all went down, and Angela was the only person who could reach me. She's an orphan as well, so she understood what I was going through. I grabbed a hold of her when I was drowning, and have been holding on ever since."

"I'm glad you had her to lean on."

"Me, too. I've made peace with my mother's passing, but I couldn't live with myself if I did to Angela what my dad did to my mom. She doesn't deserve that." He paused. "That's why I stay."

Samantha exhaled slowly. She was starting to see why Tony was so conflicted. "I understand."

"You do?"

"I do. I don't agree that it's your responsibility to take care of Angela, any more than I think it was your responsibility to save your mother, but I realize that's really easy for me to say as an outsider. I have no frame of reference for the situation you're in, so I can't even imagine how hard this must be for you."

Tony felt a release as he vented his innermost thoughts and fears to a sympathetic ear. It had been years since he'd confided in a woman other than Angela, and the heavy weight he'd been carrying around somehow felt lighter. "I hope this doesn't change things," he said.

"Why would it change things?"

"I've got a lot of baggage."

Samantha laughed. "Come on, we all have baggage. I've got a ton of it."

"You do? Like what?"

"Well, for starters, I'm somewhat of a control-freak, with a mild case of OCD."

It was Tony's turn to laugh. "Really? I hadn't noticed."

"Ha, ha. I also have an intense fear of crowds and a tendency, when upset, to drink too much."

Tony couldn't help but smile. Her laundry list of pathologies only made her more endearing. "Well, faults and all, I think you're pretty damn fantastic. I only wish we had met under different circumstances, so we could flow with what's happening between us. This doesn't seem fair to you. You deserve so much better."

"Don't worry about me," Samantha assured him. "I'm a big girl—I can handle a little delayed gratification. But I don't want to be the reason you leave Angela. I'll be here to support you in any way I can, but the decision to leave has to be yours and yours alone."

"I understand."

"But just so you know," Samantha added. "I'm not going anywhere."

"Neither am I, Sam. Neither am I…"

Chapter Eleven

*S*amantha was sandwiched between her housemates in the packed-to-capacity auditorium, waiting for the lights to go down. Soon the Rainbow Theater—UCSC's multicultural acting troupe—would be presenting a collection of short plays and skits written, directed, and performed by students of color. The highly anticipated event was a welcome splash of culture on a lily-white liberal landscape, and the community had come out in full force for opening night.

Samantha flipped through the program. Many of her friends and classmates were involved in this year's production. Her eyes scanned the page until she found Tony's name. One of his housemates, a brilliant Venezuelan siren named Charla, had written and directed one of the shorts. Despite Tony's protests that he had no desire to be on stage, Charla insisted on casting him in the lead role. Tonight was his big acting debut, and Samantha was excited to see his performance.

Over the past few weeks, Tony and Samantha's friendship had blossomed like a field of wildflowers after a spring rain.

Despite their busy schedules, they managed to see each other every day, checking in not out of obligation, but because they genuinely cared about what was going on in the other's life. They met for lunch or coffee, to smoke or study. Tony always seemed to know exactly how to track her down, and quickly became a permanent fixture in Samantha's daily routine, seamlessly filling the pockets of loneliness and empty spaces.

Samantha glanced at her watch. Fifteen minutes past show time, and grips and technicians were still running around tending to last minute details. The whole event was clearly running on people of color time—half the audience had yet to take their seats.

Faby noticed Samantha's foot tapping out a staccato beat. "What is your problem? You're acting as if you're the one about to take the stage. I'm sure your man will be fine."

"He is not my man," Samantha hissed, glancing around to see if anyone had heard. On top of the nerves she was feeling on Tony's behalf, she was also uneasy about the fact that Faby and Gabe would be meeting Tony for the first time after the show. Though she'd never admit it, their approval meant a lot to her.

"Which play is he in?" Gabe asked, thumbing through the program. Preferring sports to theater, he usually skipped out on the artsy, thespian stuff.

"The first one," Samantha answered. She was saved from

further inquisition when the room finally darkened and the emcee took the stage.

Damion's rich voice boomed through the speaker system. "Wassup my peoples—how is everyone feeling tonight?" The crowd erupted in a chorus of whoops, hollering, and applause. Damion beamed at the sight before him, a sea of friendly faces, his people, coming together to be educated and entertained. "On behalf of Rainbow Theater, I would like to welcome you to our 13th annual production. We've got a great show lined up, and hope you leave tonight having laughed, cried, and maybe even learned something. First up is a short that was written and directed by one of Rainbow's own, Ms. Charla Santirosa." Another wave of applause from the crowd. "I see you all are familiar with Charla's work. Well, without further ado, let's get to the goods. Ladies and gentleman, I introduce to you the *Modern Day Drifter.*"

The curtain rose and there stood Tony, clad in dusty blue jeans, a white t-shirt, and an ankle-length, brown, leather trench coat. He had grown out his facial hair for the role, and a five o'clock shadow and scruffy goatee adorned his usually clean-shaven face. Equal parts rugged and ethereal, he gazed out at the audience contemptuously, fully embodying the play's anti-hero, a lost man in search of his soul. He launched into his opening monologue, a scathing critique of society's descent into materialism and apathy.

"I can go for days without looking another man in the eye. I don't see the need anymore—everyone's dead inside. Dead people walking and talking, but not feeling or knowing. They surround themselves with things, pretty things, the shine blinding them to life. Life that will go on, whether they're participating or not."

He stalked back and forth across the stage, casting accusatory glances at members of the audience, as if he could see through every facade they attempted to project. Those who were not terribly uncomfortable were totally transfixed. Several scenes unfolded on stage beside him while he provided searing narrative commentary. A picture-perfect Buppy couple he tagged as hopelessly codependent. A group of student activists he dubbed as privileged and pretending. The married father of four soliciting prostitutes to help pass the time during those lengthy business trips. Tony called everyone out on their shit.

His humor and charisma transmitted well in this medium, and though he had no theater background whatsoever, he was a natural. By the final act, he had the audience eating out of the palm of his hand, the women especially. When he closed his final scene, Samantha could have sworn she heard a collective sigh rise up from the crowd. Their eyes locked as he lined up with the rest of the cast to take his final bow, a smile tugging at the corner of his mouth, breaking character for the first time. Samantha blushed bright red at his acknowledgement of her, starstruck by the sight of him up on stage, larger than life.

As the lights came on and the crowd broke for intermission, Faby turned to Samantha, stars in her eyes as well. "Girl, I totally get it."

***

Samantha welcomed the cool night air against her flushed skin as the crowd spilled onto the patio. The buzz around her was overwhelmingly positive—*Modern Day Drifter* was a hit.

Tony was beyond captivating, and seeing him up there in the spotlight, his aura magnified by a million underneath the stage lights, was making it difficult to maintain a healthy level of platonic detachment. Overcome with a desire that bordered on the unbearable, she was a puddle of lust and inappropriate thoughts. She needed to get herself under control.

Sticking a cigarette in her mouth, she rummaged around in her purse for fire. "Faby, do you have a light?"

A flicker of a flame appeared in front of her. She lifted her head to find Tony staring down at her, still in costume. He looked so impossibly sexy that her cigarette almost fell to the ground as her mouth hung open.

She grabbed her cigarette without lighting it. "Hey."

"Hey."

They stared at each other, longing to collapse into a warm embrace, but painfully aware of the many pairs of eyes watching them.

"You were great," Samantha managed finally.

"You think?" Tony had received a steady stream of accolades since stepping off-stage, but he might as well have been performing for an audience of one. Samantha's opinion was the only one that mattered.

"Yeah, it was great," Samantha repeated lamely. Why couldn't she think of anything more interesting to say?

Faby, who had been standing behind her throughout the awkward exchange, cleared her throat loudly. "I'd love a chance to tell Tony how great he was."

Samantha stepped to the side, allowing Faby to push forward. "I'm sorry. Tony, this is Faby."

"Nice to finally meet you," Faby said, extending her hand.

"Likewise," Tony said.

"Well, I have to agree with my roommate. Your performance was positively…" Faby cut her eyes at Sam. "Mesmerizing."

"Wow, I imagined you'd be a much tougher critic," Tony said with a wink. "But really, all props go to Charla. She wrote the words—all I did was speak them."

"And modest, too," Faby noted. "Now if only you could master the use of modern communication devices."

Tony laughed. "Yeah, I'm sorry our little camping adventure worried you so much. Next time I'll make sure we check in more regularly."

"Next time, huh?"

"This is my other housemate Gabe," Samantha cut in. She didn't need Faby any more in her business than she already was.

"Wassup man," Tony said with a nod.

"Good to meet ya."

"We're hosting the after-party at our house later tonight," Tony said. "You guys should come by."

"Wouldn't miss it," Faby said.

Tony glanced at Sam expectantly. "What about you Miss Samantha? Are you going to grace us with your presence this evening?"

Samantha couldn't repress a smile. Who was she kidding —there was nowhere else she'd rather be. "I think I could be persuaded to make an appearance."

"Excellent." He noticed Damion by the stage entrance, waving frantically. "I should get going—there's a ton of stuff I gotta help with backstage. But I will definitely see you all later. Enjoy the rest of the show." He turned and jogged toward the door. Samantha's eyes followed until he disappeared backstage and she could finally breathe again.

Samantha was drowning in lust, a river of longing coursing through her veins. They'd agreed to wait to be together until he resolved his situation, but it was getting increasingly difficult to be patient. How long was she going to be able to hold back? She wanted him. Badly. More than she'd wanted anything in her entire life.

Chapter Twelve

*T*he party was in full swing by the time Samantha and company arrived. The distinctive bump of hip-hop echoed down the street, a lighthouse of sound guiding party-seekers toward the evening's destination for debauchery. Groups of people lined the narrow walkway leading up to the front door, and since Faby knew everyone, it took them forever to get inside. Once they crossed the threshold, they were swept up in a wave of undulating bodies that quickly moved them into the epicenter of festivities.

With the exception of the DJ's crates and turntables set up in the far corner, the two large rooms that made up the first floor had been cleared of all furniture. The house was packed, everyone moving and grooving to the beat amidst a thick fog of marijuana smoke. As they navigated the sea of sweaty bodies, Samantha scanned the dark, crowded room for Tony. Much to her disappointment, he was nowhere to be found.

Faby pulled Carlos toward the center of the dance floor, while Samantha and Gabe pushed through to the fringes so they could engage in their favorite party pastime—people-watching. Gabe was not a fan of house parties, but he could always find a few hours of entertainment watching scantily clad co-eds shake their bon bons as alcohol gradually loosened their clothes and inhibitions. The current collection of females didn't disappoint—the warm spring evening had all the girls dressed down, and he was awash in a sea of backless tank-tops and daisy dukes. Gabe considered himself a connoisseur of the female form, and his eyes shamelessly followed each tight and toned ass that passed in front of him, his head bobbing in approval at the wide selection of outfits that required the wearers to go bra-less. There were erect nipples everywhere. "Excellent party," he mused.

As usual, the male eye candy was not nearly as plentiful or drool-inducing. Samantha was already over it and plotting her escape. "Do you see Tony anywhere? I can't see shit without my glasses."

"No, but I do see that fine little Filipina from my Race and Ethnicity section. You mind?"

Samantha waved him away. "Go on and get your mack on. I'm good."

Gabe trotted off to handle his business, while Samantha wandered around in search of Tony. The house was filled with familiar faces, but she had no desire to engage anyone in conversation. She just smiled politely and kept moving, ignoring the drunken leers and weak pick-up lines that flew at her from all directions. It never ceased to amaze her that men who were supposed to be so educated and enlightened still struggled with basic concepts like respecting a woman's personal space.

She felt someone grab her ass, and as she turned to check the offender, wet lips covered hers in a sloppy, uninvited kiss. Stunned, she pushed the assailant away. "What do you think you're doing?"

The nameless, blond surfer boy stared back at her, eyes bloodshot, the stench of tequila rolling off his tongue like noxious fumes. "I missed those lips," he slurred, leaning in for another kiss.

Samantha held him at arm's length—what had she been thinking going home with this guy? "Stop it," she stated firmly. "I'm not interested in an encore of our last meeting."

He stared right through her, the words falling on deaf ears. He obviously didn't have much experience with rejection. "Don't be mad—I would have called, but you didn't leave your number." He backed her up against the wall. "I was hoping I'd run into you again. Our night together was so hot, baby."

Samantha pushed him away again. "I am not your baby." She turned to leave, and he grabbed her wrist. "Let go of me."

Tony suddenly appeared behind surfer boy, his face twisted into a menacing scowl. Samantha wasn't aware his face could make such a hideous expression. "Is there a problem here?"

Before she could respond, Gabe appeared at her side, echoing Tony's sentiments. "Is there a problem here?"

Surfer boy released Samantha's arm, fear shining in his eyes. Both Gabe and Tony looked like they would drop him without a second thought. "No problem," he stammered, attempting to maintain some kind of macho posturing. "We were just talking." He turned to Samantha. "Call off the dogs, will ya?"

"The only dog I see here is you," Samantha spat. Surfer boy, finally getting the hint, retreated without so much as a backward glance. She turned to her would-be heroes. "While I appreciate the concern, I'm a grown woman. I don't need rescuing."

"Homeboy didn't look like he was taking no for an answer," Tony said calmly, a protective fire burning in his eyes. "I wasn't about to sit back and let some dude harass you."

"Yeah," Gabe chimed in. "What he said."

Samantha folded her arms in front of her chest. On the one hand, their chivalrous impulses were sweet. But her feminist sensibilities would not tolerate being cast as the helpless female. "I can take care of myself."

"Of course you can," the men mocked in unison. They glanced at each other in surprise, then burst out laughing.

"She's a stubborn one, ain't she?" Tony asked.

"Dude, you have no idea."

"So delighted I can give you two something to bond over," Samantha said dryly.

Tony put an arm around her. "You guys want to know the location of the secret keg?"

Gabe's eyes lit up. "There's a keg?"

Tony placed a finger over his lips and motioned for them to follow. He led them up to the third floor attic where a small group of people were kickin' back, listening to Bob Marley, and passing around a blunt. The vibe upstairs was completely different from the meat market mentality polluting the lower levels of the house. A full-size keg of Sierra Nevada sat in the corner of the room, guarded by the emcee of tonight's production, a tall, dark-skinned brotha with locks, sporting a "Free Mumia" t-shirt.

"Damion," Tony said to the kegmaster, "these are some very special friends of mine. Please make sure they get the VIP treatment."

"Sure thing," Damion replied. He poured a foam-free cup of beer and handed it to Samantha. "Welcome."

"Thanks. I'm Samantha."

Damion did a double-take, unable to hide his surprise. This pretty light-skinned girl with the magic smile was Tony's new 'friend'? No wonder homeboy was all sprung and droppin' the "L" word left and right. "*The* Samantha?" Tony shot him a cautionary glance, which Damion ignored. "So I finally get to meet the woman my boy can't seem to shut up about."

"Yeah, she goes on and on about him, too," Gabe blurted out. He lacked that social filter that prevented every random thought he had from flying out of his mouth.

A rosy glow colored Samantha's cheeks, a mixture of pride and embarrassment. "Shut up, Gabe."

Damion laughed. "Sorry, sweetheart, didn't mean to embarrass you. I just can't resist giving this guy a hard time." He slapped Tony hard on the back. "It's very nice to finally meet you."

"Likewise."

Tony ushered his guests over to the ring of sofas in the center of the room and made introductions. Tony's circle of friends was comprised mostly of graduate students, and Samantha recognized several of them as TA's for some of her classes. Samantha frequently forgot that despite his undergraduate status, Tony was five years older than her. At first she felt hopelessly young and out of place, but Tony's crew was so down-to-earth and unpretentious that the outsider feeling quickly evaporated. She appreciated their wisdom and maturity, quite the contrast to her out-of-control peers whose primary concern was who could drink who under the table. They continued to smoke and philosophize as the noise levels below rose, the crowd downstairs growing drunker and rowdier as the night wore on. Gabe eventually left to resume his search for the hottest of the half-naked hotties, but Samantha remained by Tony's side, soaking up all the knowledge being dropped by Tony and his friends.

They were an eclectic assortment of characters—artists, activists, and visionaries. Damion, Tony's best friend and wingman, was by far the most extroverted of the bunch. A master of the spoken word, Damion was impossibly smart, and he commanded everyone's attention whenever he opened his mouth. Samantha imagined he'd make a wonderful professor some day.

"That's an oversimplification," Damion argued, responding to his friend Paco's claim that money was the root of all evil. "The real problem here, the real cause of social and structural inequality, is Capitalism. Capitalism is set up to reward and promote unchecked greed. The rich cannot get richer without standing on the backs of the underclass. And who pays for their prosperity? Third world nations and the lower classes. You can't put this on one president, or even the Republican Party. Shit is built into the system. We aren't going to see lasting social change until the system—and our relationship to it—changes."

"So what do you suggest then?" Paco challenged. "Mass exodus? Conversion to Socialism? How do we take down Capitalism?"

"From the inside," Damion preached confidently. "We have to become the 'haves' in the system. And then when we've accumulated wealth and resources, we have to redistribute it in ways that benefit the good of all people, instead of using it to further our own selfish interests."

"Spoken like a true liberal," Caleb chided. Caleb, the only white male in the group, was the resident cynic. His politics were far from conservative, but he could never resist playing devil's advocate in their heated debates. Caleb believed that change could only come through conflict, so he made it his personal mission to be as confrontational as possible at all times. "Man is inherently selfish. His primary instinct is self-preservation. Your vision of a perfect world is seriously flawed in that it requires man to go against his nature."

LaDawn, a coffee-colored sista rocking an Angela Davis-type fro took issue with Caleb's observation. "*Man* may be inherently selfish, but the same cannot be said for women. Women are absolutely capable of seeing beyond their own self-interests…"

The group went around and around, the debate becoming more heated as the night wore on. Eventually, Tony got up to leave, gesturing for Samantha to follow. They made their way down to the second floor, weaving around the couples that lined the hallway in various stages of hooking up. Samantha couldn't help but wish she was one of them—after three beers, her libido was starting to kick into gear.

Tony opened a door at the end of the hall and flipped on

the light. Posters of Bob Marley and Malcolm X hung side by side on the far wall above two twin beds. The room was tiny, and with piles of books and boxes everywhere, there was barely room for the two of them to stand. Tony plopped down on his bed. "Finally, peace and quiet."

Samantha sat across from him on Damion's bed. "I thought your friends were great. They may talk a lot, but at least they're talking about things that matter. All I'm surrounded by is talk about sports, American Idol, and who's doing who."

"I know. Don't get me wrong—I love those cats. But I get weary of the intellectual masturbation. All I do is listen to these folks sit around and try to solve the world's problems from their couch. They spend so much time complaining about the need for change that they sometimes neglect the fact that real change starts within. I think that's where Caleb was going before everyone jumped all over him. We can't help anyone until we help ourselves. Folks get so caught up in the blame game, fretting over things which they can't control, that they forget that."

"Yeah, it's like Michael says—you've got to start with the man in the mirror."

"Exactly." He could always count on Samantha to know exactly where he was coming from without a lot of tedious explanation. "So, who was that guy?"

"What guy?"

"The one with his tongue down your throat."

"Oh, him." Samantha shifted uncomfortably. "He's nobody. Just a mistake I made before I knew any better."

"Look, I know I have no right to feel this way," Tony began. "But the sight of another man with his hands on you made me crazy. I wanted to knock that dude into the middle of next week."

Samantha repressed a smile. Usually jealousy turned her off, but on Tony, it was just another endearing quality. "Trust me, you have nothing to worry about. I went through a pretty bad phase earlier this year, where I was trying to fill the emptiness inside with these... encounters. I was so lonely, and I thought these men could fill the space, distract me from the ache, even if it was only temporarily."

"Because of what happened with your ex?" Tony asked.

"Yeah. Did you know I was planning to save myself for marriage?"

Tony raised an eyebrow. "Save yourself? As in your virginity?" Samantha nodded. "Wow—girls still do that?"

"Most of my friends thought I was crazy, too, but it was important to me. My older sister got pregnant when she was fifteen, and had an abortion. It changed the whole trajectory of her life. I didn't want to end up in a similar situation."

"I can understand that. So what happened?"

"I fell in love. This guy named Eric. We dated all through

Junior and Senior year and planned to stay together, even though he was going to college on the East Coast and I was coming here. He painted such a beautiful picture of our lives together that I naïvely believed he was 'the One.' On Grad night, he talked me into giving him my virginity." Samantha lowered her eyes. "And then he went away to school and cheated on me."

"Ouch. I'm sorry, Sam."

"Yeah, shit happens. Anyway, after that, I kinda swung over to the other extreme. I guess I wanted to see what I'd been missing." She shrugged. "Turns out, I wasn't missing much."

"I hear that from my female friends a lot," Tony said with a chuckle. "So what now? Still trying to fill that space?"

"No, not really. When I met you, I discovered what it felt like to be truly *connected* to another human being… It changed everything. There's only one man I can see myself being intimate with now."

Tony patted the space beside him. "Come here."

Samantha hesitated. She didn't know if close proximity was the best idea right now. She was still flush with desire after seeing him up on stage.

"What's the matter?"

Samantha shook off her lustful thoughts and joined him on the bed. "Nothing. Sorry."

Tony opened the slim wooden box on his bedside table. He pulled out a picture of himself with an older man sporting a beard so long it looked like it had been growing for decades. "This is Al," Tony explained. "I met him my first week in Santa Cruz. The man's a true nomad, just passing through town when our paths crossed. Meeting him completely changed my outlook on life."

"I remember you mentioning him before."

"Al taught me a lot of things in a short time. It was like an apprenticeship in living. We talked about my mother dying, my father leaving, everything." Tony picked up a faded picture of his parents during happier times.

Samantha gasped. The resemblance between Tony and his father was incredible. "You look just like him."

"I know." He handed her another picture of a teenage Tony with his mother and sister. "I think the fact that I was a spitting image of my pops was really hard on her." Tony blinked back the painful memories. "Anyway, Al taught me about forgiveness—how to forgive my parents, how to forgive myself. He also spoke on how important it was to nourish my soul. To figure out what made me feel alive, what made life worth living, and to surround myself with those things. He gave me this box the day he left, and to honor him and what he taught me, I use it to store symbols of life and love. Pieces of my soul."

"May I?"

Tony placed the box in her lap. "Of course."

Samantha explored the contents, moved by the trust he was exhibiting by opening his life to her so completely. She looked through all his old photos, falling in love with the little boy in the baby pictures smiling up at her. There were poems and songs he'd written; random quotes and song lyrics scribbled on scraps of paper; articles on the Caribbean torn out of travel magazines; even a Stevie Wonder CD.

Samantha held up the CD. "Stevie, huh?"

He took the CD from her and popped it into the CD player. Stevie's smooth voice filled the room. "No one puts the world into perspective like Stevie."

Samantha carefully placed the items back in the box. "There weren't any pictures of Angela in there."

Tony was shamed by her observation. "You're right. I hadn't even noticed that."

"Do you have any pictures of her?"

"Yeah, a bunch. Just not in there." He fished a photo album out of a box beside his bed and handed it to her.

Samantha flipped through the album. Lots of pictures of him with Damion, who he'd known for the better part of his life, but she had to thumb through over half the album before she found a picture of Angela. She was gorgeous. "Wow."

"Not what you expected, huh?"

"Well, I knew she was white, I just never pictured you for the blond-haired, blue-eyed type. She looks like a supermodel."

Samantha suddenly felt very inadequate. How could she compete with that?

"Angela's no supermodel," he corrected. "She's a regular girl with hang-ups and insecurities just like everyone else. Besides, true beauty comes from within—you know that."

Samantha closed the photo album. "I guess."

Always in tune where Samantha was concerned, Tony sensed her shift. Picking up his camera, he pointed it at her.

"No," she snapped, turning away. "I hate having my picture taken."

He lowered the camera to his side. "And why is that?"

"I don't know. I just do."

"Well you're going to have to make an exception for me. I need a photograph of you for the box."

Samantha blushed, desire and longing once again bubbling to the surface, begging for release. She avoided his eyes. "That's sweet, but you don't have to…"

"I know I don't have to, but you belong there. You are very much a part of my soul, Samantha. You are my future."

She looked into his eyes and saw truth and commitment shining back at her. He was her future, too, and every passing day, every shared moment of quiet intimacy like this, only confirmed it.

For the first time since finding out about Angela, Samantha felt the overpowering urge to kiss him. Knowing it was wrong, yet powerless to stop it, she closed her eyes as Tony slowly leaned forward. She felt his breath on her cheek, then his lips brushing softly against the side of her face, timidly inching closer to her mouth. Breathless with anticipation, she felt time stop—but only for a second. A loud pounding at the door snapped them both out of their spell.

"Samantha, are you in there?"

Samantha jumped off the bed, flushed and shamed. What was she doing? She threw open the door, and Faby came spilling into the room with Damion right behind her. "Hope we weren't interrupting," he said with a wicked smile.

"No, not at all," Samantha said quickly. "We were just looking at photo albums and stuff." Red-faced and flustered, she couldn't bring herself to look in Tony's direction.

"Uh huh." Faby didn't believe a word of it—you could cut the sexual tension in the room with a knife. "I think it's time for us to head home. The cops are breaking up the party."

"Oh, okay." Samantha reached for her purse. "I guess I'll talk to you tomorrow."

"Wait." Tony was staring at her with an unfiltered intensity, as if they were the only two people in the room. He handed his camera to Damion. "Will you take our picture real quick?"

Samantha's whole body responded as she was pulled into a warm embrace, Tony's hand on the small of her back, pressing her to him. Her skin was on fire in every place where their bodies touched. Thankfully, Damion was quick to snap the picture, and she was able to extricate herself from his arms before she really lost it.

"I want a copy of that pic," Samantha said, turning to leave.

"You got it."

Samantha followed Faby out, and Damion sat down, shaking his head. He'd seen something through the lens of that camera that he'd never seen before—two people who were made for each other. "You need to get down to L.A. and handle your business, before you really mess this up."

Tony stared at the ceiling. Damion was right. His self-control eroded, he no longer possessed any shreds of restraint. "I know."

"No, I don't think you do," Damion chastised. "Don't blow this dude. She's the One."

Tony let the words sink in. For the first time, he actually understood what people meant when they said that.

Chapter Thirteen

*A*s the only morning person in the house, Samantha was usually the first out of bed. Yet here it was, well after noon, and she could not will herself out from under the covers. Endless replays of the almost-kiss had kept her awake most of the night, and when she did finally drift off to sleep, she tossed and turned with lustful dreams—kissing Tony, holding Tony, making love to Tony… She had never felt this way before, and now that the sexual attraction had been engaged, she feared it would be impossible to turn off. Platonic was no longer a viable option.

She followed the aroma of freshly brewed coffee down the hallway. Faby was in the kitchen, making way more noise than usual as she slammed cupboards and banged dishes on the linoleum countertop. "What's the matter with her?" Samantha asked Gabe, who was watching cartoons on the couch.

Gabe glanced over his shoulder toward the ruckus in the kitchen. "I think she and Carlos had a fight."

"Oh. Did you have fun at the party?"

"Yeah. Tony's pretty cool, all things considered."

A large crash came from the kitchen, causing Samantha to jump. She promptly went to investigate as Gabe sat unfazed on the couch.

Samantha found Faby on her knees beside an overturned bowl of fruit. "What is going on in here?"

"I dropped the fruit," Faby muttered.

"I see." Samantha helped her scoop chunks of cantaloupe and melon into the bowl. "You okay?"

Faby dropped the bowl of soiled fruit into the sink and reached for a glass of orange juice. She finished it in one gulp, then poured another, spiking it heavily with vodka.

"Screwdrivers for breakfast, huh?" Samantha asked.

"It's been one of those days."

"In that case, fix me one too while you're at it."

The women sat down with their drinks and a plate of Faby's mouth-watering *huevos rancheros*, but neither could eat. They just sat there with long faces and heavy hearts, pushing their food around in silence. After a few minutes, Faby finished her drink and got up to make another one.

"What happened?" Samantha asked when Faby returned to the table.

"My boyfriend doesn't think I'm attractive anymore."

Samantha surveyed Faby's hourglass figure and wondered if she'd looked in the mirror lately. The girl was heavy on the curves, in all the right places, and could hold her own against any Victoria's Secret model. "What are you talking about?"

"He didn't want to have sex last night."

"Maybe he wasn't in the mood."

"Carlos is *always* in the mood. Something is wrong." Faby took another sip of her drink. "I swear to God, if he is cheating on me, I will cut his little dick off."

Samantha choked on her juice. "Let's hope it doesn't come to that."

Faby fixed Samantha with an accusatory glare. "Speaking of cheaters, you and Tony looked pretty cozy when we busted in on you last night."

"I told you, nothing happened."

"Yet."

Samantha pushed her plate away and stood up. "I'm really not in the mood for this."

Faby adjusted her tone. "Sorry, that was a low blow." She poured more vodka into Sam's glass. "Sit."

"Trust me, nothing you say can make me feel worse than I already do." Samantha dropped her head into her hands. "This situation sucks."

"What's the latest with the girlfriend?"

"He doesn't want to break up with her over the phone, so he's going to wait until he goes home after Finals."

"That's weeks away."

Samantha continued to sulk and drink. It wasn't her place to put demands on Tony—he had to do this in his own time, in his own way. "What can I say, it's complicated."

"What's complicated?" Gabe asked, sitting down beside her. He eyed her eggs. "You gonna eat that?"

Samantha shook her head and Gabe went to work, devouring everything on her plate. When he finished, he took Faby's plate and finished her food off as well. "You guys must be talking about Tony again," he said between bites.

"How'd you guess?" Sam muttered sarcastically.

"I just don't want to see you get hurt," Faby said. "Don't get me wrong—I like the guy. It's obvious you two are head over heels for each other. But he really needs to man up and handle his business. Right, Gabe?"

"Right," Gabe agreed. "But you gotta remember Fab, men are cowards. No matter how much he cares for Sam, he has to break someone's heart to be with her. Someone he loves. He's going to avoid that for as long as humanly possible."

Samantha held the sides of her head. "Aren't you guys supposed to be making me feel *better*?"

"No, sweetheart," Faby corrected. "We're real friends. Our job is to make sure you don't get hurt in the first place."

Samantha decided it was time for a subject change. "Alright, Gabe, since you're the current spokesperson for mankind — what does it mean when a man doesn't want to have sex?"

"I wouldn't know, I've never met one."

"See!" Faby shouted. "I told you that bastard is cheating on me!"

"Whoa, Carlos turned down sex? How much did he drink? Sometimes dudes can't get it up when they're faded."

"No more than usual."

Gabe frowned. "I'll keep an eye on him."

"You will?"

"You keep cooking for us like this, I'll do anything you want." He kissed Faby on the forehead and cleared the table. "I never ate this good at home."

Gabe's sudden tenderness brought a tear to Faby's eye. "I love you, Gabe."

"I love you, too, Fab. Trust me, if homeboy is cheating on you, I'll beat his ass myself. That's a promise."

Gabe and Faby's exchange struck a cord with Samantha, and she was finally able to see her situation from an outside perspective. She didn't like what she saw. "I don't want to be a cheater. I know how it feels to be cheated on—I should know better."

Faby nodded, relieved to see Samantha finally talking some sense. "Not to mention how much it will jack up your relationship karma. It's really not worth it, Sam."

"I know. The more time we spend together, the harder it gets to control ourselves."

"Then maybe you shouldn't spend so much time together."

As if on cue, the phone rang. Neither Sam nor Faby moved to answer it, afraid of who might be on the other end. Gabe finally silenced the annoying ring. "Hello. Hey, what's up. Yeah, she's right here." Gabe held the phone out toward Samantha. "Tony."

Sam took the phone. His ears must have been burning. "Hey."

"Hey. What are you doing today? We're BBQ-ing down at the beach, and I was hoping you'd come through. Bring your housemates—the more the merrier."

Samantha leapt to say yes, then looked across the table. Faby was shooting her a cautionary glance. "I don't think that's a good idea," she answered weakly.

"Come on, it's supposed to be gorgeous today. Perfect beach weather."

Samantha swallowed hard. "I don't think we should spend any more time together until you handle your situation. I don't want to risk a repeat of last night."

Tony softened his voice. "Nothing happened last night."

"Because someone stopped us," Samantha said firmly. "But it never should have gotten that far." She paused for a moment, her heart violently opposed to the words she knew needed to be said. "I think we need to slow down and take some space. Put a little distance between us."

Tony fell quiet. That was the last thing he wanted. "You're right, things went a little too far, and I take full responsibility for that. But I promise you, it won't happen again."

"I don't think either one of us can guarantee that, and you know it."

Tony knew she was right, he just didn't want to hear it. "If that's really what you want, I'll keep my distance. But—"

"It's not what I *want*. It's just the way it has to be right now."

Tony knew better than to try and talk her out of it. When Samantha made up her mind about something, she was hard to budge. "Can I still call you?"

"Of course you can."

"Good." At least he had that. "You know where I am if you change your mind."

"I know. Goodbye, Tony."

Samantha hung up the phone and finished her drink. "There, are you happy now?"

Faby put her hand on Samantha's leg. "You did the right thing."

Then why did it feel so wrong?

Chapter Fourteen

*T*ony was in a mood. He hadn't seen Samantha in a week, and the estrangement was taking its toll on him. Not having her around was like being deprived of oxygen—it impaired his ability to function. How had she managed to get so completely under his skin in such a short amount of time? During the course of many sleepless nights, a fundamental truth came into focus—he did not want to live without her.

Everything was reaching the breaking point simultaneously. Papers he hadn't even started yet were due, and he had a Statistics final to study for. He wouldn't be able to graduate if he didn't pass Stats, and the stress multiplied exponentially with each day that passed. On top of all that, things with Angela had only gotten worse. They'd had a major blowout the last time they spoke, and Tony was in avoidance mode. He just didn't have the energy to deal. Angela's calls went unanswered as he dug himself a deeper hole to hide in.

Tony dropped his backpack on the floor with a thud,

causing his roommate to look up from his book.

"Rough day?" Damion asked.

"You could say that."

"Sorry if this makes it worse, but Angela left another urgent message."

"Just one?"

"Actually four, but who's counting." Damion studied his friend. "You can't avoid her forever."

"You think I don't know that?"

"Do you? You keep postponing the inevitable, like shit is gonna handle itself, and look where it's gotten you. I've never seen you wrapped so tight."

Tony closed his eyes, his hands lightly gripping the side of his head. "I just can't deal with Angela right now."

"That attitude is what got you into this mess in the first place. This isn't going to get any easier. But at least when it's done, everyone can move on, instead of lingering in this hellish limbo." Damion set his book aside. "I ran into Samantha at Oakes today."

"You did? What did she say? Did she look okay?"

"She was trying to play it off, but I could tell she was sad. She asked about you."

"What did you tell her?"

Damion shook his head. Tony's disinterest in Angela could only be matched by his obsession with all things Samantha.

"That you'd been in a terrible mood and were insufferable to live with."

"Thanks."

"Well, it's the truth. It's springtime, and your ass is about to graduate. You should be on top of the world, but instead you're moping around the house, slamming doors, and throwing tantrums like a two-year-old. It's getting old."

Tony stood up, determination shining in his eyes. "I'm going to call her."

"Angela?"

"No, Samantha."

"What are you going to say to Samantha? That you love her and miss her, but not enough to get your shit together and come correct?"

Tony stopped dead in his tracks, whipping around. "I thought you were on my side."

"I *am*. I want to see you get the girl—no doubt about it. But you're going about this all wrong. I looked into that girl's eyes today—she's hurting. Until you can offer her something to take that pain away, leave her alone. She's a good woman and deserves better. You both do."

Tony stomped off down the hallway, fuming. He never meant for things to get so out of control. Who knew you could fall in love so fast? It certainly hadn't happened like that with Angela. He'd been foolish to think he could backburner such a firestorm of emotions. He hadn't wanted to hurt anybody, yet somehow managed to hurt everybody.

Dialing the familiar number, he waited patiently for her to answer, a huge knot forming in his stomach.

"Hello."

"Hey Angela, it's me."

Angela pressed pause on her Pilates DVD, amazed that her MIA boyfriend had finally decided to return her calls. She took a deep breath, attempting to bracket her rage. If they started out arguing, the conversation would go nowhere fast. "I've been leaving you messages for days."

"I know. This quarter is killing me. So much to do before graduation." Tony paused, his gut twisted by the string of half-truths he was forced to utter. "I'm sorry."

Angela chose not to acknowledge his weak apology. "What's the date of your graduation? I really should book my flight soon."

"You don't need to book a flight. My last final is on Wednesday, and then I'm coming home."

Angela instantly brightened. "You are? That's a great idea. Then I can ride back up with you for graduation and save some money. We haven't taken a trip together in forever—this could be just what we need to reconnect."

Tony didn't have the heart to correct her assumptions. What he needed to say, he had to say in person. "Yeah, we can talk more about all that when I get home."

"I can't wait to see you, baby."

"Me, too," he choked out. "Look, I'm in danger of failing Stats, so I better get to this study group meeting."

Angela was already racing forward in her head, plans for his homecoming and graduation celebration taking shape. All previous anger had been forgotten. "Kick ass on your finals, babe. I love you."

"Love you, too."

Tony hung up the phone, disgusted with himself. Did he even know how to tell the truth anymore?

Chapter Fifteen

*I*t was the weekend before graduation, and though they should have been studying for finals, hundreds of students had converged at La Bahia apartment complex for the last big rager of the year. Ninety percent of La Bahia's occupants were college students, and to commemorate year's end, the residents had turned the building into a huge, rave-like super-party. Each apartment hosted a different theme, with everything from hip-hop to techno represented. There was even an apartment on the second floor stocked with every board game imaginable—from Chess to Scrabble to LIFE to Connect Four. Eighties music set the tone here, as people waited around to get in on the next round of their favorite childhood game, nostalgia and alcohol mixing to form a giddiness that infected everyone who walked through the door.

There was a keg on every floor, and for five dollars you could purchase a blue plastic cup and drink to your heart's content, though many party-goers, preferring not to stand in the long lines for the keg, had brought their own liquor. Bahia babes—party hostesses wearing barely-there fluorescent tube tops and miniskirts—circulated with trays of JELLO shots, and spirits were high as everyone welcomed a break from the stress and studying, reality placed firmly on hold for one night.

As Samantha navigated the congested hallways, her ass was grabbed for the fifth time in two minutes. A group of guys had lined up along the impassable corridor, brazenly copping a feel every time a fine woman passed by without a male escort. Samantha would have gladly returned the favor with some unsolicited contact of her own to the jerk's groin, but amidst the sea of pervs, it was impossible to figure out which perv had accosted her. She cut her eyes at each one of them, ignoring their leers, propositions, and lame innuendo as best she could. This was the precise reason she avoided parties like the plague.

What am I doing here? Under normal circumstances, she would have skipped the end-of-the-year bash altogether, especially since Faby, her wingwoman, was out of town attending her cousin's *quincinieta*. But Samantha was hoping to run into Tony, who had vanished after she'd asked for some space. Samantha hadn't intended for her request to come across as an ultimatum, but Tony had obviously interpreted it as such. She had totally underestimated how much she'd miss him.

As the crowd got denser and drunker, Samantha began to regret her decision to come. She was never going to find him in this madhouse. Besides, Tony was almost as antisocial as she was—the odds that he was actually in attendance were slim. He was much more likely to be parked at the beach, strumming a guitar in the back of his van. She would give anything to be transported to such a sublime moment.

Samantha climbed the stairs to the third floor, where her friends Mike and Kyle were hosting La Bahia's official Stoner's Suite. The duo supplied a significant portion of the student population with weed, and their place was easily the most crowded spot in the building. The hotboxed living room offered visitors a contact high upon entry, with smooth reggae grooves playing in the background, lulling the occupants into a lethargic haze. Samantha figured if Tony was in the building, he'd make it to Mike and Kyle's eventually.

She was about to knock when the door suddenly opened, a cloud of sweet-smelling smoke billowing into the hallway. A small group of people spilled out, almost knocking her over.

"Excuse me," giggled a red-eyed blond, pushing past Samantha.

Samantha stepped inside and greeted the crowd of familiar faces lounging around in various stages of baked. Kyle immediately came over and scooped her into a bear hug. "Samantha Merrick," he exclaimed, lifting her off the ground.

"Where you been girl?"

Samantha laughed. Kyle was a cutie, but such a player. "I've been around."

Kyle looked her up and down. "That's a damn lie. You've been hiding, depriving us all of this beautiful face." He shook his head and brought her hand to his lips. "So selfish."

Samantha smiled. The boy was smooth. With his impish grin and British accent, he somehow managed to make the cheesiest lines work. No wonder he got so much play—women were a sucker for guys with accents. "I'm here now, aren't I?"

Kyle ushered her into the crowded living room. "Yes, you are. Stay awhile."

Samantha took a quick inventory of the room—no Tony. She let Kyle pull her onto the couch, situating her squarely on his lap. He produced a three-foot glass bong from behind the couch and packed it. "You wanna hit this?" he asked.

Samantha bent over the bong and placed her lips inside the cool glass ring. She took a deep inhalation as Kyle lit the bowl, the water in the base bubbling. A curl of smoke crept up the cylinder, and when the cylinder was full, Samantha signaled for Kyle to remove the bowl. Sucking in a deep breath, the smoke flew up the bong and disappeared into her mouth. She strained to hold it in for a moment, then exhaled, erupting in a violent cough as the last bit of smoke passed over her lips. "I think I just broke my lungs," she sputtered.

Kyle handed her his beer, the closest thing he had to water. "Hit it again."

Samantha pushed the bong away. "No, I'm good."

"Come on."

Samantha shook her head. "No, really." She leaned back, letting a wave of calm and cool tingling wash over her. She loved that moment when the high first kicked in. A thin veil of sleep descended, tugging at the corners of her eyelids, blurring the lines between conscious and unconscious. Everything slowed down, and she felt all tension and anxiety melt away as she sank deeper into the couch.

"That's some good shit," Samantha mumbled.

Kyle finished off the bowl, blowing sweet smoke into her face. "Train wreck, sweetheart. The skunkiest of the skunk. You really need to hit this again."

"I'll be comatose if I hit that again," she said, giggling.

"Isn't that the point?"

Samantha faded into the scenery as groups of people flowed in and out. The snippets of conversation she overheard in her moments of lucidity were hilarious.

"If you're so convinced God is a woman, please explain to me why she gave y'all periods?"

"I'm telling you, if you blend the mushrooms up in a smoothie, you can barely taste the cow shit..."

"And then that mofo tried to wronghole me after I specifically told him my booty was off limits!"

Her surroundings became more and more surreal as the evening progressed. Shots of Jaegermeister, followed by more rounds of puff puff pass... She was feelin' good, and after a while she didn't even mind the soft caress of Kyle's hand on the back of her arm. Closing her eyes, she pretended it was Tony's touch sending delightful tingles up her spine.

"Hey Samantha."

Samantha opened her eyes to find Damion standing over her. She sat up, ripping herself from Kyle's wanna-be embrace. "Hey." Instantly alert, her guilty eyes darted around the room. "Is Tony with you?"

Damion smiled. He was glad to see Samantha hadn't lost her focus. "As a matter of fact, when I left him, he was upstairs looking for you."

Samantha sprang up off the couch, suddenly reenergized. Not only was he here, he was looking for her! She planted a grateful peck on Damion's cheek. "Thank you," she whispered, before hurrying off.

A thorough canvas of the third floor yielded no Tony. Frustrated, she stepped out onto the roof to escape the suffocating heat in the congested stairwell. The cool night air hit her like a bucket of ice water, brisk and sobering. She stumbled toward the railing and peered over the edge. The balconies below were packed with people, laughter and revelry echoing throughout the courtyard and back alley. Turning her eyes skyward, she caught a sliver of the moon trying to burn though the dense cloud cover. Despite the chill, it was a beautiful night.

"I was hoping you'd make your way up here."

Samantha whirled around to find Tony emerging from the shadows. He stopped about ten feet away from her, hands stuffed in his pockets. They stared at each other, the space between them a canyon of longing, regret, and unexpressed sentiments. Samantha leaned against the railing for support, willing her feet to stay rooted, instead of carrying her into his waiting arms. "Hey."

"Hey." He joined her at the railing. "This is an excellent people-watching spot. You can observe all the illicit activity down below virtually undetected."

"So I see."

Tony folded his hands in front of him. "How have you been?"

"Okay. You?"

"Miserable," Tony confessed, staring into the building across the way. A couple was cuddled up on the couch watching a movie. The image was like a sucker-punch to the gut. "It really sucks not having you around."

Samantha nodded. With no idea where to begin saying all the things that needed to be said, she turned her attention to the various scenes playing out on the balconies below. A dominos tournament was in progress on one of the larger patios, and Samantha could tell from the familiar scent in the air that they were smoking more than cigarettes down there. On one of the fire escapes, a couple was making out. The guy was sucking shamelessly on the girl's breast like a newborn infant, and the girl had her hand in his pants. They didn't seem at all concerned that someone could walk up on them at any moment. Samantha then shifted her gaze to another couple in the midst of a heated argument. Upon closer inspection, she realized the guy in question was Carlos. But the girl was not Faby.

"I can't believe this," Samantha exclaimed.

"What?"

She pointed in the direction of the arguing couple. Carlos had his hands on the girl's shoulders, and she was trying to push him away. "Carlos is down there fighting with some chick."

Tony zoned in on the altercation. "Oh shit."

"Faby was right—that bastard is cheating."

The word was like a whip cracking against the side of Tony's face. He flinched. "You don't know that for sure."

The girl below burst out crying, and Carlos pulled her into his arms. When she turned her face to look up at him, Carlos kissed the girl full on the mouth.

Samantha headed for the stairs, enraged. How could Carlos do this to Faby? After two years! "This is some bullshit!"

"Samantha, wait. Are you sure you want to get in the

middle of this?"

Samantha stopped and turned around. "I just caught that prick cheating on my best friend. I *am* in the middle of this." Carlos was going to bleed when she got her hands on him.

"I'm just not sure this is the best time or place to—"

Samantha couldn't believe her ears. "What are you talking about? You don't actually expect me to sit here and do nothing, do you?"

"Of course not. I'm just saying, you don't have all the facts."

"All the facts? I have two eyes that just saw that asshole kiss another woman! Those are all the facts I need." Samantha didn't have many friends, and was fiercely loyal to the few she did have. "Why are you defending him? Is that some kind of cheater code? That you protect each other?"

Tony recoiled as if he had been slapped. There was no mistaking the venom and disgust in her voice. "Ouch."

Samantha felt weeks of unexpressed anger surge to the surface. What she had just witnessed brought her face to face with reality, triggering a minefield of emotion. "What the hell is wrong with me?" All of a sudden, there was another couple screaming into the night. "Cheating is one of the most disrespectful things you can do to someone you claim to love. Have you ever been cheated on? Have you? Well I have, and I can tell you this much—it is a betrayal that totally cripples a person's ability to trust. It's wrong Tony, on so many levels, and I don't want any part of it."

"But we're not cheating."

"It's emotional cheating—it's worse!" Samantha could feel herself starting to lose it. "Do you realize how frustrating this is? I didn't know it was possible to feel like this. I thought soulmates only existed in books and movies. Then you show up, reading my mind, making me feel safe, making me believe… You're one of the best things that's ever happened to me, but because you have a girlfriend, it feels dirty. I want to shout from the rooftops how I feel about you, but instead I'm ashamed to speak your name. Do you realize how much I hate this? Do you?"

Tony watched the picture of his fairytale ending start to crack. "I'm starting to," he said softly.

Samantha continued, her momentum fueled by a cocktail of emotions—guilt, anger, shame. The alcohol in her system effectively dulled any ability she had to self-censor, and the accusations were flying out of her mouth. "I want to believe that you love me, but if you really loved me—"

"I do love you."

"But you belong to someone else."

"I don't *belong* to anyone."

"Then why do you tiptoe around Angela like you do? Is she really that fragile? How come she has so much influence over how you live your life? She leads you around by the balls and you just let her. For all your talk about seizing the moment and living life to the fullest, I never imagined you could be such a fucking coward."

Her words flew at him like machine-gun fire, every hurtful phrase a direct hit. There was nothing he could say in his defense. She was right—he was a coward. "I don't want to hurt anyone."

"You're hurting me!" Samantha yelled. Tears spilled from her eyes and she turned away, determined to hide her pain.

Tony reached out to comfort her, but she pulled away. "Don't," she snapped.

He started to tell her about his plans to go home and handle things, but was afraid his assurances would sound contrived. He had never seen Samantha so angry—her body was actually shaking with rage. "Maybe I should just go."

"Maybe you should."

Tony stared at the back of her head. For the first time since their trip to Big Sur, she was shutting him out, and he hated it. "I know you think these are just words, but I do love you Samantha, more than you could possibly know."

Silence.

"I'm going to make this right, you'll see. We *will* be together."

Samantha blinked back angry tears. Words. Tony always said the right words, but she was tired of his empty promises.

She stared over the railing, saying nothing. Carlos and his mystery chick had disappeared, and the crowds below appeared to be thinning out.

When she finally turned back toward the stairs, Tony was gone.

Chapter Sixteen

*T*he room was spinning, and she could not make it stop. Sprawled across the bed in Kyle's room, head hanging over the side, Samantha reached for the wastebasket and drew it closer. She wanted so badly to throw up. Maybe if she got some of this poison out of her system, she could finally pass out and put an end to this miserable evening.

After Tony left her on the roof, Samantha searched the building in vain for Carlos's cheating ass, anxious to discharge some of her festering anger. Questions tormented her. Were all men lying, cheating cowards? Was she being played for a fool, yet again? And what business did she have falling in love with another woman's boyfriend anyway? She didn't know who she was more angry with—Carlos, Tony, or herself.

She eventually ended up back at Kyle and Mike's, where the group had moved on from Jaegermeister to tequila. Unable to locate Carlos, Samantha turned her urge for destruction inward, and Kyle was more than happy to provide all the Cuervo she needed to numb out the self-loathing brought on by her most recent reality check. She continued to drink from her bottomless shot glass until her sense of humor returned.

Samantha had been slipping in and out of consciousness for God knows how long before she asked Kyle if there was somewhere she could lie down. She had been fine until that last bong rip, but now it was spin city for days. Samantha took a deep breath and tried once again to close her eyes—she didn't want to be awake anymore. Hell, she didn't want to be alive anymore.

Someone slipped onto the bed beside her and started rubbing her back. When she failed to stir, the hand moved past the dip of her lower back and began to caress her ass. Samantha rolled over.

"You up?" Kyle asked, resting his hand on her exposed midriff. Face inches from hers, he reeked of liquor and cigarettes.

"Yeah," she whispered. "Barely."

"You're more than welcome to crash here tonight. There's plenty of room."

Samantha nodded. She couldn't even think about moving, much less leaving. Besides, she was pretty sure her blood-alcohol level was way over the legal limit, so driving herself home was out of the question. "Thanks," she mumbled, closing her eyes. *Please leave me alone.*

No such luck. Kyle slipped his leg between hers, pushing them apart. He pressed his body against her, grinding a sizeable erection against her thigh.

Samantha turned toward him. "Kyle, I don't—"

Kyle covered her mouth with his, silencing her. His tongue forced its way past pursed lips, his insistence and urgency crushing her head against the pillow. Clumsy hands tugged at her clothing, until he was able to push aside the fabric of her bra to reveal a nipple that, much to Samantha's irritation, was erect. Rolling the hard nub between his fingers, he lifted her shirt, fully exposing her chest. As he brought his mouth down to her breast, her back arched involuntarily to meet him.

The spins had started again, and Samantha was lost in warm kisses and tingling sensations. She didn't care about Tony's girlfriend anymore, she just needed to be with him, just this once. Clinging tightly to the body that writhed above her, she surrendered to the kiss.

Kyle groaned and climbed on top of her. Suckling the left breast, and then the right, he slipped a hand between her legs. "God, you are so fucking wet," he gasped. Excited, he slipped a finger inside of her.

Samantha opened her eyes. She was so dizzy. *Wait, this isn't Tony.* "No," she whispered, pushing his hand away. *Where am I?* "Stop."

Kyle covered her mouth again, swallowing her protests. He tried to slip her jeans off, but they were skintight and practically glued to her body. He jammed his hand once again down her pants, rubbing his finger back and forth over her clit. She began to wriggle beneath him.

"You like that, don't you?"

Samantha's legs fell apart. Having lost all motor skills, she had no energy left to fight him. She was too drunk to care about what he was doing to her, much less stop him.

Someone knocked hard on the locked door, interrupting them. Kyle bolted upright, adjusting Samantha's blouse as she lay lifeless on the bed. "Who is it?"

"Is Samantha in there?"

Kyle cursed and opened the door. Finding Samantha unconscious on the bed, the button of her pants unsnapped, sent Tony into a rage. He charged into the room, fixing Kyle with a murderous glare. "What is going on in here?"

"Nothing man," Kyle replied. His eyes darted around the room, as if he were looking for a hole to hide in. "She's been passed out the whole time. I was just checking on her."

Tony scooped Samantha into his arms. Whooping Kyle's ass would have to wait—he needed to get Samantha home. "If you ever touch her again, I'll kill you," Tony warned. He pushed past Kyle, knocking him back against the dresser.

Samantha did not move or stir as he carried her down the stairs, out of the building, and up the street to his bus. He couldn't help but feel responsible for her condition, and was livid about the scene he had just walked in on. Damion was right—his inaction was hurting people, hurting the people he loved. This wasn't fair to anyone.

Samantha started to show signs of life when he placed her in the bus. Rolling her head to the side, she peered at him through swollen eyelids. "You came back."

"Of course I came back," he said, buckling her seatbelt. "I wasn't going to leave you like this."

"I love you, Tony," she said dreamily.

Tony started the bus. "I love you, too."

Swimming in dreams of daring rescues and great escapes, Samantha leaned her head against the cool window and passed out.

Chapter Seventeen

Samantha slowly opened her eyes. A searing pain sliced through her temples and exploded into a dull pounding sensation. She squinted at the unfamiliar walls in front of her, not recognizing the faded wood panels. Rolling onto her back, her eyes lifted and Bob Marley came into focus. She was in Tony's bed.

The house was alive with sounds of activity—blaring music, snippets of conversation in the hall, the creaking of floorboards as people moved around in the massive Victorian. Her weary eyes finally landed on Tony's motionless form. He was sitting on Damion's bed, watching her.

The sun was high in the sky, filling the room with warm sunlight. "What time is it?" she asked groggily.

"A little past noon."

Samantha struggled to sit up, wincing as the movement sent shooting pains through her head. She swung bare legs over the side of the bed, alarmed to discover she wasn't wearing any pants. The only thing she had on was one of Tony's t-shirts.

Samantha scratched her head. The last thing she remembered was lying down on Kyle's bed. "How did I get here?"

"You don't remember?"

She shook her head. It felt like there were rocks tumbling around between her temples. "Ouch."

"What's the last thing you *do* remember?"

Samantha recalled their argument on the roof at La Bahia. The hurt and disappointment from the previous night came flooding back as she dislodged the memory. "I remember us fighting… and you leaving. Then I went back to Kyle and Mikey's to drink some more."

Tony's jaw clenched. "And then?"

"I was starting to spin, so I asked Kyle if I could lie down. That's the last thing I remember." She glanced around the room. "I have no idea how I got here."

"You must have blacked out," Tony said stiffly. "Otherwise you might remember your boy Kyle trying to date rape you."

Shock, and then disbelief passed across Samantha's face like fast-moving clouds. "What are you talking about?"

"Let's just say that when I found you, it definitely looked like I had interrupted something. But you were out cold. I don't even want to think about what might have happened if I hadn't busted in."

Samantha worked backwards in her mind, trying to fill in the details of that lost time. She caught a flash of Kyle kissing her—sloppy lips slobbering all over her face. She hadn't felt threatened so much as annoyed. But that was all she remembered. Everything else was a black hole. "I can't believe you came back... After the horrible things I said to you."

He handed her a bottle of water. "I should have never left you alone in the first place."

"I'm a big girl."

"A big girl that almost got herself into a situation," he snapped, a protective paternal fire flaring up. "I wish you'd find a better coping mechanism than drinking yourself into unconsciousness."

Samantha narrowed her eyes. "I'm not your girlfriend — it's not your job to take care of me. Next time you're struck with a chivalrous urge, feel free to skip the knight-in-shining-armor routine. Save yourself some trouble." She stood abruptly and her head exploded in pain. She brought a hand to the side of her face and sat back down.

"Look, I don't want to fight, Sam. There's something I need to tell you."

Samantha downed half the bottle of water. She'd need several more gallons before she felt properly hydrated. "I'm listening."

"I'm going home to see Angela. To end things."

Now he had her full attention. "What? When?"

"Wednesday, after my last final."

"What about graduation?"

"I'm hoping to be back by then, but if I miss it, I miss it. I don't need to walk across a stage to know I accomplished something."

Samantha felt a pang of guilt about the pressure she had placed on him. Obviously, her tantrum had accelerated things. "Look, if you're doing this because of what I said last night... I'd had a lot to drink and wasn't exactly thinking clearly."

"You don't have to sugarcoat for me, Samantha—you meant every word. And you were right—I've been acting like a coward. I should have ended my relationship as soon as I realized I was falling for you. This conversation with Angela is long overdue. Believe me, I would leave today if my degree wasn't on the line."

Blood was pumping through Samantha's veins hard and fast. Despite her weakened physical state, she was on the verge of actual elation. This was really happening—she was finally going to be with the man she loved.

Tony watched the webs of fear and mistrust vanish from Samantha's eyes and his heart lifted. He sat beside her, and her head naturally fell to rest against his shoulder. He placed a hand on her leg.

"I'm so sorry," she whispered.

"Me, too. For everything. I should have left you alone until I was free to be with you. I messed everything up."

Samantha squeezed his hand. "This doesn't feel messed up to me."

Tony smiled. Slipping an arm around her waist, he kissed the side of her head. "One more week and this will all be over."

One more week.

Chapter Eighteen

Somehow, everyone managed to backburner the emotional drama long enough to finish their respective papers and cram for tests, and they all made it through finals in one piece. Samantha did her part to keep the peace by keeping her discovery of Carlos's infidelity to herself—for the time being. In the cold, sober light of day, Samantha realized that maybe this wasn't the best time to blow her best friend's life apart. Faby was really struggling in her Critical Theory class, and needed to ace the final to pass. Taking her out of commission at such a crucial moment in the quarter could jeopardize her grade, and Samantha didn't want to risk making a bad situation worse.

Not that conscious and calculated deception was easy. Samantha had never been a very good liar, and she hated every second of it. But strangely enough, the ruse did have one positive effect. Having to face Faby every day while harboring such a huge secret helped Samantha develop a greater understanding for what Tony must be going through.

If keeping the truth from someone you love is only done to spare them pain, did the ends justify the means?

In Samantha's mind, right and wrong had always been clearly defined, instinctual even. But she was learning that sometimes the lines between right and wrong blurred, requiring a degree of moral flexibility. Samantha kept trying to imagine how she would feel if she were in Tony's position. Would she want to end a five-year relationship over the phone? And what if the roles were reversed—how would she like being dumped long distance? Tony was doing the best he could under the circumstances—she could see that now. But instead of being supportive, she had thrown a tantrum like a spoiled child. If he missed his graduation because of her pseudo-ultimatum, she'd never forgive herself.

Her head jerked toward the window when she heard the familiar rumble of Tony's bus pull into the driveway. She met him at the door and collapsed into his arms, intoxicated by his scent as he planted a soft kiss on her forehead. Samantha longed for the day when she would be able to lift her head and bring her mouth to meet his.

"I can't wait until I'm able to give you a proper greeting," he whispered, reading her mind.

Samantha released a long sigh. "Me, too." Pulling away, she regarded him seriously. "Are you sure you want to do this now?"

Creases wrinkled Tony's brow as he studied Samantha's face. "Why? Have you changed your mind about wanting to be with me?"

"No, of course not."

"Then what's with the long face? Don't freak out on me now, Sam. Not when we're so close to having it all."

His gaze was intense, steady, conviction shining in his eyes. When he looked at her like that, she had no choice but to believe him.

"I'm not freaking out," Samantha assured him. "I'm just more sympathetic to your situation now. I keep trying to put myself in Angela's shoes. I feel bad for her, for both of you. I know how difficult this trip is going to be, and I don't want to make light of it."

"I appreciate that, but like you guys keep telling me—it's time for me to man up." He squeezed her hand. "When are you going to tell Faby about Carlos?"

"As soon as she gets home. She's on campus turning in her last paper as we speak."

"Good. I know how hard it's been to keep such a huge secret, but you did the right thing."

Samantha wasn't sure if she agreed with him, but appreciated his attempt to absolve her. "It's all going to be over soon," she whispered, trying her hardest to focus on the positive. "For both of us."

Tony folded her into another embrace, his hand resting gently on the nape of her neck, fingers tangled in her hair. "As much as I hate to leave you—the sooner I go, the sooner I can get this over with."

"I know." A tight fear gripped her. What if, despite his promises, he didn't come back? The thought of losing him sent waves of panic rippling through her.

Tony held her face between the palms of his hands, bringing his face within an inch of hers. "I *will* be back."

Her lower lip quivered as she blinked back tears. She tried to answer, but was so choked up that the words stuck in her throat.

Tony leaned forward and brushed his lips against hers. It was the whisper of a kiss, but he lingered just long enough to ignite a sensual flame that spread like an Arizona wildfire through every inch of her body. The hair on her arms stood on end, jolted to attention by the current of energy passing between them. For a moment, Samantha forgot where she was as he maintained dangerously close proximity, the circumstances that rendered such a kiss forbidden far from her mind. The flesh of her bottom lip felt singed where they had touched, and she would have given anything for him to quench the fire with a flick of his tongue. But how could she survive another taste without giving in to the irrepressible urge to devour?

Tony backed away, slightly off-balance. A rush of pure

adrenaline surged through his body, more powerful than any drug he'd ever experienced. From just a kiss. He couldn't imagine what it would be like when they finally made love.

"I should go," he stammered.

"I know."

But neither of them moved. The force drawing them together did not want to be severed. He finally tore his eyes from her face and ordered his feet to move, one in front of the other, down the walk toward the van.

As he watched Samantha grow small in his rearview mirror, the euphoric love fog lifted and was replaced by an intense dread. Tony felt like he had to be strong for Samantha, but inside, he was terrified of what waited for him in Los Angeles. Could he really do it? Could he really leave Angela?

He was about to find out.

Chapter Nineteen

*S*amantha barely had time to process Tony's departure before Faby came home, her cheating boyfriend in tow. She cursed silently when Carlos walked through the front door behind Faby. She had managed to avoid him since the party, and the sight of him made her sick to her stomach.

Carlos headed for the kitchen, a case of Coronas under his arm. "Hey, Sam."

Samantha ignored him, wondering if she should wait until Gabe got home to talk to Faby. What if things got out of hand? She didn't know if she could break up a fight between the two of them by herself.

"I am so glad this quarter is finally over," Faby said, plopping down beside her on the couch. "Did Tony take off?"

"Yup, about an hour ago."

Genuine concern colored Faby's expression. "How are you holding up?"

Samantha shrugged. "I'm okay. It's a little frightening how much I miss him, but hopefully he won't be gone too long."

"It's good to see him finally do right by you."

Carlos sat down beside Faby, draping an arm around her shoulder. Samantha immediately jumped up, not wanting to share air, much less furniture, with the lying bastard.

"Faby, I need to talk to you." She grabbed her friend's arm and yanked her away from Carlos's slimy embrace. "Alone."

Samantha dragged Faby down the hall and closed the door. "There's something I need to tell you."

"So I see," Faby said, taking a seat. "What's up?"

"Please don't hate me for not telling you sooner," Samantha started, wasting no time. "But I saw Carlos with another woman last weekend."

The color drained from Faby's face. "You what?"

"At La Bahia. Tony and I saw him kissing some chick."

Faby's face hardened into a stone mask. "Are you sure it was him?" Her tone was surprisingly calm considering the bomb Samantha had just dropped.

"Yeah, I'm sure. I'm sorry, Fab."

Faby turned on her heel and charged back into the living room. The next thing Samantha heard was a loud crash.

"You crazy bitch!" Carlos screamed. When Samantha reached the living room, she found Carlos crouched on the floor holding the side of his face. Blood trickled down his cheek from a cut just below his eye. Faby was standing over him with the Dustbuster, preparing to bring the appliance down on his head for a second time.

"Faby, stop!" Samantha yelled. Faby hesitated for a moment, and Carlos took the opportunity to tackle her onto the couch.

Carlos pinned Faby beneath him as she kicked her legs and tried to hit him with closed fists. "What the hell is wrong with you?"

"Who is she?" Faby demanded. "Who is this whore you're fucking?"

"What are you talking about?" Carlos asked, feigning complete innocence.

"Give it up, Carlos," Samantha said. "I saw you on the patio at La Bahia." She stood over them and pulled at his arms. "Let her up."

When Carlos loosened his grip, Faby brought her right knee up hard into his midsection. He doubled over in pain.

"I don't know what Sam thinks she saw," Carlos said, gasping for air. "But it's not what it looks like."

"Are you calling my best friend a liar?"

"I know what I saw," Samantha said.

Carlos paled—he was cornered and caught. "I swear to God, she means nothing to me. I love *you*, Fabiola."

"You *love* me?" Faby asked incredulously. She threw the remote control at him, followed by every book on the coffee table. Carlos deftly dodged the flying objects. "Were you thinking about how much you love me when you were fucking that bitch?"

Samantha tried to position herself between the warring couple, then thought better of it when she almost got beamed by a flying ashtray. Faby was out of control, turning every household item that wasn't bolted down into a weapon.

Gabe walked in just as Faby picked up his beloved Playstation. Surveying the wreckage, he immediately placed himself in the line of fire. "Faby," he said, holding up his hands. His voice was calm, but firm, as if he was negotiating the release of a hostage. "Honey, put down the Playstation."

Faby blinked, snapping out of her violent rage. Regaining her composure, she lowered the Playstation, unharmed, to the ground.

Gabe breathed a sigh of relief. "What the hell is going on in here?"

Faby, who had yet to shed a single tear, turned cold, unforgiving eyes on Carlos's cowering form. "This asshole decided to flush a two-year relationship down the toilet so he could get in the pants of some tramp."

Carlos tried to advance. "If you would just let me explain."

"Explain? I could give a fuck about your explanations. Get out."

Faby's words had an unquestionable finality about them. She stomped off to her room without so much as a backward glance.

Carlos tried to follow, but Gabe barred his way. "You need to leave," Gabe warned. "Don't make me throw you out, because I will."

"This isn't how it looks."

"Uh huh. Save it for someone who gives a damn." Gabe showed Carlos to the door, then slammed it in his face.

"I am so glad you came home when you did," Samantha said, stacking the strewn books neatly on the table. "You know she whacked him upside the head with that Dustbuster."

Gabe laughed. "That's my girl." He checked the cables on the Playstation before placing it back on the TV stand. "Carlos is lucky this didn't go down in the kitchen or he would've been dodging plates and knives instead of books and pillows."

"No kidding."

"She gonna be okay?"

"I hope so. I've never seen her go off like that. She could have really hurt him."

"Would have served him right." Gabe gestured toward Faby's bedroom. "You gonna check on her?"

Samantha shook her head. "I'm probably the last person she wants to talk to right now. Seeing as how I'm one of those cheaters and all."

"Huh? That's not even the same thing."

"I doubt Faby sees it that way. She's better off with some

space and privacy to process things. She knows where we are when she's ready to talk."

"If you say so." Gabe got up and headed for the kitchen. "You want a beer?"

"I would love a beer."

Samantha sat back on the couch, looking around at their trashed living room. She really hoped, for Tony's sake, that things with Angela went better.

Chapter Twenty

*T*ony had worked himself into quite a state by the time he reached the 10 West toward Santa Monica. Seven hours alone in the car had given him plenty of time to run through all the scenarios of how the break-up could play out, and most of them did not end well. Now that he was in the home stretch, his heartbeat was racing, thumping hard against the walls of his chest. His sweaty palms slipped on the steering wheel, beads of perspiration rolling down the side of his face as the cool night air rushed through the open window. He tried to calm himself by taking slow, deep breaths, but was soon gasping for air. Pulling off at the next exit, Tony headed for the nearest payphone.

Damion answered on the third ring. "What up."

With shaky hands, Tony struggled to light a cigarette. "I think I'm having a panic attack."

"What? Where are you?"

"At an AM/PM on Centinela. I am literally two exits away from the crib, and I had to stop." Tony took a drag off his cigarette, the short, raspy breaths beginning to slow as the nicotine worked its way through his system. "I don't know if I can do this, man."

"Stop being so dramatic."

"I'm serious, D—I can't fucking breathe!"

"You need to focus on the big picture," Damion said. He was starting to sound like a broken record. "You say you want to be with Samantha? Then get your black ass back in that car and handle your business playa, cause you can't have it both ways."

Tony slammed the phone down. He wasn't trying to have it both ways—all he wanted was Samantha. Nothing had been the same since she stumbled into his life, and the sooner he could get back to her, the better. He was just trying to find a way to inflict the least amount of damage on Angela in the process. Why couldn't everyone understand that?

Just after midnight, Tony finally reached the faded stucco apartment complex he used to call home. Most of the lights in the four-story building were off, including the lights in his apartment. He was tempted to stay in the van until morning, anything to avoid having to go inside. But once again, he caught a flash of Samantha's tear-streaked face as they said goodbye, and the promise he'd made to her. This had to end tonight. He grabbed his duffel bag and headed inside.

Tony was greeted by the strong scent of patchouli incense

in a dark house. Everything was exactly as he'd left it. He glanced around the room at the life they'd created together. Furnishings were sparse, but tasteful. A tan leather sofa they'd acquired from a yard sale in La Brea; a red velvet beanbag from a thrift store on Haight Street. Framed photographs of the two of them during happier times lining the mantel above the fireplace. So many memories. They had been happy once; he couldn't deny that. But those memories had been made during another life.

Tony had moved so many times after his mother died that he'd learned the benefits of traveling light. As a result, Angela had taken sole responsibility for making their house into a home. The antique mirror in the hallway, an ornate iron planter, bamboo plants placed in the corners for luck—that was Angela's taste, Angela's touch. He did a quick inventory and realized that aside from a footlocker and some records, there wasn't much of himself left in the apartment. He wondered if that would make packing up and leaving any easier.

The dim glow of flickering candlelight illuminated the bedroom doorway at the end of the hall. Tony made his way toward the light, cursing as the floorboards creaked under his weight. He couldn't turn around and run now—she had to know he was home.

When he reached the bedroom, he found a sight that once upon a time would have made him weak in the knees.

Angela was sound asleep on the bed, wearing nothing but an emerald green silk nightie. The delicate fabric hugged every curve, just barely containing her ample bosom that rose and fell with each inhale and exhale. Her wavy blond hair was fanned across the pillow, shimmering like gold in the candlelight. She was as beautiful as ever, but just didn't light his soul on fire the way Samantha did. Blowing out the candle, he backed out of the room and headed for the couch, thankful for the reprieve. He would deal with things in the morning, after a good night's sleep.

"Why didn't you wake me?"

Tony opened his eyes to find Angela standing over him, hands planted firmly on her hips. The room was still dark, not a hint of daylight present in the sky. "What time is it?" he asked, sitting up.

"I was sure the sight of me in this get-up would make it impossible for you *not* to wake me," she said, gesturing to the form-fitting nightie. She looked him up and down, the blue of her eyes clouded by pain and confusion. "But instead, the suspicious behavior continues."

Tony rubbed his eyes. "Suspicious behavior?"

"Avoiding my calls, being generally vague and evasive. Come on, Tony, I wasn't born yesterday. You're cheating on me, aren't you?"

Wham—just like that. Tony blinked and stared at her dumbfounded. No time to plead his case, spin things, or cushion the blow. Damion was right—women must have a sixth sense about these things. "You have to admit, things between us have been strained for a while now."

Angela didn't even bat an eye. "I'll take that as a yes."

"No, technically, I haven't cheated."

"Technically? What the fuck does *technically* mean?"

"That it's been strictly platonic. Samantha and I haven't slept together."

A light bulb went on in Angela's head as she slowly began connecting the dots. "Wait, back up—*Samantha?* As in Sam, your new camping buddy?"

Doh! He walked right into that one. "It's not how it looks."

Angela shook her head in disbelief. "This is such bullshit. Yeah, we hit a rough patch. But instead of trying to work on it, you just gave up. Like what we've built here isn't worth fighting for. I guess cheating makes it a lot easier for you, huh? Instead of having to do any actual communicating or compromising, like people do in *real* relationships, you set it up to where I have no choice but to leave you." She leveled him with a disgusted glare. "You are such a coward."

Tony flinched. *Yep, that seems to be the consensus.* "I'm telling you, I didn't cheat."

"Oh shut up," she snapped. "This has been going on for

months. You've been lying to me for months."

"I… It's…" Tony was fresh out of excuses. It was time for him to take responsibility for his actions. "I'm sorry. I swear, I didn't set out looking for this. It just happened."

"What just happened? I thought you said it was strictly platonic." Angela scrutinized her lover as he avoided her eyes. "Wait a minute—don't tell me you're in love with her?"

The longest pause in the history of pauses. Tony looked up to see tears trembling on the rims of Angela's eyelids, anticipating his response. The words barely made it past the lump in his throat. "I think I am."

Angela squeezed her eyes shut as her worst fears were confirmed. This wasn't some drunken fling—this woman meant something to him. He *loved* her? What? How was that possible? She didn't want to hear anymore or know anymore. This couldn't be happening.

Angela ran from the room and Tony followed, only to have the bedroom door slammed in his face. He jiggled the locked doorknob. "Please open the door."

Something crashed against the wall and shattered into pieces. Sounded a lot like the vase he had given her for their second anniversary. Tony could hear her sobbing and pounded his fist against the immobile wooden barrier. "Angie, please!"

Things continued to crash and slam in the bedroom. After a few minutes the door opened and Angela shoved an armful of clothes into his chest, hangers poking him in the chin. Then she threw a large bag filled with his belongings into the hallway. "Get out of my house," she said, her voice cold and unforgiving. "Get your shit, and get the fuck out."

Tony dropped the armload of clothes and attempted to grab her shoulders. "Angela, please calm down."

She pushed his hands away with surprising strength, knocking him off balance. "Don't touch me, don't you ever touch me." Angela picked up the pile of clothes from the floor and headed for the balcony. Before he could stop her, she tossed them over the side.

Tony watched as clouds of fleece and cotton floated toward the ground. "What the hell is wrong with you?" he yelled, swept up in the emotion of the moment. He was wide awake now.

Seeing red and seeking to destroy every last trace of him, Angela scanned the room for more of his stuff. "I told you to get out." She spotted a crate of records beside the entertainment center. She picked it up and headed for the balcony.

Tony cut her off and snatched the crate of priceless vinyl out of her hands. "Damnit, Ange, this is not a scene from *Waiting to Exhale*—knock that shit off. Can't we talk about this like civilized human beings?"

"Oh, so *now* you wanna talk?" She whirled around to face him. "Get out!" Since the patio door was still open, her screams echoed throughout the silent courtyard. Lights flicked on in several of their neighbors' apartments.

Tony had an aversion to drama, and did not appreciate the Springer-like scene unfolding in front of him. Angela was completely unhinged, and if she kept carrying on like this, someone was going to call the cops. "Alright, I'm going to leave," he said, backing away, the crate of records tucked safely under his arm. "But this is not over. Whether you believe me or not, I care about you." He took a step forward. "If you'd only let me explain."

"Go to hell," she spat, hatred in her eyes.

Tony dropped his head, defeated. He had never seen her so angry—he was actually afraid. "I'll be at my sister's when you're ready to talk."

The door slammed behind him, causing the entire building to shake. He ignored the disapproving stares from the multitude of neighbors peeking through closed blinds or standing in open doorways watching him depart. They had woken the whole building with their yelling. When he reached the ground floor, Angela appeared on the patio and hurled the bag he'd left behind over the balcony.

No, that hadn't gone well at all.

Chapter Twenty-One

Samantha watched Faby pour cake mix into a shallow baking pan. Faby came from a long line of strong silent women who found solace in the kitchen. Cooking was a coping strategy, as pain and sorrow was transformed into regenerative nourishment. Since her break-up with Carlos, Faby had been cooking up a storm—pies, tamales, casseroles —the fridge was packed with leftovers. She would start on the *Arroz con Pollo* as soon as Gabe got back with the missing ingredients, and dessert—pineapple upside-down cake—was on its way into the oven.

Samantha swiped a finger full of batter from the ceramic bowl. "I'm going to add another ten pounds to the freshman fifteen I gained last year if you keep this up."

Faby set the oven timer and began rinsing the chicken breasts. "I'm just glad there's someone around to enjoy it," she said, lips drawn in a tight line. "My appetite is pretty much nonexistent."

Samantha hated seeing Faby like this. Her vibrant nature snuffed out by betrayal, a fog of stoic depression lingered in its place. At first Samantha was content to leave her be, but after a week of manic cooking and very little venting, Samantha was becoming concerned. Faby without her fire and flair was like Mr. T without his mohawk—it just felt wrong.

"We should do something tonight," Samantha suggested. "Get out of the house. We could catch a movie, shoot some pool—whatever you want."

"What I *want* to do is go out and key that motherfucker's car." A malicious flame sparked in Faby's eyes as she brought the knife down across a breast of chicken, slicing it in half.

"We could do that," Samantha said. Finally, signs of life. She grabbed the near-empty bottle of tequila and poured the last shot, pushing the glass toward the center of the table. "I'll flip you for it."

"Please—I need this way more than you do." Faby swallowed the shot and reached for a slice of lemon. "Where the hell is Gabe anyway? We sent him to the store hours ago."

Gabe appeared in the doorway with a bag of groceries under his arm. "I was trying to give you some time to sober up before round two," he said.

"Oh shut up and give me my tequila," Faby barked, taking the bag from him. "Did you get everything on the list?"

"Yup."

"Thanks." Faby tore open the bottle of Jose Cuervo, and filled both shot glasses to the rim. "Bottoms up," she said, throwing her head back. The copper-colored liquid disappeared down her throat.

Samantha quickly followed suit. Who was she kidding —she was in as bad of shape as Faby was. Graduation had come and gone with no word from Tony. Samantha thought for sure he would have called to check in, but days passed and nothing. That couldn't be a good sign. What if he'd changed his mind? What if he wasn't coming back?

Samantha cut another lemon into six wedges. She should have known it was too good to be true. With very few exceptions, Samantha found men to be fundamentally unreliable. They always left when she needed them most, just like her father did when she was a little girl. She thought Tony was different, but maybe she was wrong. Maybe in her quest to kill the loneliness, she had imagined the whole connection. It wouldn't be the first time her heart had lied to her.

"Jesus, it's barely four o'clock," Gabe said, watching Samantha take another shot. "I know why Faby's lushing it up, but what's your excuse? Sympathy drinking?"

"Tony still hasn't called," Faby volunteered, suddenly chipper.

"Really? What's up with that?"

Samantha glared at him. "If I knew the answer to that question, do you think I'd be knocking back shots of tequila?"

"My bad, no need to bite my head off," Gabe said. "I'm just trying to gauge if I should go to Costco for the next liquor run."

"That is a great idea," Faby said, as she resumed her slicing and dicing. "What took you so long anyway?"

"I stopped by 24 Hour Fitness to pick up my paycheck and ran into Carlos."

Faby paused, knife in mid-air. Just hearing his name conjured up murderous impulses. "Did you talk to him?"

"I had to, he followed me out to the parking lot."

"You should have dropped a free weight on his foot," Samantha said. "Then he couldn't have followed you anywhere."

"What did he want?" Faby asked.

"He wanted to know if you'd calmed down," Gabe reported. "He wants you back. Apparently he's miserable without you."

"He should have thought of that before he went and stuck his dick in someone else," Faby mumbled, unimpressed.

"That's what I told him." Gabe poured himself a shot of tequila. "I don't think he's going to give up though."

Faby added the chunks of diced chicken to the vegetables sautéing in the frying pan. "He will stay the hell away from me if he knows what's good for him." The meat sizzled as the kitchen filled with the aroma of onions and garlic. "All my life I watched the men in my family cheat on their wives. I did not go away to college so I could turn into my mother."

An hour later, after yet another satisfying meal, the trio laid around in their respective food comas, passing the bottle of Cuervo between them. Halfway through the bottle, Faby finally started to open up.

"You know, I really wanted to bash his head in," Faby said.

"You *did* bash his head in," Samantha said with a giggle, her face warm from the alcohol. Of the three of them, she had the lowest tolerance. It didn't take much to get her wasted.

"Yeah, I guess I did hit him pretty hard. I think that's what's bothering me. In that moment I was so blind with rage that I actually wanted to kill him." Faby stared straight ahead at the wall, as if a movie only she could see was being broadcast on the pale surface. "I could have really hurt him."

"He deserved it," Samantha insisted.

"Maybe so, but I didn't know I had that kind of hatred in me. I thought about growing old with this man, having his children one day, and it all disappeared in an instant. How does that happen? How does love turn to hate so quickly, so totally?"

"You know what they say," Samantha mused. "You can never hate someone the way you hate someone you once loved."

"Ain't that the truth."

"I knew this one girl back in high school," Gabe chimed in. "Sweet, innocent, mild-mannered preacher's daughter. She'd never so much as uttered a curse word, much less had a bad thought about someone. Then one day she discovered her boyfriend, who she'd given her prized virginity to, had cheated on her."

"Been there," Samantha said, followed by a drunken hiccup.

"Yeah, yeah, we know. My point is, that quiet church girl snapped like a twig when she found out, and after a varsity football game, she tried to run him down in the parking lot with her car."

"Shut up!" Faby yelled.

"Swear to God. He managed to jump out of the way, and she drove right into the visiting team's bus. Airbags deployed, totaled her car. No one ever saw it coming."

Samantha took the bottle of tequila out of Gabe's hand. "I wish I'd mowed Eric down with my car. He deserved that, and so much more." She took a swig. "On second thought, I wish I'd castrated him first, *then* run him over."

Faby took the bottle from Samantha. "I love that story," she said, feeling a surge of female solidarity. "I hope that boy crapped his pants right before he saw his life flash before his eyes. What was her name?"

"Whose name?" Gabe asked.

"Church girl."

"Oh. I think her name was Sarah."

Faby raised the bottle of tequila in the air. "To Sarah!"

"I wonder if that's what happened to Tony," Samantha

whispered, mostly to herself. "What if Angela flipped and did something to him."

The laughing stopped as the three of them pondered her hypothesis.

"Does this Angela chick have any crazy in her?" Gabe asked.

Panic started to crest as Samantha recalled the stories Tony had shared with her about Angela. "Tony referred to her many times as being unstable…"

"I'm sure he's fine," Gabe said quickly.

"Then why hasn't he called?"

Her desperate query was met with uncomfortable silence. No answers were forthcoming—at least any she wanted to hear.

Samantha headed outside for a smoke, once again assaulted with fears, doubts, and chest-clenching anxiety. Something was wrong—she could feel it. She'd never had a problem getting inside Tony's head before, and could not understand why he'd fallen off like this. For the first time since they'd met, she felt disconnected, plunged back into the soul-numbing loneliness that had plagued her much of the year. She didn't want to be lost again. She didn't want to be alone.

"Please come back, Tony," she whispered into the unforgiving night. "Please come back."

Chapter Twenty-Two

*F*or days Tony's calls to Angela went unanswered. In a way it was fitting that his trademark method of avoidance was now being used to punish him. And it was working—he felt terrible. In all the scenarios Tony had run through, he never imagined he'd be shut out so thoroughly, denied the opportunity to explain and make amends. He needed for Angela to know that he still cared for her, that he never meant to hurt her, how sorry he was for all of it. But she didn't care. From what he could tell, she never wanted to speak to him again.

A lifelong friendship reduced to ashes, just like that. The magnitude of his loss was finally starting to hit him. Not that he'd expected Angela to congratulate him and wish him well as he embarked on his new relationship, but he had hoped that after the initial hurt subsided they would be able to maintain some kind of a friendship. Long before they became lovers, Tony and Angela had been friends. Best friends. Their shared history had to count for something.

The smell of freshly baked cookies filled his sister's tiny studio, and despite his terrible mood, Tony had to smile. Chocolate chip cookies had been their mother's specialty, her cure-all for everything from bad dreams to broken hearts. Some of his fondest memories were of late nights around the kitchen table with Mom and Ashley, talking about life and love over warm cookies and cold milk. There was something comforting about the sight of his apron-clad sister removing a pan of cookies from the oven. A throwback to simpler, happier times.

"When did you take up baking?" he asked, impressed with his sister's newfound skill. Ashley had always rebelled against anything that smacked of domesticity. "Those don't smell burnt at all."

"It's not like it's hard to pre-heat an oven and set a timer," she said, pouring two tall glasses of milk. "I just wish I could do more to help with this Angela situation."

"You and me both. I don't know what else to do, Sis. Angela is determined to avoid me. She's been calling in sick to work, and from what I can tell, she hasn't been back to the apartment in days. I've called most of her friends, but everyone claims they haven't seen her."

"Maybe you should just go back to Santa Cruz," Ashley suggested. "Give her some time to calm down. This must be a lot to absorb all at once."

Tony would have loved to go back to Santa Cruz.

Knowing Samantha was back home waiting for him was the only light at the end of this long, miserable tunnel. He'd tried to call to let her know what was going on, but no one had answered, and he hadn't tried again. Hearing her voice would have gone a long way toward soothing the turmoil in his heart, but calling to cry on her shoulder would be selfish when all he had to offer was more delays. He needed to make a clean break with the past before making any more plans for the future. The overlap he'd allowed had done enough damage.

"I can't go back until everything here is settled," he explained. "Until I know Angela is going to be okay."

Ashley cast a sympathetic glance at her brother. He was trying so hard to do the right thing, but like most men, he was utterly clueless. "Sweetie, I know this is not what you want to hear, but it is going to be a very long time before Angela is okay."

Tony was not ready to accept that reality. He couldn't be responsible for ruining someone's life. He would not turn into his father. "It's nice to just sit here and talk like this," he said, trying to push the negative thoughts to the back of his mind. "Thanks for letting me crash."

"Any time brother—that's what family is for," Ashley said, patting his hand. "Stay as long as you need to."

A loud pounding on the front door interrupted their quiet bonding moment. Tony raised an eyebrow. "You got a bootie call you forgot to mention?"

Ashley removed her apron and unconsciously fluffed her hair. "No."

Tony followed his sister to the door, wondering who had the nerve to show up unannounced at this late hour. They were both surprised to find Angela, distraught and disheveled, on the other side of the door.

Tony's heart broke when he saw her standing there, a frail version of her former self. He took a tentative step forward. "Hey."

Angela stared blankly at Tony, then turned her attention to Ashley. "I hope it's not too late," Angela said, clutching the doorframe for support.

"Of course not," Ashley replied, gesturing for Angela to come in. "How are you doing?"

"As well as can be expected, seeing as how my whole life just got blown apart." Angela took a few steps into the apartment, then collapsed.

Tony rushed to her side as Angela crumpled into his arms. She reeked of alcohol, legs jello beneath her. He helped her to the couch while Ashley retreated to the kitchen for some water. Angela had been taking a fairly strong antidepressant for several months, and was not supposed to mix the pills with alcohol. "How much have you had to drink?"

"Not nearly enough," Angela slurred. Tears quickly filled her eyes as she gazed up at him.

Tony pressed a glass of water into Angela's shaky hand,

his gut twisting into knots. He couldn't stand to see women cry. "Drink this."

Angela pushed the water away. "What does she have that I don't have?" she asked, her voice thick with desperation. "Because whatever it is, I can change. I know I can change... Just please... Please don't leave me."

Tears streamed down Angela's face, her body shaking in seizure-like convulsions. Seeing her like this brought back too many memories—sleepless nights in crowded apartments, listening to his mother cry herself to sleep on the other side of the wall. Tony had been here before. He was all too familiar with the signs of an impending breakdown.

Tony glanced helplessly at his sister, who was standing in the doorway in the midst of her own déjà vu. Ashley never realized how much Angela resembled their mother. The two women looked nothing alike physically, but in terms of demeanor, they might as well have been twins with their almost endearing helplessness and quiet frailty. *No wonder Tony feels so responsible for Angela's well-being,* Ashley thought. *He's still trying to save Mom.*

Tony cradled Angela in his arms, continuing to rock her back and forth while she repeated the phrase "please don't leave me" over and over. This is what he had been afraid of, this is what he'd lacked the courage to face. And it was a hundred times worse than he'd imagined it would be.

With his sister's help, he was able to get Angela home and into bed. She had managed to cry herself to sleep in the car, and was dead to the world as he carried her up the stairs to their apartment. After tucking her in, he collapsed on the couch next to his sister, battling his own emotional exhaustion.

"Maybe I should stay here tonight, just to make sure she's okay," Tony said, glancing toward the bedroom.

Ashley frowned. "Look, I'm no psychologist," she began, "but the two of you have this major codependency thing going on."

Tony rolled his eyes. "Geez, you're starting to sound like Damion."

"Well, he's been known to be right on occasion," she said with a smile. "Seriously though, it's time to be realistic about this. You're leaving. It's not your job anymore to take care of her. Angela is going to have to learn how to take care of herself now."

"But how can I leave her like this?"

"What choice do you have, Tony? And what about Samantha? Remember her, the love of your life? Do you think she's going to wait forever?" She rested a hand on his leg. "You need to choose. You can't be with them both."

"I've made my choice," Tony stated firmly. He lowered his voice, afraid he might wake Angela. "I chose Samantha."

"Then go be with Samantha," Ashley urged, always the calm, cool voice of reason. "You've done all you can do here."

Chapter Twenty-Three

Samantha had been sitting by the phone for six days, anxiously awaiting word from Tony. His absence was paralyzing, as if life were completely on hold while they were apart. She couldn't eat, sleep, concentrate—she was completely useless. As each day turned into night and back into day again with no word from Tony, Samantha started to fear the worst. Maybe he wasn't coming back. Maybe it had all been a dream.

Curled up on the couch on the afternoon of the seventh day, wrapped in a blanket of insecurities, Samantha stared lifelessly at the TV as an old *Friends* rerun came back from commercial. *Friends* was one of her favorite shows, but not even Chandler Bing's wicked sarcasm could get her to crack a smile today. She was about to lap Faby in the race to hit rock bottom.

Samantha had almost nodded off when she heard a familiar rumble pull into the driveway. She sat straight up. *Was that... Could it be?* She ran to the front door and was shocked to find Tony strolling up the front walk, a large duffel bag slung over his shoulder. His eyes lit up when he saw her standing in the doorway. "I was hoping you'd be home."

Samantha flew off the porch, down the steps, and into his arms. Dropping his bag at their feet, Tony lifted Samantha off the ground and swung her around in a half-circle as she clung tight to his neck.

"I missed you so much," Samantha whispered, as waves of relief washed over her. "I was beginning to think you weren't coming back."

Tony set her down. "I'm sorry it took me so long."

"It's okay, you're back now." She touched the side of his face. "How'd it go?"

"It's over."

Samantha caught her breath. How long had she waited to hear those words? "Really?"

"Yeah. Angela and I... we're done. I'm a free man."

Before she could respond, Tony brought his mouth down to meet hers. With a hand on the small of her back, Tony drew Samantha closer until their chests and hips were touching. His tongue gently pushed past petal-soft lips, sucking the breath right out of her as she went limp in his arms. Samantha's body melted into his as she yielded to the pent-up desire and passion coursing through her veins.

"Are you for real? Are you really here?" Samantha

gasped, pulling away and touching his face. "Is this really happening?"

Tony took her hands in his and kissed them. "Yes. And I promise you, I'm never going to leave your side again."

Samantha let the words sink in. This was really happening. They were finally going to be together. She wanted to do cartwheels of joy, but noticed something in Tony's face that dampened her celebratory mood. He looked like he'd aged several years in the week he'd been gone. "Are you okay?"

Tony kissed her again and squeezed her tight. "A lot better now that I'm back where I belong."

They went inside, and Tony caught Samantha up on everything that had happened. Though his narration of the events was flat and dispassionate, his eyes told a different story. Samantha could see the pain and guilt he carried, as if part of him was still in L.A. with Angela. She took his hand, interlacing fingers with his. "I'm so sorry."

"It's okay," he whispered, emotionally spent from having to relive the whole terrible ordeal. "The split was inevitable —we were staying together for all the wrong reasons. What did my sister say? Oh yeah, that we were codependent." He pulled Samantha to him, encircling her with his arms. "Don't get me wrong—it was hard. One of the hardest things I've ever had to do. But the pain doesn't come close to overshadowing the genuine elation I feel knowing that I'm finally free. Free to love you and be with you—mind, body, and soul."

"Mind, body, and soul..." Samantha repeated softly, still rooted in a faint shadow of disbelief as she just wasn't used to having her dreams come true.

"I love you so much," Tony said, kissing her again. He'd probably kissed her over a hundred times since he'd arrived —he just couldn't get enough. "With every breath, with everything that I am. Shoot, the way I feel right now makes the word love feel hopelessly inadequate. We transcend language. We're on a whole other level, babe." The sentiments rolled effortlessly off his tongue. They were the easiest, most honest words he had ever uttered.

"I love you, too," Samantha whispered, gazing into his eyes. The line between fantasy and reality had disintegrated —she was living a dream. "I've never felt this happy in my entire life. I didn't know it was possible to feel like this. I keep waiting to, I don't know, wake up or something."

Tony gathered Samantha into his arms again, deciding to forgo words altogether and show her how much she meant to him. Carrying her to the bedroom, he took his time removing each article of clothing, gradually becoming familiar with the parts of her he had yet to know. He drank her in with all his senses, delighting in every taste and touch, the scent of her skin an aphrodisiac, every curve a work of art. Tony wanted to give every inch of her body his full attention, to atone for the months of torturous neglect. Tonight, he would make up for lost time. He wouldn't rest until she was seeing stars.

Samantha was no virgin, but she made love for the very first time that night. Nothing could have prepared her for the sensory explosion she experienced every time Tony touched her. She rose to him, opened for him, excited and nervous as the unimaginable became reality. Those were really his hands on her hip; that was really his mouth on her breast. Tony was as in tune with her physically as he was mentally and spiritually, and it didn't take him long to bring her to the brink of orgasm. She was loving every second of it until Tony dove down between her thighs, his mouth seeking another pair of lips.

Reflexively, Samantha clamped her legs shut. "What are you doing?" she asked, suddenly self-conscious. She'd never let a man go down on her before.

"Just trust me," Tony whispered, pushing her legs apart. He kissed a trail from her belly button down to the soft patch of hair between her legs. "You are so beautiful."

Samantha gasped as he flicked his tongue against her swollen clit. Leaning back, she tried to relax and surrender to the moment. She had never been with an older man before, and Tony knew exactly which buttons to push to keep her hovering on the edge of ecstasy, her whole body overcome by the continuous tremble of a low-grade orgasm, begging for full release. Samantha clutched a pillow to her face to muffle her moans and groans.

When Tony finally made his way inside her, Samantha understood what it meant to truly become one with someone. Being with Tony came as naturally as breathing, and they fit together perfectly in every way. She couldn't feel where she ended and he began—it was one breath, one heartbeat, one heart. Two halves melded together to make a new and improved whole. They were *meant* to be together.

Every repressed feeling they shared rushed in as the emotional floodgates burst, infusing them with the most overwhelming sense of joy either one had ever experienced. They made love all through the night, their desire for each other insatiable, until finally collapsing in the wee hours of the morning, exhausted and spent, tangled in each other's arms.

Chapter Twenty-Four

Samantha opened her eyes the next morning to find Tony staring down at her with awe and admiration. A smile spread across her face. "Well, I guess I didn't dream you," she mumbled sleepily as he leaned down to kiss her good morning.

"This is better than a dream," he mused, drawing her close. "Last night was..." He shook his head, a flash from the previous night's sexcapades derailing his train of thought. "Last night was incredible. Girl, you took me places I ain't ever been before."

A blush crept into her cheeks. "But I didn't even *do* anything. You did all the work."

"Sweetheart, that was not work. I *wish* I could get paid to make love to you all day. If that were the case, I'd be putting in for overtime. My ass would never call in sick."

Samantha giggled. "You are too much."

Tony mimicked a soldier-style cadence. "Anthony Carteris reporting for duty, ma'am!" He slipped a hand between her legs, excited to feel wetness. "How would you like it this morning, Ms. Merrick? A little doggy-style perhaps?"

"Mmmm, sounds good," Samantha purred, making room for him between her legs. "I love a quickie in the morning."

Four hours later, the two of them came up for air.

"We can't do this all day," Samantha insisted, recovering from yet another mind-blowing orgasm. They had run through the entire box of condoms Tony brought, and didn't even bother using one the last two times.

"Why not?" He rubbed her hypersensitive clit, causing her to slap his hand away. "I haven't had this much fun in ages."

Samantha tried to free herself from his vise-like grip, but he wasn't about to let her up. "I have to be at work in two hours."

"Shhh," he said, squelching her protests with a kiss. "No talk of the real world just yet."

As much as Samantha would have loved to spend the day frolicking between the sheets with Tony, she had already called in sick several times over the past week. "Babe, my boss is gonna have my ass if I take another day off."

Reluctantly, Tony released her. "You're right, I'm sorry. What can I say—I'm just trying to make up for lost time."

"I know, but we have the rest of our lives for that. Besides, I only have to work a four-hour shift today. I'll be home by six."

"And I'll be waiting," Tony said.

Samantha's shift at the coffee shop flew by. She hummed softly as she fixed mochas and lattes for impatient patrons, a dreamy smile on her face as she reminisced about the previous night's explosive consummation. Co-workers who were not used to seeing Samantha exhibit such cheer were perplexed by the way her attitude had gone from cranky to lovestruck overnight.

Samantha was able to get off early, and when she returned home, she found both her housemates gone and Tony hard at work in the kitchen. She paused for a moment in the entryway to watch him. The man knew his way around a kitchen. He was bent over the sink washing dishes, his back to several pots and pans simmering on the stovetop, each emitting a flavorful odor. The dining room table had been set, a bottle of wine sitting beside two place settings. Several lit candles cast a warm glow throughout the room, creating the perfect mood lighting for a romantic dinner for two.

Samantha removed her jacket and joined him in the kitchen. "What's going on in here?"

Tony turned, startled. "Hey," he said, a bright smile lighting his eyes. "You're home early."

"Hope that's okay."

"Of course it is." Tony leaned down to steal a kiss. "I was so overwhelmed with missing you that I developed Faby's cooking disorder."

Samantha laughed. "Where are Gabe and Faby anyway?"

"Out for the night."

Samantha raised an eyebrow. "Really? How'd you manage that?"

"I gave Gabe some cash to take Faby out for dinner and a movie. Thought we could use some alone time."

Samantha surveyed the elaborate spread. "You did all this for me?"

"For *us*. We have a lot to celebrate."

"We certainly do." Samantha smiled again. Her cheeks were starting to hurt from the perma-grin she'd been wearing since Tony returned. She peered curiously into the large pot on the stove, the familiar aroma tickling her nostrils. "Oh my God — is that what I think it is?"

Tony smiled at her knowingly.

Samantha's eyes grew wide with amazement. Tony had prepared her favorite Filipino dish. "Where did you learn to make *adobo*?"

"Well I *am* half-Filipino."

"Yeah, so am I, and I can't cook shit." She reached for the ladle, her tastebuds tingling at the thought of the meal ahead. "May I?"

"Please."

Samantha fished a piece of chicken out of the pot and sampled Tony's spin on the popular Filipino dish. No one's version of *adobo* had ever come close to her grandfather's recipe, but Tony had created a close second.

Tony gazed down at her with expectant eyes. "So how is it?"

"It's delicious." She laid the spoon down. "You never

cease to amaze me."

"And to think, I'm just getting started."

Samantha pointed to the second covered pot. "What's in there?" she asked.

"Greens. And cornbread in the oven. Had to represent for our Black side, too," he said with a wink.

They sat down to enjoy the feast Tony had prepared. Samantha was blown away by his romantic gesture—she thought stuff like this only happened in the movies. "I can't believe you had time to do all this," she said, fixing a second helping of *adobo*.

"That's not even the half of it," he reported. "I also found a job."

Samantha stared at him, stunned. "You did? Doing what?"

"Bartending at the Crow's Nest."

"You're serious about staying in Santa Cruz?"

"Of course I am—I told you I wasn't leaving you again. All I have to do now is find a place to live."

"You don't want to stay in the house on West Cliff?"

"Naw. Damion is moving back to L.A. at the end of July, and I'm not trying to share that tiny room with anyone else. It looks like I'll be scoping out some new digs." Tony flashed a bright smile her way. "Know of anyone who might be looking for a roommate?"

Samantha shook her head. "Not really. But I'm sure you

can find someone on Craigslist."

"I don't want to live with just anybody though," Tony hinted. "Any potential roommate has to meet certain criteria."

"Such as?"

"Let's see. About 5'5 with brown eyes. Long, curly hair. The most curvaceous booty a brotha has ever seen. Know of anyone who fits that description?"

"I might," Samantha replied, blushing. The thought of making a home with Tony was something ripped out of her wildest dreams. It never even crossed her mind that they might be moving too fast. "I need to run it by Gabe and Faby, but you're more than welcome to stay here with me if you like."

"I think I'd like that very much."

Samantha felt her pulse quicken, a rumble of passion in her gut. Would he always affect her like this? She wanted to crawl across the table and rip his clothes off. With her teeth.

As if reading her mind, Tony stood and walked over to her, a wicked gleam in his eyes. "Soooo, you ready for dessert?"

Chapter Twenty-Five

*F*or the first time, Samantha was truly excited about what tomorrow might bring, as if anything was possible. They let their dreams run wild as they talked about the trips they'd take, the cities they'd live in, the children they'd have. Tony painted an amazing picture of their lives together, and his enthusiasm was infectious. Travel figured prominently into the master plan, and Tony was anxious to take advantage of his newfound freedom. He had already compiled a list of places for them to visit, and their first outing—a trip to Sykes Hot Springs—was planned for the following weekend.

"Are you sure you can't find anyone to cover your shifts next week?" he asked. "I don't have to start my bartending gig until Thursday after next, and I'd love to spend a few days camping along the Oregon coast, maybe even head up to Seattle. You'd love Seattle."

"I'm sure I would," Samantha replied. She'd always wanted to visit the Pacific Northwest. "But I've called in so many favors lately—the other baristas are tired of covering for me."

"I thought Teresa was looking for extra shifts? Isn't she trying to save up for some big trip to Europe next summer?"

"Yeah, but she also met a guy recently, and you know how that goes. I'm not the only one all sprung and in love anymore."

Tony threw down his magazine in mock frustration. "Damnit, the world is supposed to be revolving around *us*. What is wrong with these people, didn't they get the memo?" He sat up. "You should just quit your job."

"How am I going to pay my rent and afford all this travel if I do that?"

"Don't trip, I got you," Tony said.

"I couldn't let you do all that."

"Why not? This is our life now, our path. Me and you against the world. I'm the one that's done with school and free to work full-time. I have no problem stepping up and taking care of things. Besides, it would only be temporary, until we could find you a job with more flexible hours."

"Like what?"

"Like Tony's personal sex slave."

Samantha smiled as he tackled her onto the bed. "Hmmm, that sounds intriguing. Does that position come with benefits?"

"But of course." Tony slid his hand under her shirt to play with one of her nipples. "Would you like to see a sample of the benefits package?"

Samantha leaned back as Tony covered her with kisses. *So this is what love feels like,* she thought. Being with him was so *easy.* Samantha had always been somewhat of a loner, and even her closest friends eventually got on her nerves after awhile. But Samantha never felt like she needed space from Tony. They had sequestered themselves to her room the past few days, completely cut off from the outside world, and within the confines of these four walls, Samantha was totally content. As far as she was concerned, there was no reason for her to ever leave this bed.

If only things could have stayed that way.

The phone rang, but Samantha made no effort to answer it. The only person she had any interest in talking to was laying beside her, and she'd left strict instructions with her housemates that they did not want to be disturbed. Which is why she was surprised to hear a soft knock at her door a few minutes later. "Hey Sam." It was Gabe. "You guys decent?"

Samantha sat up and adjusted her clothing. "Yeah, come in."

Gabe poked his head inside. "Tony, the phone's for you. It's Damion."

"I'll be right back," Tony said to Samantha, following Gabe into the living room.

Samantha waited about ten minutes, and when Tony didn't return, she went to see what was going on.

Tony was sitting on the edge of the couch, head in hands, the phone at his side. Samantha stopped dead in her tracks

—something was wrong, very wrong. "What's going on?"

Tony lifted his head to reveal a face drained of all color. There were tears in his eyes. "It's Angela. She's in the hospital."

Samantha's hand flew to her mouth. "Oh my god—what happened?"

"Damion didn't have many details, but apparently she overdosed last night. My sister called from the hospital and asked him to track me down." He looked up at Samantha, heartbreak in his eyes. "I need to go. Be there."

"Of course," Samantha said. "Do you want me to go with you?"

"Uh, that's probably not the best idea right now."

"Of course not. I'm sorry." Samantha dropped her head, at a complete loss for words. She didn't know what to feel or say, or how her attempts to comfort him would be received. So she stood there, helpless and in shock, until Tony reached out, wrapped his arms around her waist, and buried his head in her chest.

Within the hour, Tony was packing up the van once again. They'd been living in a dream, but now it was time to wake up. Samantha looked sadly around the room at their makeshift love nest, hugging a pillow to her chest. That morning, the most pressing thing on their minds was finding somewhere that would deliver breakfast in bed. Everything had changed so fast Samantha was suffering from emotional whiplash. How long was he going to be gone this time? She was beginning to feel like their union was cursed—every time they tried to take a step forward, something got in the way.

Samantha noticed the corner of Tony's treasure box sticking out from under the bed. She picked it up, running her hand over the intricately carved lid. He couldn't have meant to leave it behind.

Samantha walked out to the van and placed the box on the seat beside him. "You left this by the bed."

"I know." He handed it back to her. "This box is my most prized possession, and I'm leaving it here with you, where it belongs. Where it's safe." He wiped a tear from her cheek. "This absence is only temporary. I'll be back before you know it, babe."

Samantha avoided his eyes. She had promised herself she wasn't going to cry. "I'm just going to miss you so much."

"I know... Me, too." He pulled her into his arms, resting his chin on the top of her head. "You just focus on one thing, okay?"

"What's that?"

"That I love you, and plan on spending the rest of my life with you. Nothing can get in the way of that. Nothing."

And just like that, he was gone.

Chapter Twenty-Six

*T*ony stepped off the elevator and headed for the nurse's station. He hated hospitals. The sterile white corridors and overpowering stench of antiseptic did nothing to mask the debris of death and disease that hung heavy in the air. He hadn't set foot in a hospital since the night his mother died, and sure enough, the echo of footsteps in a hollow hall brought back every painful memory he fought so hard to suppress. His mother had been gone five years, but the ache of missing her hadn't dulled with time. Not even a little bit.

"Excuse me," he said, approaching the nurse behind the switchboard. "Can you tell me what room Angela Anderlini is in?"

"221," the nurse said without looking up. "The doctor is with her right now, but you're welcome to wait in the lounge with the rest of the family."

The rest of the family? Were Angela's grandparents here? Angela hadn't spoken to either of them since they banished her from the house for daring to fall in love with a Black man. Tony wasn't sure he could deal with them on top of everything else. They'd always said Tony would ruin Angela's life, and now he'd gone and proven them right.

He entered the lounge and found his sister Ashley huddled in the corner with some middle-aged black man he'd never seen before. When Ashley saw Tony, she abandoned her conversation mid-sentence and hurried toward him. "I'm so glad you're here."

"I got here as soon as I could," Tony said, giving her a hug. He eyed the scrawny brotha with the unkempt afro suspiciously. "Are the grandparents here?"

"They were," Ashley confirmed. "But they got into it with Angela's mom and left."

"Angela's *mom*?" Tony asked, eyes darting up and down the hall. Every time that woman showed up, she brought trouble with her. Tony and Angela had taken her in several times over the years to help her get clean, only to find themselves robbed blind for their trouble. The last time anyone had seen Angela's mother, she was working a corner in Venice trying to support her drug habit. "Let me guess, Mr. Shifty over there is with her."

"Yeah, his name is Darius. Genice is in with the doctor."

The door to Angela's room swung open and the doctor emerged, followed closely by Genice Anderlini, Angela's absentee, crackhead mother. Tony bristled at the sight of her, his bullshit radar on high alert. Granted, the woman didn't *look* high or strung out, but Tony knew that where Genice was concerned, looks could be deceiving.

Genice marched right over to him, cold blue eyes piercing. "Nice of you to finally make an appearance."

Tony rolled his eyes. Coming from a woman who'd chosen drugs over her only daughter, the sanctimonious air was laughable. "No disrespect, Mrs. Anderlini," Tony said, fighting to hold his tongue and temper, "but have you even seen your daughter in the past three years?" He brushed past her and caught up to the doctor. "Excuse me, can I get an update on Angela Anderlini's condition?"

"And you are?"

"My name is Tony, sir. I'm her, uh… I'm Angela's boyfriend."

"Ah yes, she's been asking for you." The doctor closed the chart and tucked it under his arm. "Miss Anderlini was admitted to the hospital late last night, after being found unconscious in her apartment by her mother. The tox screen shows that Angela consumed a large quantity of antidepressants while drinking alcohol—a very dangerous combination. Her vitals are strong, and there doesn't appear to be any damage to her organs, so we expect her to make a full recovery. But we can't release her until she's been assessed by the staff psychiatrist, and we are certain that Angela is not going to try and harm herself again."

"What do you mean—'try and harm herself again?'

"Angela's mother seems fairly certain this was a suicide attempt."

The doctor's words knocked the wind right out of him. "I had no idea."

"Are you happy now?" Genice asked, coming up behind

him. "You see what you've done? This is all your fault."

Tony whirled around to face her, his cheeks hot with rage. "And I'm sure your stellar parenting skills had absolutely nothing to do with it," Tony snapped. "You wanna toss blame around, Genice? Why don't we talk about why Angela needed to be on antidepressants in the first place!"

"Look, I realize I'm no candidate for mother of the year," Genice said, playing up her distress for the doctor's benefit. "But I love my daughter. And while you were up in Santa Cruz doing god knows what, Angie and I were rebuilding. She's forgiven me. That's what she called to tell me after she took all those pills—that she'd forgiven me." Genice burst into tears as her pimp boyfriend draped an arm around her shaky shoulders.

Tony watched unmoved as Genice's crocodile tears mixed with cheap mascara to form dark streaks on her cheeks. He wasn't buying this sudden show of motherly concern. Genice had sold her soul to the crack devil years ago and was always running a scam—he didn't trust the woman as far as he could throw her. "I'm not buying it," Tony said, his instinct to protect Angela reignited. "I wouldn't put it past you to try and cash in on this tragedy."

"You worthless, two-timing bastard—how dare you talk to me like that!" Genice got up in his face, spraying him with spit and whiskey-tainted breath. "Who the hell do you think you are?"

Ashley, who had been watching quietly from a distance,

decided to intervene. She placed a hand on Tony's arm. "This isn't helping Angela."

Tony took a step back. As much as he wanted to lay the blame for this situation at Genice's feet, deep down Tony knew what the true catalyst of this disaster was. This time he was the one who had abandoned Angela and broken her heart. Genice was right—this was all his fault.

"I'd like to see her," Tony said, turning his attention back to the doctor.

The doctor paused for a moment, expecting to hear an objection from Angela's mother. Surprisingly, there wasn't one. "If she wakes up," the doctor cautioned, "please try not to upset her."

Tony took a deep breath and pushed open the door. Angela was sound asleep, her skin a ghastly pale. The rhythmic beeps of the monitor reverberated through the eerie stillness, causing Tony to shiver. He really hated hospitals.

Slipping into the seat beside Angela's bed, Tony took her hand. Gone were his reservations and petty criticisms. He couldn't remember anymore the laundry list of reasons why she had not been good enough. All he knew was that he loved this woman, and desperately needed for her to be okay. Bowing his head in the darkened room, he did something he hadn't done in years. Five years, to be exact. He prayed.

"I know you only seem to hear from me when I need

something," Tony began in a soft whisper, seeking out his forgotten God. "But I messed this one up good, and don't know where else to turn. Angela needs to be okay. Whatever I have to do, I'll do it. Just please, let her be okay."

Angela began to stir and rolled her head toward him. "Tony," she whispered.

"I'm right here," he said, squeezing her hand.

Panicked eyes darted around the room. "Where am I?"

"You're in the hospital. Your mother brought you in."

"What happened?"

Please try not to upset her. "Shhh, don't talk. You need your rest. I'm here now, everything's going to be okay." He brushed the hair back from her forehead tenderly.

Angela's eyelids came down like a heavy curtain as she struggled to keep them open. "Promise me you won't leave again…" she whispered, before slipping back into unconsciousness.

"I promise," he winced, knowing in his heart that he meant every word.

❧

When Tony finally left Angela's side for a long overdue smoke break, Genice slipped into her daughter's hospital room. "So, how'd it go?"

"He bought it," Angela reported, smug satisfaction replacing the distraught pseudo-breakdown ruse she'd been keeping up. "Tony will think twice before ever trying to leave me again."

Chapter Twenty-Seven

*T*ony stared blankly ahead. He had been sitting in his bus chain-smoking for almost an hour, trying to figure out how things had gone so terribly wrong. Consumed by guilt, the walls of his life pushed in on him. A suicide attempt? Seriously? He couldn't wrap his head around the latest turn of events.

The auburn sky was dusted with clouds as the sun disappeared behind the building, the last traces of day vanishing into night. The last time he watched the sun set, he had been cuddled up under a blanket with Samantha, planning their lives. Those quiet moments of perfection felt like they happened ages ago, in another life. So close to having it all, he'd held the holy grail of his existence in his hands. But now he had to let go. How was he going to let her go?

Ashley's cell phone sat beside him on the passenger seat. He needed to call Samantha and give her an update, but couldn't move. With all the information he was being forced to process at once, his brain had short-circuited, a numbness descending over him. He just needed for everything to stop—no more life-shattering revelations, no more drama. Just a few moments of silence so he could try and figure out what to do with the rest of his life.

Tony never imagined something like this could happen. He knew Angela would take things hard, but to actually try and kill herself? Maybe if he'd shown more compassion, or hung around a little longer to help her through it… But no, Tony had acted with nothing but selfishness at every turn, and now he had to suffer the consequences.

He was startled out of his guilt-fueled trance by a sharp tap on the window.

"Earth to Tony," Ashley repeated. "Unlock the door."

Tony opened the passenger door so Ashley could climb in. "How'd it go?" she asked.

"I haven't called yet."

"Oh." Ashley placed the phone on the dash. "You shouldn't be sitting out here beating yourself up—this is not your fault."

"Come on, you were there—she was falling apart and I just left."

"At my urging," Ashley reminded him, trying to deal with guilt pangs of her own. "Trust me, bro, I am sitting right beside you on the guilt train. But the truth is, neither one of us is responsible for Angela's actions. In the end, she was the one who decided to take those pills." Ashley stopped, not wanting to come off as too preachy. The last thing her brother needed was a lecture. "You should call Sam."

Tony continued to stare straight ahead. "I know."

After a few minutes, Ashley decided to leave Tony alone to brood—it was obvious he needed some space. "I'm going to get something to eat at the cafeteria. I was just checking to see if you were done with my phone."

Ashley's parting words penetrated his moody fog. "Oh, right. Sorry." He grabbed the phone and flipped the lid up. "Just give me a few minutes."

"No problem. Take your time."

Tony dialed Samantha's number. She picked up on the second ring. "Hello?"

"Hey, it's me."

Samantha sat up. She had been camped out by the phone, anxiously awaiting word. "Thank God—I've been so worried about you. Is Angela okay?"

"She's going to be fine," Tony said quietly. "But things are pretty bad." He struggled to force the words out, words he didn't even want to know, much less speak aloud. "She tried to commit suicide, Sam."

Samantha's jaw dropped. "Oh my God."

"Yeah, my sentiments exactly."

"But she's going to be okay?"

"Physically, yes. But emotionally…" He paused. "She's

still rather fragile."

"I don't know what to say," Samantha whispered. "I'm so sorry."

"I know, me, too."

Silence. Time was standing still for them again, but not in a good way.

"I know I said I'd be back," Tony started. "But I don't know how I can leave her like this. Not right now."

"Of course." Tears started to roll down Samantha's cheeks as she stifled her sobs. She was devastated, but determined not to show it. She had to be strong for her man. "I completely understand."

"You do?"

"Of course I do. We're talking about someone's life here."

"I just don't know what I'd do if something happened to her," Tony said.

"I know."

"I love you, Sam."

Samantha smiled—it was amazing how three little words could bring such comfort in even the darkest of times. "I know that, too."

"Alright, well, I should get back inside. I'll call you in a few days."

Samantha's heart sank. A few days? Why was he shutting her out? "I'm here whenever you need me," she managed to choke out.

The line went dead. Samantha stared at the phone in her hand—did he just hang up on her?

Whatever Tony was going through, apparently he wanted to deal with it alone.

So much for me and you against the world.

Chapter Twenty-Eight

*T*ony poured himself a cup of coffee and sat down with the morning paper. He had brought Angela home from the hospital a few days ago, and life was slowly returning to normal. Well, as normal as things could be for someone who suddenly found himself trapped in a life he didn't want.

The doctors no longer felt Angela was a threat to herself, but thought it was best if someone was around to watch her. Since Genice couldn't be trusted with the care of a houseplant, much less an emotionally unstable human being, Tony agreed to move back in. He had intended to sleep on the couch for the duration, but on their first night home Angela woke up in a panic, screaming his name. She wasn't able to sleep through the night without him by her side, so against Tony's better judgment, he returned to their bed. He just couldn't bring himself to deny her anything right now.

Angela refused to talk about the overdose outside of her therapy sessions. As far as she was concerned it was a terrible "accident," and any attempt by Tony to broach the subject triggered an immediate shutdown. Eventually, he stopped bringing it up, praying it was being adequately dealt with in therapy. The last thing he wanted to do was make things worse —he'd done enough damage.

"Any special requests for dinner?" Angela asked, coming up behind him. She was dressed in a navy pantsuit, a brown leather briefcase in her left hand. "I'm going to swing by the store on my way home from work."

Tony forced a smile, struggling to hide his own intense depression. "Whatever you want is fine with me."

"Maybe I'll stop by the Fish Market and pick up some Ahi. How does that sound?"

"Sounds fine."

"Great. I'll see you tonight then." Angela bent down to give Tony a kiss and couldn't help but notice how he stiffened whenever she got close to him. Tony was going through the motions, trying his hardest to be there for her, but it was obvious his thoughts were elsewhere. Angela blinked back tears as she brushed her lips against his and retreated.

Angela was a firm believer in "out of sight, out of mind." After all, isn't that what had happened to her? Tony never would have ended up in another woman's arms if she'd been there to take care of his needs. Now that Tony was back home where he belonged, it was only a matter of time before they got their relationship back on track. Angela was certain she could make him forget all about this Samantha person.

Tony heard the front door close and allowed himself to relax. When Angela said she wanted to go back to work, he'd been ecstatic, thankful for the much-needed break from the constant pretending. Living with Angela again was like having a noose around his neck. With each day that passed, the rope tightened, and now he could barely breathe. How much longer until he suffocated?

Grabbing the cordless phone, he stepped onto the balcony and lit a cigarette, tapping his foot impatiently as the phone rang and rang.

"Hello."

"Finally," Tony said, taking a seat in one of the faded plastic patio chairs. The ashtray was overflowing with cigarette butts —he'd been averaging a pack a day since returning home.

"Finally indeed—I was about to send out a search party," Damion scolded. "I really wish you'd get a damn cell phone."

"Come on, man, you know I have no desire to be that reachable."

"Right, right. So how's it going?"

Tony took a long drag off his cigarette. "Hell on earth, my friend, hell on earth."

"Is Ange home from the hospital yet?"

"Yeah, they discharged her on Friday. She actually decided

to go back to work today."

"Really? She must be feeling better then."

"I guess."

"So what's the plan? How long are you going to stay down there?"

"Not sure. Her doctors think it's best if someone is around to watch her, so I can't exactly leave."

"Wait, hold up—you moved back in?" Damion asked. "Isn't that sending mixed signals?"

"What was I supposed to do? What if she tries that shit again? Whether I like it or not, Angela is my responsibility."

"What about Samantha?"

Just hearing her name filled Tony with the most overwhelming sense of longing. Next to losing his mother, being away from Samantha was the worst pain he'd ever had to endure, even worse than almost losing Angela. Their souls had merged when they consummated their love, and without her, Tony felt half-dead inside. He just did not know how to reconcile his intense need to be with Samantha with the guilt he felt over leaving Angela. "I haven't talked to her in over a week."

"What? Why not?"

"I don't know what to say."

"And you think saying nothing is a solution? She must be going crazy over there!"

"I just need some time to figure out what to do. Cut me

some slack here—it's not like I could have anticipated things going down like this."

"Still…"

"Look, if you're so concerned about Samantha's well-being, can you do me a favor and check on her? You know, see how she's doing, make sure she's okay…"

Damion shook his head. When was Tony gonna learn that avoidance mode was not the answer? "She needs to hear from *you*."

"She will. Tell her I'll call as soon as things stabilize."

"Alright, man, I'll swing by her place on the way home from work tonight."

"Thanks, Dame."

"No problem. Hang in there, buddy."

"I'm trying."

Chapter Twenty-Nine

*S*amantha was a mess. Between the anxiety, insomnia, and gut-clenching paranoia, she was pretty much on edge twenty-four hours a day. All around town, normal college students were out and about enjoying the best of what summer in Santa Cruz had to offer, her housemates included. Gabe had headed out bright and early to De La Veaga for a round of frisbee golf, and Faby was at the beach working on her tan. A healthy dose of sunshine probably would have done Samantha a lot of good, but she had placed herself on house arrest until she heard from Tony. She just knew the second she left the house, he'd call.

Samantha missed Tony so much it physically hurt. Apparently that was the flipside of loving someone more than life itself—when you couldn't be with them, it impaired your ability to function. And that was precisely the situation Samantha found herself in—unable to function. Now that she'd had a glimpse of how things could be, she couldn't imagine her life without Tony in it. She didn't want to. So instead, she channeled all of her energy into the futile task of pining, moping, and waiting.

The doorbell rang and Samantha bolted upright. "Tony," she gasped, racing to the front door.

But it wasn't Tony she found on her doorstep. Instead Tony's best friend Damion stared back at her. Samantha instantly feared the worst. "Oh God, what's happened now?"

Damion saw the panic on her face and quickly put her mind at ease. "Oh no, it's nothing like that—everything's fine," he said quickly. "Well, obviously not fine, but nothing *else* has happened." He stuffed his hands in his pockets. "Tony asked me to stop by."

"You talked to him?"

"Yeah, earlier today. They released Angela from the hospital, and he's been staying with her, to keep an eye on her. That's why he can't call."

"He found time to call *you*."

Damion scrambled to find an excuse for his buddy's inexcusable behavior. "He's just trying to be discreet. He doesn't want to agitate Angela."

Samantha adjusted her tone. "I'm sorry, I didn't mean to snap at you. It's just that everyone else is out partying their lives away while I've been holed up in this house holding some freak phone vigil." She gestured for him to come in. "How is he?"

"Wracked with guilt, miserable, and missing you," Damion said, taking a seat on the couch. He noticed the cluttered surroundings. Empty beer bottles and coffee mugs littered the coffee table, and celebrity gossip magazines covered the floor. It looked like someone had been camping out on the couch. "How are *you* doing?"

"About the same," Samantha confessed. "Not knowing what's going on down there has been the worst, but I'm trying my hardest to be patient."

"You should be a candidate for sainthood," Damion said. "You've been incredibly patient. Tony is lucky to have you."

"I appreciate you saying that, but let's be real—I'm hardly a saint. I'm a homewrecker who drove a woman to attempt suicide." Samantha shook her head as tears welled up in her eyes.

Damion placed a hand on her leg. "Hey, this is not your fault."

"Yes it is. If I hadn't pressured him, he wouldn't have felt the need to fast-track the break-up. Maybe if we'd taken things a little slower..."

"There is no way either one of you could have known something like this was going to happen."

"But it *did* happen. And now... God, what now?"

Damion placed an arm around her shoulder. He didn't have any of the answers she needed. *Damn you Tony*, he thought. *You should be here comforting your girl, not me.*

"You know the worst part?" Samantha continued. "As much guilt as I'm feeling, I know it's only a fraction of what Tony must be feeling. He must be going through hell right now, and I can't even help him." She punched the sofa cushion in frustration.

"I'm sorry, Sam. I wish there was something I could do to help."

"There is something you can do. Tony may not be able to call me, but you have his number, right?"

"Yeah, but..."

"Can you call him for me, Dame? Please. I need to talk to him."

Looking into Samantha's tear-filled eyes, he didn't know how he could say no. "Alright," he said, reaching for his phone. "Let's give Tony a call."

Tony was lost in the most incredible dream. He and Samantha were backpacking through the Amazon rainforest, swimming in rivers and communing with wildlife. Sweat glistened on her skin as she traipsed through the jungle in a tank top and cut-off shorts, her hair loose and wild. As he watched her toned legs navigate the rough terrain, he couldn't resist the urge to lay her down and make love to her right there in the middle of the forest. Capturing her supple lips, he pulled Samantha to him, feeling her nipples harden against his bare chest. His hands slid down to her waist, pushing her shorts over voluptuous hips. She laid back and opened for him, just like she always did... He was about to enter her juicy wetness when—

Ring!

Tony opened his eyes, scanning the room for the offensive sound. He snatched the phone off the counter. "Hello."

"Wassup, it's D—is Angela around?"

"No, she's still at work." Tony cursed Damion's timing. He only got to see Samantha in his dreams, and was not happy about having that time cut short. "Have you seen Sam? How is she?"

"Why don't you ask her yourself," Damion said, handing Samantha the phone.

Samantha mouthed the words 'thank you' to Damion as he stepped outside to give her some privacy. "Hey," she spoke into the phone. "I hope it's okay that we called—I really needed to hear your voice."

"No, it's okay. It's good to hear your voice, too." A little too good—Tony was two seconds away from hopping in the car and driving back to Santa Cruz. "I'm sorry I haven't called."

"Damion told me things have been hectic. How have you been holding up?"

"It's been rough. I have to watch everything I do, everything I say, cause I don't know what's going to set her off. The last thing I want to do is trigger another breakdown."

"Is she seeing someone?"

"Yeah, she sees a therapist twice a week, but I have no idea what kind of progress is being made. Angela refuses to talk about it with me—she's in denial that any of it happened."

"So what now?"

Tony swallowed hard. What Samantha needed, he couldn't give her just yet. "As much as it kills me to be away from you,

I can't come back yet. I can't risk this happening again. I—"
He heard Angela's key in the lock. "Good to hear from you,
man—thanks for checking in," he said loudly as Angela came
through the front door. "Tell the peeps I said what's up."

"Let me guess, Angela just walked in."

"Yup."

"I love you," Samantha whispered.

"Same here. Aight, man, peace."

The call disconnected. He was gone.

Samantha joined Damion on the porch and handed his
phone back. "Thanks," she said, putting on her very best
brave front.

"You feel better?"

"A little bit. Angela came home so we got cut off."

Damion stole a glance at Samantha as she stared off
down the street, her thoughts and heart hundreds of miles
away. He'd never seen someone simultaneously exude such
strength and vulnerability. "Now that your vigil is over, you
wanna get something to eat?"

Samantha shook her head. "I'd be terrible company."

"Let me be the judge of that." Damion bumped her hip
with his. "Come on, you can't live on beer and potato chips. We
can grab a couple of burritos from Taqueria Vallarta. My treat."

A burrito from Vallarta did sound good. "Alright," she
reluctantly agreed. "Let me grab my purse..."

Chapter Thirty

"My doctor thinks you should be in therapy with me," Angela blurted out over dinner.

Tony almost choked on his steak. For the past month he and Angela had been living under the same roof and sleeping in the same bed, yet somehow managed to get by without once discussing the status of their relationship. As far as Tony was concerned, his primary objective was to get Angela back on her feet and eventually broker a more peaceful separation. Angela, however, was intent on acting as if they had never broken up in the first place. Their apartment was a veritable minefield of tough talks and explosive confrontations they were both determined to avoid. But joint counseling? He didn't need to pay some shrink $100 an hour to tell him his relationship wasn't working.

"Does your therapist understand that we're not a couple anymore?"

Angela engaged her selective hearing and pretended not to hear him. "He's fairly confident that with proper mediation, we can get to the root of our issues, and then take purposeful strides toward resolving them."

Tony took a swig from his beer, siphoning off some liquid courage. "Angela, we need to talk."

She stood up and began to clear the table. "We can talk in therapy..."

✺

Therapy was torture. Being stripped naked and held under a microscope was not his idea of a good time. It didn't help that the therapist bore a striking resemblance to Angela's grandfather. Tony wondered if Angela noticed the similarity, or if in a strange way drew comfort from it. Unfortunately, the doctor elicited the same response from Tony as her grandfather did—defensiveness as a result of feeling unfairly judged. Tony had zero incentive to share anything personal with the man.

After sitting through several sessions punctuated by awkward silence and Tony's stoic uncooperativeness, the therapist went for the jugular. "So Tony," the doctor started, without the slightest bit of pretense, "tell me about your mother."

Tony cut his eyes at Angela. "What about her?"

"You seem to have a lot of repressed anger. Are you angry with your mother?"

The muscles in Tony's jaw clenched. "Why would I be angry with my mother?"

"You tell me. Do you feel like your mother abandoned you?"

"My mother didn't abandon me, she died," Tony snapped.

He snatched his jacket from the back of the chair, fighting to keep a lid on his rage. "I'm sorry, but there is no way in hell I'm gonna sit here and let some quack disrespect my mama." He stormed out of the doctor's office and slammed the door behind him.

Angela had barely buckled her seatbelt before Tony went tearing out of the parking lot. They drove in silence for several miles before she dared to speak. "You're not even trying," she said, her lower lip protruding.

"What did you tell him about my mother?"

"He's my therapist, Tony—I tell him everything."

"Like what?"

"It's just this theory I have," Angela mumbled under her breath.

Tony pulled the car over. He wasn't coordinated enough to drive and argue at the same time. "What theory?"

Angela stared out the window, avoiding his eyes. She had pushed him too far and she knew it. "Nothing."

"No, please enlighten me. I'd love to hear what my mother has to do with any of this."

Angela took a deep breath and proceeded with caution. "You seem to have some unresolved feelings about your mom's death, and I think, because I remind you of her, that you tend to displace your anger toward her onto me."

Tony lit a cigarette, even though he knew the smell of smoke made Angela sick to her stomach. "That's ridiculous."

"You started shutting me out after she died."

"No, actually, you were the one person I *didn't* shut out."

"You know what I'm talking about—you shut down emotionally." She rolled her window down, allowing some fresh air to circulate. He was so fucking passive-aggressive. "Sure, you let me comfort you, but you never wanted to talk about what you were *feeling*. We used to talk about everything —no holds barred. We used to have so much fun. But lately, it's like you're just going through the motions." Angela paused, suddenly nostalgic for the good ole days when they'd had an ample supply of passion and laughter between them. "This past year has been hard on me, too, you know. It seems like no matter what I do, nothing is good enough. But not once did I think about leaving you. I'm committed to hanging in there and sticking it out, even when it's hard, because that's what you do when you love someone."

Tony was unmoved. "One question, Ange. If you love me so much, then knowing what I've been through, why in the world would you make me re-live the worst thing that's ever happened to me? Do you really want to end up like my mother?" The words burst forth with such force it startled them both, the first uncensored sentiment to come out of his mouth in weeks.

"Right Tony, because of course, once again, it's all about you!" Angela burst into tears. "See, this is why we need a therapist—I can't talk to you when you're like this."

"When I'm like what?"

"When you're yelling at me!" she screamed. She glanced around frantically, eyes wide like a caged animal. "Will you just take me home? I want to go home."

Tony pulled back into traffic. So now he was the one with the emotional problems? He couldn't live like this. Angela was no closer to taking responsibility for her actions than she was after the overdose. He didn't know how much more of this he could take before he lost his damn mind.

Twenty minutes later Tony came to a stop in front of their apartment building. "You're not coming up?" Angela asked, as the VW bus idled curbside.

"No, I'm gonna drive around for a bit, maybe stop by my sister's."

"Tony, I—"

"I'll be home in a few hours, okay? I need to clear my head."

Tony sped off as Angela stared down the road at his retreating tail lights. He slammed his fist against the steering wheel, the rage inside screaming for release. Angela was a master at pushing his buttons, at somehow finding a way to make everything his fault. It had been bad before, but now that his ability to defend himself had been neutralized by her fragile mental state, their relationship had a completely different dynamic. One in which he felt powerless and trapped.

He located a pay phone and dialed Samantha's number.

She was the only thing his crazy life that made sense.

"Hello."

"Faby, it's Tony. Is Sam home?"

"How are you gonna hang up on someone mid-conversation, and then not call back for weeks," Faby snapped. Samantha, who was in the kitchen, hurried toward the phone.

"I'm calling now," Tony said. He really wasn't in the mood to get cussed out again. "Is she home or not?"

Samantha snatched the phone out of Faby's hand. "Tony?"

"Yeah, it's me." It felt so good to hear her voice, although he wished it wasn't steeped in fear and panic. "I'm sorry I haven't called."

"It's okay," Samantha said, heading to her room to escape Faby's prying eyes. Actually, it *wasn't* okay. Rather far from okay as a matter of fact. But she had to keep reminding herself that it was her impatience, selfishness, and desire for Tony that had set this chain of events in motion. "How are things going?"

"Terrible," he said. "She's making me go to couple's counseling."

"Couple's counseling? Isn't that for couples?"

"I know, I know. I'm just trying to get her healthy, and if joint therapy will help her come to terms with this break-up, then I'll do what I have to do. But my heart hasn't changed Sam—you're still the one I want to be with."

Samantha relaxed a bit, thankful for the reassurance.

"Well, how is therapy?"

"It's a joke. I got fucking ambushed today. The doc wanted to probe my mommy issues—like I'm the one who needs therapy."

"Ouch."

"Yeah, Angela's got the victim role down pat, so of course everything is *my* fault. I realize I'm hardly blameless, but I didn't mean for any of this to happen."

"I know."

"I hate that I have to put you through this, Sam. You deserve so much better."

"Don't worry about me, I'm fine. I'll wait for you, however long it takes to sort this out. We'll get through this."

Tony was reminded again of all the reasons he loved Samantha—her grace, her compassion, her strength. Women like Samantha were rare, and he had no intention of letting her go.

The operator's voice rudely cut into their conversation. "Please deposit forty-five cents for the next three minutes," the voice warned.

"Damnit," Tony cursed, rifling through his pockets. "I'm out of change."

"It's okay. I'm just glad I got to hear your voice."

"I won't be able to call very often, but whenever I get a chance, you'll hear from me. I promise."

"I'll be waiting," Samantha said. "I love you."

"Love you, too."

Chapter Thirty-One

Summer was in full swing, and at Faby's urging, Samantha had traded in her phone vigil for a more effective distraction—party-hopping. With Faby's extensive social network at their disposal, there was no shortage of BBQ's and house parties to choose from, and the girls were living it up. Samantha was still averse to crowds, but she had to admit that getting out of the house and keeping busy made time move quicker. Every day that came and went was one day closer to being reunited with Tony.

Tonight they were going to a full-moon bonfire at Seabright Beach, and Samantha had been looking forward to the gathering all week. Santa Cruz was somewhat of a hippie haven, and while she had no intention of turning in her carnivore card, certain rituals did resonate with her. Anything that celebrated Mother Nature was well worth her time and energy, and she couldn't wait to dance in the moonlight with the rest of her sister-folk.

Samantha helped herself to a handful of chips and a

Heineken. The bonfire was handled potluck-style, and there was quite a spread laid out to supplement the smell of *carne asada* coming off the grill. While the women organized the feast, the guys broke down palates to feed the fire, the soothing sounds of reggae floating in the air. Summer had officially arrived.

"Here, try this," Faby said, thrusting a red plastic cup into Samantha's hand. "Melinda made a wicked batch of Sangria."

Samantha took a sip and sucked on a Sangria-soaked peach. "Wow, that is damn good."

"Yup, and there's more where that came from. We're getting fucked up tonight, girlfriend!" Faby surveyed the selection of shirtless bachelors. This was the first time in years that she'd been single, and she was having a blast getting her rebound on. "Oooh, Adrian's here. How do I look? I'm not all windblown, am I?"

Samantha looked Faby up and down. She had on a burgundy crop top that complemented her skin tone perfectly, and skintight denim capris. Her hair was loose and hung down to the middle of her back in carefree waves. "Haven't you seen the latest Victoria's Secret catalog? The windblown look is in."

"Seriously, Sam," Faby said, with a hint of self-consciousness.

"I'm just playing. You look great, like you always do."

Faby licked her lips as Adrian made his way down the sand dune, his tanned physique on display. "Good, cause with all these fish in the sea, I'm fixin' to go fishin'."

Samantha was happy to see Faby had gotten her groove back—she was too much of a catch to waste time mourning the loss of a loser like Carlos. "Sounds like a plan. Just send up the bat signal if you need to be rescued."

As Faby made a beeline for her prey, Samantha took her drinks and headed in the opposite direction, away from the growing crowd. Taking a seat just above the water's edge, she closed her eyes, tuning everything out but the sounds of the ocean. The rolling of the surf had its own special rhythm, flowing in and out, in and out. Tony had taught her how to breathe with the waves, so she took a moment to synchronize her breath to the sound of the sea. In moments, the ocean began to work its magic, calming her nerves and soothing her soul.

An amused voice interrupted her quiet meditation. "Double-fisted, huh?"

Samantha opened her eyes and found Damion standing over her, his tall frame blocking out the setting sun. His locks were tied back beneath a blue bandana, and his white linen shirt, unbuttoned to his navel, exposed a sculpted chest. Samantha pushed aside an inappropriate thought—she never realized Damion was rocking such a hot bod underneath all those clothes. "What can I say—I've always been somewhat of an overachiever."

Damion laughed. "Well, it's good to see you out among the living. Mind if I sit?"

"Not at all. Pull up some sand."

Damion took a seat beside her. "It's going to be an amazing sunset."

"Every sunset is amazing," Samantha mused. "Like God himself is up there painting the sky."

Damion smiled. Samantha was just as Tony had described her—an earthy bohemian goddess. He could tell that buried underneath all that sarcasm was a poet's soul. "People don't take enough time to appreciate the simple things, do they?"

"No, they don't. Case in point—how many people over there are actually taking the time to watch the sunset?" She cast a glance over her shoulder at the bonfire revelers. "I count about five. Everyone else is too fixated on getting drunk and high to notice one of nature's most astounding miracles unfolding before them." Samantha looked down at her two adult beverages. "Not that there's anything wrong with getting drunk and high, but people gotta learn to multi-task."

Damion laughed again. "Have you ever seen the green flame?"

"Huh? What's the green flame?"

"At sunset on a really clear day, right after the sun disappears below the horizon line, supposedly you can see a green flame spark up at the point of exit."

Samantha was intrigued—she'd seen hundreds of sunsets and never heard of this phenomenon. "Really? I've never seen it."

"Me either. It's pretty rare cause the conditions have to be just right, but that doesn't stop me from looking for it every time I see the sun set."

They both squinted at the horizon in intense concentration as the sun quickly vanished from sight. "Did you see it?" Damion asked.

"Nope. You?"

"Nope. One of these days." The sky deepened into a vibrant red, then began to fade into purple. "So which are you—a cynic or a romantic?"

Samantha fished another piece of Sangria-soaked fruit out of the cup. "Why can't I be both?"

"Because the two modes of being are in conflict with each other."

"Maybe I like conflict."

Damion raised an eyebrow. "Do you?"

A thoughtful pause. "No, not really." Samantha stretched her legs out in front of her. "I used to be a romantic, but now I'm just jaded. I'd totally given up on ever falling in love again until Tony came along, but look how well that turned out. I'm starting to think the notion of happily ever after is a myth."

"There's still hope for a happily ever after with Tony."

Samantha glanced away from the sky long enough to catch Damion's eye. "Do you really believe that, or are you just trying to make me feel better?"

"I really believe it. Tony loves you, in a way he will never love Angela. As soon as he can get Angela well, he'll find a way out." Damion removed a glass pipe from his pocket, the bowl packed with a nug of Santa Cruz's finest herb. He passed it to her, along with a red lighter.

"Thanks," Samantha said as she took a hit. She passed the pipe back. "What's your take on Angela? Do you think therapy will help?"

Damion let out a long, slow exhale, a thin stream of smoke passing over his lips. "As you know, I've known Angela half my life. The three of us have been kicking it since middle school. But between you and me, I never thought those two were a good match."

Curious to hear Damion's take on things, Samantha leaned forward. "Really? Why not?"

Damion passed her the pipe again. "Angela has a lot of issues, and after everything Tony went through with his mom, the last thing he needs is another high-maintenance woman to take care of."

"Was it really that bad with his mom? He mentioned her battles with depression, but never goes into much detail."

"Yeah, it was pretty bad. It wasn't just depression—there were also these fits of outright hysteria. I'm pretty sure she was bipolar. She'd cry and yell and scream, with no apparent provocation, and when she wasn't lashing out, she would spend days in her room, not speaking to anyone, damn near comatose. Tony had always been a mama's boy, but after his dad took off, he became man of the house, too. He was the one who had to deal with his mother's illness and look after Ashley. Because he had to shoulder such grown-up responsibilities at a young age, he was pretty much robbed of his childhood.

"When his mom died, as painful as that was for all of us, it also meant that Tony was finally free to have a real life, you know, travel, get out of L.A. That's why I encouraged him to come to school here—I thought a change of scenery would do him some good. But any freedom he gained when his mother passed was immediately lost when Angela and all her drama became the center of his world. It is creepy how similar the two women are."

"They say men gravitate toward women that remind them of their mothers," Samantha said quietly.

"That may be true, but patterns can be broken. Angela may have been the woman he chose back then, but she's not the One. Tony has grown and matured since they first got together, especially since coming to Santa Cruz. Trust me Sam, you are exactly the kind of woman Tony wants and needs. He'll get out of this and come back to you, I'm sure of it."

Samantha hoped and prayed that Damion was right.

Four cups of sangria later, Samantha was feeling it. When the sun went down, the temperature on the beach dropped twenty degrees, the ocean whipping a chilly breeze across the sand. But between the roaring bonfire and the flush of sangria, Samantha was anything but cold. The sounds of UB40 pumped out of the boombox as Samantha joined the circle of women dancing in the moonlight, their cups of sangria raised high as they serenaded la luna.

"*Red, red wiiiine*," they sang at the top of their lungs. "*Goes to my head…*"

Samantha closed her eyes and swayed to the music. She loved being drunk. When she was drowning in alcohol, she just didn't give a fuck. About anything. It was the only time she could look at her mess of a life and actually laugh, a nice change from the constant ache she had to endure when she was sober.

Samantha felt someone come up behind her, large hands resting on her hips as they moved to the music. She turned to face the bold stranger, his hazel eyes peering out from under long, dark lashes. *Yum*, she thought, as the handsome boy pulled her closer. She threw her arm around his neck and proceeded to grind her pelvis against his, dirty dancing the night away as the mix CD transitioned into the hook-up anthem of the summer, Kevin Lyttle's "Turn Me On."

Before the song reached its first chorus, Samantha felt a hand on her arm. "Can I talk to you?"

Samantha spun around to find Damion looking down at her, a mask of disapproval hardening his usually kind features.

"I'm kinda in the middle of something," she said, turning her back on him.

"Yeah, I can see that. This will just take a minute." Damion pulled Samantha away from her dance partner, leveling him with a look so cold it could have frozen the ocean, cautioning him not to follow.

Samantha yanked her arm free, irritated and slightly belligerent. She did not appreciate being spied on and chastised by Tony's friends. She was a grown woman and Tony, well, Tony wasn't here. "I am not a child," she informed him. "And you are not my daddy."

"Fair enough. But what do you think you're doing? Besides drinking too damn much."

"I was dancing. Last time I checked, dancing was not a crime. It's not like I'm shacking up with my ex-boyfriend or something."

Point taken, Damion thought, toning it down a notch. Why was he coming off like some jealous husband? Samantha was right—she was a grown woman and didn't need a chaperone. "Look, I'm just trying to make sure you don't do something you regret."

"You know what I regret?" Samantha asked, her voice raised. "I regret falling in love with a man who was totally unavailable. I regret letting my guard down, foolishly thinking I could have it all. That's what I regret."

Damion reached out to comfort her. "Samantha…"

"No, leave me alone," she snapped, pushing his hand away. "I wish everyone would just leave me the hell alone!" Samantha took off running down the beach.

Damion started after her, but Faby appeared at his side and stopped him. "I got this one," she said. "You're the last thing she needs right now—all you do is remind her of Tony."

Damion stared helplessly down the beach, straining in the dark to see where the two women had gone. He hadn't meant to upset Samantha, but he had. She was obviously in a lot of pain, and for some reason, Damion was overcome by the urge to swoop in and make it all better. Where was this surge of protectiveness coming from? And why did it feel like more than brotherly concern?

Chapter Thirty-Two

*A*ngela scanned the crowd of people at the Marina del Rey Cheesecake Factory, looking for her mother. She was at the bar nursing her signature cocktail—a dirty martini. Angela climbed onto the barstool beside her. "Hey, Ma."

"Hey honey," Genice said, giving Angela a kiss on the cheek. "Hope you don't mind that I got started without you."

"Not at all." Angela caught the eye of the handsome bartender. "Can I get a Grey Goose and tonic?"

"Sure thing."

Genice elbowed her daughter in the side. "He's cute. You should get his number."

"I already have a man."

"Sweetheart, there is absolutely nothing wrong with having a Plan B. A girl should have options." Genice drained what was left of her martini and ordered another. "Besides, it's not like Tony has been a picture of fidelity. You're entitled to a revenge fling—it's only fair. It might even make you feel better."

"I'm not interested in revenge sex—Tony is enough for me."

"If you say so." The bartender returned with their drinks and even though she was twice his age, Genice couldn't resist flirting. When Genice was younger, she had been a dead ringer for Marilyn Monroe. Never one to downplay her favorable attributes, she capitalized on the resemblance, commanding a sizeable fee from johns who desired the pleasure of her company so they could fulfill some kind of starfucker fantasy. In her glory days, Genice made more money on the street in a week than most people made in a month. And though her looks had started to deteriorate with age, her confidence and powers of persuasion still operated at full force. She leaned forward on the bar, her ample cleavage on display. "Are you in the industry, honey?" she asked, batting her eyelashes.

The bartender tried to keep his gaze at eye level, but Genice's lovely lady lumps were too much of a temptation. "Um, yeah, kinda. So far I just have a few commercials under my belt."

"Do you have an agent?"

"No… Haven't had much success landing an agent yet."

"Well I may be able to help you out—I'm an agent."

"You are?"

"Yes, sir. I recently got a client some extra work on *Desperate Housewives*." Genice fished around in her purse. "Darn it, my business cards must be in my other bag. How do you feel about reality TV?"

"As long as it pays, I'm game. Just trying to get my foot

in the door."

"Well, I'm certain I can help with that—you've definitely got the right look. Why don't you give me your info and I'll call you to set up a meeting."

The bartender's eyes glazed over as if his fairy godmother had just materialized. He jotted down his cell and email on a napkin. "Here's all my info. I'd love to talk to you more about this."

"I'll call you," Genice said with a wink as the plastic box on the bar started to vibrate, alerting them that their table was ready. "*Ciao.*"

Genice tucked the napkin into Angela's purse as they made their way to the hostess stand. "In case you change your mind."

Angela shook her head. The effortlessness with which her mother was able to conjure up lie after lie was astounding. The waitress showed them to their table and Angela started perusing the Cheesecake Factory's monster menu.

"So how are things going at home?" Genice asked after the waitress took their orders. "Is Tony coming around?"

Angela slathered butter on a piece of sourdough bread. "No, he's still distant. He can barely look me in the eye anymore. I thought for sure couple's therapy would help, but it was a disaster. He doesn't seem to have any interest in reconciliation."

"Is he still in contact with that tramp in Santa Cruz?"

"I don't think so. If he is, he's going to great lengths to

hide it."

Genice tapped her hot pink acrylic tips on the table. "Hmmm, I thought for sure that suicide scare would whip him into shape. How's the sex?"

Angela avoided her mother's eyes. "Nonexistent. He sleeps beside me every night with his back to me, facing the wall. He is completely unresponsive to any attempts at intimacy."

"Well there's your problem—you have to remind the boy what he's missing. Never underestimate the power of the pussy, my dear." Genice sipped her drink thoughtfully. "I wonder if Darius can get us a little something to help things along."

"Mother!" Angela shrieked, appalled at the suggestion. "I am not drugging my boyfriend!"

"Will you keep your voice down—I'm just trying to help. If memory serves me, I remember you stating quite clearly that you would do *anything* to get Tony back."

"I would do anything... And I have. That fake overdose worked exactly like you said it would. But I refuse to resort to the aid of some date-rape drug to get my man into bed. He'll come around. I know he cares about me. If he didn't, he wouldn't have come back."

Genice started to lecture her daughter on the danger of mistaking pity for love, but thought better of it. Who was she to rob Angela of her delusions? Besides, Angela was much more useful to her in a vulnerable state. If things got back on track with Tony too quickly, Angela may not need her anymore, and Genice wasn't about to let that happen. She had an important business venture to get off the ground and was counting on her daughter's moral, and financial, support to make it happen.

"I'm sure you're right," Genice said, as the waitress approached with their meals. "Tony would be a fool not to see what a jewel he has in you."

Chapter Thirty-Three

*A*s the weeks passed, Samantha started to realize that this situation with Angela could drag on indefinitely. Eventually it got to the point where Tony's infrequent phone calls and Damion's gallant attempts to cheer Samantha up did little to console her. Dreams deferred faded into distant memories as her faith in happily ever after once again began to waver.

Thankfully Samantha had a buddy to mope around and be miserable with. She and Faby were quite the pair. Paralyzed by their depression, they spent entire days on the couch drinking, smoking weed, and watching TV. Soap operas, followed by talk shows, then re-runs of classic 90's sitcoms like *Friends* and *The Simpsons* before the prime time line-up began. One mindless exercise after another—wash, rinse, repeat.

Faby tossed the remote aside. "Four hundred something channels and not a damn thing on." She rolled her head toward the entertainment center and gave the DVDs a once over. "You feel like watching *Chasing Amy*?"

"Sure." An empty pizza box sat on the table beside the

empty bottle of vodka. They were running low on supplies. "Too bad we can't get liquor delivered like Domino's Pizza."

"For real. They'd be making a grip off us right now."

Samantha picked up the cordless phone and dialed Gabe's cell again. It went straight to voicemail. "Where is he? Do you think he's avoiding us?"

"And why would I do that when you guys are such a barrel of fun," Gabe said, coming in from the garage. "Don't tell me you haven't moved all day."

"I moved," Faby insisted. "We ordered pizza, and I had to get up to let the delivery guy in."

"We need you to go on a liquor run," Samantha explained. "We drank all the beer. And vodka. And what was left of the tequila."

Gabe pulled a bottle of Smirnoff out of his bag and set it on the table. "Two steps ahead of you."

Faby hopped up to grab the cranberry juice from the fridge. "You are the best," she said, giving him a kiss on the cheek.

"The very best," Sam echoed.

Gabe sat down beside Samantha on the couch. "How long are you two planning to carry on like this?"

"What do you mean?"

"Like those two lushes from *Absolutely Fabulous*."

Samantha shrugged. "What can I say, misery loves company."

"So join us," Faby added, setting an empty glass in front

of him. She filled it three quarters of the way with vodka and added a splash of cranberry juice for flavor.

"No thanks, it's a little early for me. I want to hit up the gym later." He grabbed the remote and turned to SportsCenter. "Damn, the Giants lost."

Faby passed Gabe's drink to Samantha and made one for herself. There was no such thing as too early when one was trying to drown their sorrows.

The binge drinking and chain smoking continued for another week before Samantha's body started to rebel. Deep down she knew drinking and getting stoned every day was a terrible coping mechanism, but it was so effective in numbing the pain. Everyone has their limits though. When Samantha started waking up every morning sick to her stomach, it finally occurred to her that maybe it was time to slow down.

Samantha emerged from another morning spent bent over the toilet to find Damion posted up in her living room. "What are you doing here?"

"Faby let me in," Damion replied. "I was wondering if you wanted to join me for breakfast. My treat. I'm craving sourdough pancakes from Zachary's, but I hate eating alone."

Samantha winced—Zachary's was Tony's favorite breakfast spot. "Thanks for the invite, but I'm gonna have to pass. Not feeling well."

"Yeah, I see." Brows furrowed, Damion studied her. "Don't take this the wrong way, but you look like shit. You got the flu or something?"

"Naw, I'm just a bit hungover." Samantha poured herself a glass of water and popped an Aleve. "There was a party at 728 California last night, and you know how they get down over there."

"Yes I do, and that's why I don't go there anymore." They both laughed. "Seriously though, a good meal might help. Get some food in your stomach to soak up all that alcohol."

Samantha made a face, battling another wave of nausea. "Ugh, just the thought of food makes me want to throw up."

Damion frowned. "Maybe you should think about slowing down—no one should be this hungover on a freakin' Tuesday."

Samantha folded her arms. "You're doing it again."

"Doing what?"

"That overprotective dad thing. I've told you a hundred times—I'm a big girl. You don't have to worry about me." She sat down beside him. "As sweet as it is that you care enough to worry."

"Don't misunderstand," Damion said. "I have every confidence in your ability to take care of yourself. I just get off on riding to the rescue and playing hero—it's part of my Superman complex." He puffed his chest out, imitating Superman's trademark stance. "My mom thinks I should be in therapy, but I can't afford it."

Samantha laughed. "You are a fool." She had to admit that she found Damion's presence comforting. She'd grown fond of the brainy thespian, with his quirky, offbeat sense of humor. Even in her darkest moments, Damion always found a way to get a laugh out of her. "Can we raincheck breakfast?"

"Of course," Damion said, rising to leave. He gave her a kiss on the forehead. "Get some rest, and call me if you need anything."

"I will."

Damion showed himself out, trying to get a handle on his disappointment. Though Tony had asked him to keep an eye on Samantha, Damion was seeking her out more and more these days, without Tony's prompting, because he genuinely enjoyed her company. With her quick wit and compassionate heart, Samantha was an excellent sparring partner in their lively debates, and she was the only woman besides his mama who laughed at all his corny jokes. And unlike a lot of her peers who were so focused on appearances, Samantha was refreshingly down-to-earth. The girl didn't have a superficial bone in her body, and Damion was starting to see how special she was. He knew in his heart that he would rather throw down before letting anyone, including Tony, hurt her.

Damn, he was falling for his best friend's girl.

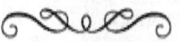

Samantha awoke to a loud banging on her door. Pulling the covers over her head, she attempted to block out the streaks of daylight that filtered through the closed blinds. "Go away!"

Gabe came in and yanked the blankets off her bed. "You're going to be late for work."

Samantha reached for the covers and lay back down. "I called in sick."

"You did? Are you sick?"

"Yes," Samantha snapped. "I'm sick of people hovering, asking if I'm alright. Why can't everyone just leave me alone?" She rolled onto her side, turning her back to Gabe.

Gabe placed a hand on her hip and rolled her toward him. "Look, I'm worried about you. You've been in bed for three days. I've never seen you so twisted up over some dude."

"Tony is not just some dude; he's the love of my life."

"Well, I wish he'd start acting like it."

"Out," Samantha ordered, pointing to the door. "I am not in the mood for another round of Tony-bashing."

"Hey, I'm not here to bash—I feel for the guy, I really do. But this has been going on for months, Sam. These are supposed to be the best years of our lives and you're carrying on like somebody's widow. How long do you plan to put your life on hold waiting for him to come back?"

It was a question Samantha had asked herself many times

over the past week. She was trying her hardest to be patient, but the Fate that brought them together was now conspiring to keep them apart. "Maybe when *you* fall in love, you'll understand what I'm going through. But until then, please keep your opinions and pop psychology to yourself. It's not helping."

"I'm just—" He stopped, once again treated to the back of Samantha's head. "You know what, forget it. Between your depression and Faby's PMS, I can't do anything right." He stood to leave. "I can't wait until you guys are back to normal."

Gabe's comment about Faby's PMS caught Samantha's attention. As was common with women who lived together, the two of them had synchronized cycles long ago. It dawned on Samantha that she hadn't gotten her period in a couple of months. Not since…

Oh God. Samantha jumped out of bed and began getting dressed.

"Now that's more like it," Gabe said, stepping out of the way as she hurried around the room. "You going to work?"

"No, I just remembered an errand I have to run," she said rushing past him. "I'll catch up with you later."

Chapter Thirty-Four

*T*ony knew something was up the moment he entered the dimly lit apartment. Angela had gone to great lengths to set the scene for a romantic interlude—the soft glow of candlelight, a full course meal on the dining room table, the smooth voice of Al Green in surround sound. Tony had just wandered into Seduction Central.

He tried to back quietly out of the room and flee unnoticed, but his escape plan was foiled when Angela appeared in the kitchen archway with a bottle of champagne. The short silk robe she wore showed off long, shapely legs, and her golden tresses hung loose around her shoulders. Against his will, Tony felt the stirring of desire down below. Angela had always been supermodel gorgeous—all hills and curves. But while she still had the ability to rouse him physically, emotionally he only had eyes for one woman—Samantha.

"What's all this?" Tony asked, setting his gym bag on the couch.

Angela poured them each a glass of champagne. "Things

have been so tense lately. I thought we could use a break from the pressure of trying to fix everything all at once. Maybe if we focus on reconnecting on a basic level, as man and woman, some of the other issues will sort themselves out." She tugged at the sash around her waist and the robe fell open, exposing her magnificent nakedness. With a gentle shrug of her shoulders, the robe dropped to the ground.

Tony averted his eyes as she came toward him, willing his hormones to settle. "Sex isn't going to solve our problems," he said as Angela ran her hands across his torso. She always smelled like flowers, and he was awash in the scent of jasmine, his favorite of her many perfumes.

Angela planted feathery kisses along the nape of his neck. "How will we know unless we try?" She pressed her large, firm breasts against his chest. "I know you want me... I know you've missed me."

Angela reached into his shorts and took his semi-erect penis into her hand. It grew harder with her touch. Encouraged, she dropped to her knees and took him into her mouth, moving her head up and down as he moaned softly. Slowly, Angela felt the balance of power start to shift.

Tony pulled away. "Stop."

"Why?" Angela asked. She reached again for his penis, which now stood at full attention. "You used to love it when I gave you head."

Tony adjusted his shorts and backed away. "Just... stop. I never should have let you do that."

"Why not?"

"Because it's wrong."

"Wrong? Since when is it wrong for two lovers to pleasure each other?"

"Angela, we've been over this—we are not a couple." He turned on the lamp in the corner, flooding the room with light. "I don't think of you that way anymore."

Humiliated, Angela snatched her robe from the floor and covered herself. "I don't understand. We have over a decade of history between us. We've been together for *five years*. How can you stand there and tell me you feel *nothing*?"

Tony was actually feeling a lot of things—fear, shame, pity, disgust—but unfortunately for Angela, nothing that resembled motivation to give their doomed relationship a second chance. He'd had it with playing house, and refused to give her false hope by letting his libido get the best of him. "You're right — we go way back, and because of the depth of our shared history, I will always love you and care about what happens to you. But I'm not *in love* with you anymore."

"But how do you know for sure," she pleaded, tears filling her eyes. "If you would just meet me halfway, I know we could get it back."

Tony shook his head. "It's over, Ange. All this denial is

just postponing the inevitable." He cupped her face gently. "I can't love you the way you want me to, and we both deserve better."

Angela pushed his hand away. "You may think you can do better, but you're it for me. If I can't have you, I don't see the point in going on."

A strong sense of panic gripped him. Was that an empty threat, or had he pushed her too far, too soon? "Angela, don't talk like that."

"Why not—it's the truth. Life isn't worth living without you."

Before Tony could start to backpedal, Angela ran from the room and locked herself in the bathroom. He banged on the door, begging to be let in, but she ignored his frantic pleas. Tony heard her rifling through the medicine cabinet, and began ramming the door with his shoulder. Splinters of pain shot through his arm with each hit, but he continued to throw his body against the locked door with all the force he could muster. The technique worked great in the movies.

Finally, the door to the tiny bathroom yielded to his repeated assault. The edge of the door clipped Angela on the shoulder as it flew open, knocking her off balance, the handful of pills she clasped falling to the ground.

Tony grabbed her shoulders, shaking her. "What are you doing?"

"What do you care?" she screamed back, struggling to get free. "This will put us both out of our misery." She beat her fists against his chest as he fought to restrain her. Eventually she wore herself out and collapsed in a sobbing heap onto the bathroom floor.

Tony held her close while she cried, but Angela was inconsolable. For hours she repeated her pathetic loop, begging him over and over not to leave, as if sheer repetition could turn fantasy into reality. She finally drifted off to sleep around midnight.

After Tony put her in bed, he went through the house and threw out every bottle of pills he could find. Then, after taking several shots of Jack Daniels, he poured every last drop of alcohol down the drain. It just wasn't safe to have any booze or pills lying around. Satisfied that the house had been thoroughly suicide-proofed, he laid down on the couch, exhausted. He knew now what needed to be done. He just hoped he had the strength to do it.

Chapter Thirty-Five

Samantha tossed her keys on the counter, turning the doctor's words over in her head. Pregnant. With Tony's baby. She didn't know how to begin processing this information. What was she going to do about school? She was only twenty —how was she going to handle being a *mom*? She could barely take care of herself, much less a little baby…

Though she felt utterly unprepared for motherhood, Samantha knew abortion wasn't an option. She came of age watching her sister struggle with persistent guilt and regret after aborting her baby, and Samantha had no desire to follow in her footsteps. Besides, this was Tony's child, their love child. The fear and disorientation that resulted from having her whole life turned upside-down was nothing compared to the love she already felt for this miracle growing inside her. The timing was terrible, but she couldn't deny that starting a family with Tony was something she had dreamed about. And now that dream was going to become a reality.

Samantha rubbed her belly. Tony would have to come

back now—this changed everything. Angela's problems would surely take a backseat to this latest development. *They were going to have a baby.* Samantha needed to get a hold of Tony and tell him the news.

The doorbell rang, interrupting her daydream. It was Damion.

"That's crazy," she said, ushering him inside. "I was just about to call you. I need to talk to Tony. It's urgent."

"Sam, uh, that's kinda why I'm here…"

The tone of his voice said it all. This wasn't one of Damion's brotherly check-ins—he was here to deliver bad news. "What's the matter? Did something happen to Angela?"

"Tony asked me to come by," Damion stammered, clearly uncomfortable. "To give you a message."

"What message?" Samantha's pulse quickened—she had never seen Damion so unnerved. "For God's sake, spit it out already."

Damion took a deep breath. "Tony's not coming back, Sam. He's decided to stay with Angela."

Samantha's heart stopped as Damion's words detonated. She couldn't possibly have heard him correctly. "What?"

Damion's face was a mask of sheer agony, as if someone were forcing him to swallow ground glass. "Angela isn't doing well, and Tony needs to be there for her. He realizes it isn't fair to string you along like this, so he's decided to cut you loose." Damion braced himself, fully expecting Samantha to lash out and strike him. "I'm sorry, Sam."

Samantha placed a hand on the doorframe for support. "I don't believe you. Why couldn't Tony tell me this to my face?"

"He felt it was best this way."

"Best for who?" Samantha felt another wave of morning sickness crest and bolted for the bathroom. Damion followed close behind, but she slammed the door in his face.

After a few minutes of violent wretching, Samantha sat back, wiping her mouth. There was a soft tap on the door. "Are you okay in there?"

Samantha opened the door. "No, I'm not okay—this whole thing is making me sick to my stomach." She snatched the cell phone from Damion's hip and attempted to access his address book.

"Give me the phone, Sam."

"Not until I talk to Tony."

"He doesn't want to talk to you."

"Tony is not the only one with wants and needs," she snapped. Samantha was severely gadget-challenged, and couldn't figure out how to pull up the contact list on Damion's fancy iPhone. She threw the device at him in frustration. "Dial the fucking number."

"He told me not to—"

"I don't give a damn what he told you, dial the fucking number!"

Realizing that Samantha wasn't going to believe it unless she heard the words from Tony himself, Damion did as he was told. Tony answered on the second ring.

"You did not just send your boy over here to break up with me," Samantha yelled, her voice shaking with rage. "What the hell is wrong with you?"

"You shouldn't have called here."

"And you shouldn't have sent someone else to do your dirty work." She was met with stony silence. "So it's true, you've decided to stay with Angela?"

"Yes."

Samantha studder-stepped backwards as if she'd been dealt a heavy blow. This couldn't be happening. "And what about us? What about the plans we made?"

"It's not gonna happen, Sam. It was fun while it lasted, but it's best if you to forget about us and move on."

Fun while it lasted? Who was this man, and what had he done with Tony? "But there's something I need to tell—"

"I wish there was another way, but there isn't. Please don't call here again." The line went dead.

Samantha stared at the phone in disbelief. Never in her wildest dreams did she think Tony was capable of such cruelty. But clearly she didn't know him at all.

"Are you alright?" Damion asked softly.

In the wake of Tony's cold-hearted dismissal, she had

forgotten Damion was standing there. She felt another wave of nausea coming on. "Just go, Damion," she said, heading back to the bathroom. "Your work here is done."

Damion pulled away from the curb, thoroughly disgusted with himself. Why had he let Tony put him in the middle of this? In the past month he'd come to care a great deal about Samantha, and would never forget the look on her face as she ordered him out of the house. Total devastation. Damion hated that he had any part in causing her that kind of pain. But Tony was right—he had to break Samantha's heart to set her free. From what Damion could see, that mission had been accomplished.

Once again, he dialed Tony's number. "It's done," Damion reported. "She threw me out."

"Does she hate me?" Tony asked.

"Yeah man, she hates you."

"Good. Will you look in on her in a couple of days?"

"I'll try, but she pretty much hates my ass, too."

"Sorry about that, man."

"Don't worry about it," Damion said. "I just wish we could have gotten your happy ending."

"Me too, homie. Me, too."

Samantha paced back and forth in her bedroom, trying to figure out her next move. The shock had worn off, and now she was just confused. This didn't make sense. The man she had just spoken to sounded nothing like the Tony she knew and loved. She refused to believe that the last few months had been a lie, that the love they shared was all in her head. There had to be more to the story; there had to be a reason why Tony had acted so cold.

If he thinks this is the end of things, he is sadly mistaken, Samantha thought. She had way too much on the line to give him up without a fight.

Chapter Thirty-Six

*M*aybe *I should just swing by her house,* Damion thought, as he paced back and forth in his tiny room. He felt terrible about the part he played in Tony's little break-up plot, and was desperate to make amends. Samantha refused to take his calls, but Damion was undeterred. Samantha's friendship meant the world to him, and he was ready to do whatever needed to be done to win her forgiveness.

Damion was startled out of his deliberations by a sharp rap on his bedroom door. "Come in!"

Samantha burst in, a backpack slung over her left shoulder.

Damion stared at her—shocked, but elated. His fear that she was never going to speak to him again was apparently unwarranted. "Man, is it good to see you. Are you okay? I've been trying to get a hold of you for days. Have you gotten my messages?"

Samantha looked around the room. "Yeah, I got them."

Damion could tell from Samantha's icy monotone that she was still pissed, but he didn't care. He was just glad she was there. "I owe you a huge apology."

Samantha's gaze settled on him, her eyes devoid of any emotion. Damion was going to have to jump through some hoops to gain his sought-after absolution.

"I never should have agreed to be Tony's mouthpiece," Damion continued, anxious to plead his case. "That was between the two of you, and it was not my place to get involved."

"You got that right."

"What can I say—I messed up. Big time. But please, let me make it up to you. Whatever I can do to make this right, I'll do it. Anything you want."

Samantha took a seat on Tony's bed, her knees suddenly weak. All of Tony's stuff was exactly as he'd left it—boxes of books, a closet full of clothes. It sure *looked* like he'd planned to return. Surrounded by all his things, the past few days seemed even more surreal. Samantha hugged a pillow to her chest, the faint trace of his scent tickling her nostrils. Closing her eyes, she breathed in memories of happier times. Maybe it had all been a bad dream...

"Samantha?" Damion asked. "You still with me?"

Samantha set the pillow aside. "You're willing to do *anything* to make this right?"

"Yes," Damion said. "Just tell me what you need."

"I need you to take me to L.A. to see Tony."

Damion sat down across from her. "Come on, Sam—you know I can't do that."

"Why not? You did his bidding. Now it's my turn."

Damion rubbed his eyes. How did he end up in the middle of this? Oh, that's right, Tony put him there. "It's a bad idea," Damion argued, trying to dissuade her.

"That's for me to decide." Samantha stood, firm in her resolve. "Look, I'm doing this with or without your help, so either you take me, or I'll find some other way. But I'm going to see Tony tonight."

Damion could see the determination shining in her eyes. Trying to steer Samantha away from this course of action would be an exercise in futility. "When do you want to leave?" he asked.

"I'm packed and ready to go right now."

Damion glanced at the clock. If they left now, they could probably make it to L.A. before nightfall. He reached for his overnight bag. "Alright, looks like we're going on a little road trip."

They made it to L.A. in good time. Samantha didn't speak much during the six-hour drive, preoccupied with her own thoughts, but at least her hostility toward him appeared to have waned. Though Damion had reservations about this particular mission, he was thankful for the opportunity to redeem himself in Samantha's eyes. Besides, Samantha had every right to confront Tony and demand an explanation. He should have had the balls to break it off face to face in the first place.

Damion had called ahead to let his mother know they were passing through town, and when the weary twosome arrived on her doorstep, she had a home-cooked feast of greens, cornbread, and gumbo waiting for them, which they devoured gratefully. Born and raised in Mobile, Alabama, Corinne Waters had perfected the art of southern hospitality; it wasn't long before she had Samantha smiling and laughing, the gloomy cloud over her head temporarily lifting. Damion smiled at the sight—it looked like a little TLC from Mama Waters was just what the doctor ordered.

After enjoying a delicious meal, Damion refocused on their primary objective. While the two women chatted and cleared the table, Damion stepped onto the porch to call Tony. He cursed silently when Angela answered the phone.

"Hey stranger," Angela greeted warmly. "When are you coming home? We miss you down here."

"I actually just got into town," Damion replied. "Decided to bring a carload down before the official move."

"And when's that?"

"A couple of weeks."

"Well, I hope everything goes smoothly. Here's Tony."

Tony stepped onto the patio for some privacy. "Wassup man."

"Yo, can you get away for a bit? I need you to swing by the house."

"Whose house?" Tony asked. "Where are you?"

"I'm at my mom's," Damion explained. "Samantha's with me."

"What?" Tony glanced over his shoulder to make sure Angela wasn't within earshot. "What were you thinking bringing her down here?"

"She was coming to see you with or without me. I figured it would be better if I was here to run interference."

"Shit," Tony cursed. "Fuck."

"Look, you need to come over here and deal with this."

"What am I supposed to tell Angela?"

"I don't know, but think of something and get your ass over here. Samantha isn't going anywhere until she speaks to you." Damion hung up.

Tony lit a cigarette and began to pace. There was a reason he had delegated the break-up duties to Damion—there was no way Tony could look Samantha in the eye and tell her he didn't love her. Samantha would see right through him. *Damnit.*

The patio door slid open. "Is everything okay?" Angela asked.

"Yeah, I gotta swing by Damion's and help him move some furniture."

Angela eyed him suspiciously. "Can't it wait until morning? It's pretty late."

Tony put out his cigarette and headed for the front door.

"It's not that late." He slipped on his jacket. "I'll be right back."

Angela reached for her coat. "Wait, I'll go with you. I can visit with Corinne and catch up. She probably whipped up one of her famous feasts in honor of Damion's visit, and I'm sure there's plenty of leftovers we can take off her hands." Angela glanced toward the kitchen. "Do you think it's tacky if I show up with my own Tupperware?"

"Corinne's gone to bed," Tony improvised. "She's down with the flu. I'm just gonna help Damion unload this dresser, then come home."

"I can still keep you company on the drive," Angela offered.

"No, that's okay. I'll be back before you know it." Tony gave her a quick kiss on the cheek and hurried out the door.

Angela waited for him to drive off, then followed.

Chapter Thirty-Seven

*T*ony pulled up to Damion's house in Culver City, his stomach twisted in knots. Samantha was probably gearing up to tear him a new asshole, and he couldn't blame her. This was all his fault. Coveting her affection when he was in no position to reciprocate, he had woven a tapestry of dreams, which he was now going to shred into a million pieces. Samantha had trusted him, only to have her heart broken in ways that would likely have ripple effects on all her future relationships. Yes, he fully expected a verbal beatdown, and deserved everything she chose to throw at him.

Tony wasn't surprised that Samantha had been able to strong-arm Damion into bringing her down. Samantha was willful and headstrong, and Tony knew she wouldn't take this lying down. He just wished he'd had more time to strengthen his resolve before having to face her. Not only was Samantha determined, she was smart. She'd pick up on any weakness in his story, and if she sensed his hesitation, she would persist.

Tony didn't want Samantha to waste any more time waiting for him—at least one of them deserved to be happy. He was going to have to deliver the performance of a lifetime to pull this off.

Samantha came down the walk to meet him. His pulse quickened as his eyes locked on her shapely silhouette. Tony had underestimated what a powerful effect her physical presence would have on him. Taking a deep breath, he put his game face on. He had to focus and suppress the surging lust. Cold, hard cruelty was needed to seal the deal. There was no time for nostalgia; this was goodbye.

Samantha stopped in front of him, arms folded across her chest. "You came."

"Damion made it sound like I didn't have much of a choice. I couldn't exactly have you showing up at my place." Tony shoved his hands in his pockets and glanced up the street. "You shouldn't have come down here."

"What, did you really think I'd let you blow me off like that?"

Tony had always found Samantha particularly striking when she was angry, and was having a difficult time staying in character. "Look, I'm sorry I was short with you on the phone, but you could have saved yourself a trip. Nothing you say is going to change anything—I've made my decision, and I'm staying with Angela."

"But why?" Samantha's voice cracked for the first time,

revealing her true level of distress. "Because she tried to kill herself? Do you really want to spend the rest of your life with someone because of guilt and some twisted sense of obligation?"

"That's not the reason I'm staying," Tony lied. "Angela is an important part of my life. I love her. This whole situation really clarified things for me."

"Oh really? That's not what you were saying a week ago."

"I was confused. It's no secret that when we met, Angela and I were having some problems. And then you came along, and you were everything Angela wasn't—spontaneous, new, exciting. But I was wrong to mistake the allure of newness, with love."

Samantha rocked backward, pain and confusion written all over her face. "Are you saying you never loved me?"

Tony fought to keep his voice even. It was killing him to have to utter all these hurtful lies. "I thought I did, Sam. I wanted to. But I think it was more infatuation than the real deal. I'm sorry."

"You're full of shit," Samantha spat. "I don't know why you're saying these terrible things, but I don't believe you."

"You're young," Tony said. "I wouldn't expect you to understand the bond two people develop when they've been together as long as Angela and I have."

Samantha's face reddened with anger. "Don't you dare patronize me," she hissed. "This isn't about me being young and naïve. It's about you being a coward and a liar."

Tony shrugged. "Call me all the names you want—it isn't going to change the fact that we're over."

They stared at each other a long while. Samantha scanned Tony's face for a glimpse of the man she had fallen in love with, but all she saw was a cold, heartless shell. In that instant, every ounce of love she felt for him morphed into a searing hatred.

"Well, if you're done," Tony said finally, "I should get going. Angela is at home waiting for me."

"Yeah, go ahead and leave," Samantha said with a wave of her hand. "You men seem to be good at that."

Chapter Thirty-Eight

*A*fter Tony drove off, Samantha sat down on the porch, head in hands. She had been such a fool. She had trusted Tony, allowed herself to love him, and he had ended up being no different than all the other lying, cheating men she'd been involved with. She couldn't believe she had been so wrong about him.

There was no way she was going to tell him about the baby. At first, she thought it might make a difference, but after the conversation they just had, it was clear he had moved on. Besides, unlike Angela, Samantha didn't want a man who was only staying with her out of duty or obligation. She had too much pride for that.

A pearl-colored sedan pulled up in front of Damion's house. The driver sat motionless behind the wheel, staring at Samantha. Unnerved by the driver's menacing presence, Samantha stood to take refuge inside the house. The driver got out of the car and revealed herself. Angela.

Fucking fantastic, Samantha thought. She was still reeling from her conversation with Tony, and now she had to deal with Angela, too? The Universe seemed determined to punish her for the part she'd played in this love triangle.

Samantha approached Angela cautiously and the two women faced off on the sidewalk, quietly sizing each other up. From the way Tony and Damion spoke of her, Samantha imagined Angela as a frail, weak, unstable mess. But the woman that stood in front of her was anything but helpless and weak. She looked like she was ready to kick Samantha's ass into next week.

"I take it you know who I am," Angela said finally.

"Yes," Samantha answered, at a complete loss for words. She hadn't expected to ever come face to face with Angela, and didn't know if she should hate her, pity her, or apologize. "What are you doing here?"

"I felt it was time the two of us had a little chat," Angela said sweetly. "Seeing as how we have so much in common." Angela glanced toward the house. "How is Mama Waters doing? Did she cook for you guys? Please tell her I send my love."

Samantha's dislike of Angela was instantaneous, activated by her dismissive, condescending tone. She had no desire to engage her in conversation—polite or otherwise. "You're obviously here to mark your territory," Samantha said, cutting to the chase. "Well, you can save your breath—Tony and I are finished."

Samantha turned to walk away, but Angela grabbed her

arm. "Where do you think you're going? I'm not done with you yet."

Samantha drew in a deep breath. The last thing she wanted was to get baited into a catfight, but if the girl put hands on her one more time… "Like I was saying," Samantha snapped, yanking her arm from Angela's grasp. "There is no need for violence. Tony and I are history. Game over. You won."

"And you think it's that simple, huh? That you can slide in, sleep with someone's man, and then go about your merry way? Actions have consequences, you homewrecking slut."

"Fine," Samantha said, throwing up her hands. "Say what you need to say and get it off your chest. But I'm not going to fight with you."

Angela looked Samantha up and down with distaste. "I can see what Tony saw in you. He's always been an ass man. But don't kid yourself, that's all you were to him—a piece of ass."

Samantha rolled her eyes. "Are you finished?"

"You're so pathetic, chasing after a man who clearly doesn't want you," Angela continued, blind to her own deep hypocrisy. "What did you think, that you'd come down here and Tony would drop everything and come back to you? Get a clue sweetheart—he used you. *I'm* the one who has his heart. *I'm* the one he came home to."

Samantha shook her head in disbelief. This was definitely not the fragile woman she had envisioned. Angela was no victim—she was a fighter. *Fuck being cordial*, Samantha thought. *The gloves are coming off.*

"You're the one who's in denial Angela. Tony was happy in Santa Cruz. The only reason he came back is because you swallowed a bottle full of pills."

Without missing a beat, Angela hauled off and slapped Samantha hard across the face.

Samantha held a hand to her cheek. "Wow, looks like I struck a nerve."

"The only thing that matters is that he came home—back to me, back to our bed. Tony makes love to me every night, and now, we're going to have a baby." Angela waited for the news to register, pleased to see the shock and devastation on Samantha's face. "I can see he neglected to mention that little tidbit."

"This has got to be some kind of joke," Samantha said, more to herself than anything. What was he, the most fertile man on the planet? Samantha was starting to understand the reasons for Tony's abrupt change of heart. He had slept with Angela, gotten her pregnant, and sealed his own Fate. No wonder he couldn't look her in the eye. That worthless, two-timing bastard.

"No joke," Angela gloated, rubbing her belly. "And there is no way you can compete with that, so why don't you take your slutty ass back to Santa Cruz and leave us the hell alone!"

"Gladly!" Samantha yelled, her emotions getting the best of her. "You can have him! But remember Angela—once a cheater, always a cheater."

Unable to take their anger out on the true guilty party, the women turned their fury on each other. Angela tried to slap Samantha again, but Samantha caught her arm mid-swing. The two women struggled, and it wasn't long before Angela had a handful of Samantha's hair.

"Get off me!!!" Samantha screamed, her shrieks echoing down the quiet street.

Damion came racing out of the house and immediately placed himself between the two women.

Samantha lunged at Angela. "Bitch!"

"Whore!" Angela yelled back.

"Ya'll need to calm the fuck down before someone calls the cops," Damion chastised. "Angela, what are you doing here?"

Angela's entire demeanor changed now that she had an audience. Her voice softened, tears sprang up in her eyes, and her lower lip protruded ever so slightly. "I just wanted to put a face to the name," Angela pouted. "I wanted to see the other woman with my own eyes, and tell her to back off and leave us alone. Tony made his choice."

"You're right, he did, and he chose you. Why can't we just leave it at that?"

"How can you stand there and defend her?" Angela asked, tears rolling down her face. "I thought you were my friend."

"I am your friend. But the person you should be taking your anger out on is Tony. He hurt *both* of you. Coming over here to kick Samantha's ass is not going to solve anything."

"I see how it is," Angela said, her voice thick with feigned hurt and betrayal. "Just keep your trampy friend away from my man, okay? It's over." Angela got into her car and sped off.

Damion turned his attention to Samantha, who was shaking with rage. "Are you okay?"

"I'm fine," Samantha said, unable to hold back the tears any longer. "You were right—coming down here was a terrible idea."

Chapter Thirty-Nine

*A*fter an amazing homemade breakfast of banana pancakes, hash browns, and grits, Damion and Samantha got ready for their trip back to Santa Cruz. Having found all the answers she came for, Samantha was anxious to return to her life. The farther she got from Tony and Angela, the better.

"I've packed a couple of sandwiches and some snacks for you," Damion's mother explained, handing him a medium-sized cooler. "Now you won't have to waste your money on greasy fast food when you get hungry later."

"Thank you so much for everything, Mrs. Waters," Samantha said, hugging the woman goodbye. Between the home-cooked meals and sage counsel, the hospitality at the Waters home had been off the chain. "I'm sorry I brought all this drama to your doorstop."

"Drama? Please child, that was nothing. I was glad for the company. Feel free to stop by and visit anytime, you hear?

You family now." She folded her baby boy into a warm embrace. "And you… Promise you'll drive safe and mind the speed limits, okay?"

"Yes ma'am," Damion said. He gave her a kiss on the cheek before getting into the car. "I'll see you in a few weeks, Ma."

They were about halfway home on the long, lonely stretch of the I-5 when Damion's car started to overheat. Damion pulled off at the next exit, a bare bones truck stop that just barely met the gas-food-lodging quota. Thankfully, there was a mechanic on duty at the service station who promised a diagnosis within the hour. They ducked into the adjacent IHOP to escape the blistering desert heat and await the verdict.

"I hope it's nothing major," Damion muttered after the waitress refilled his cup of coffee. "These roadside mechanics are notorious for padding their estimates and recommending unnecessary repairs."

"Whatever the cost, I'll pay for half," Samantha offered.

"You don't have to do that."

"Yes I do. This never would have happened if I hadn't made you drive me down here."

"If it helped you achieve some kind of closure, it was worth it," Damion said softly.

Samantha stared out the window and resumed her quiet

brooding. She had the strong, silent routine down pat, and it was driving Damion crazy. How was he supposed to help her if she wouldn't open up about how she was feeling?

Damion couldn't *believe* Angela had played the pregnancy card. He let Samantha think it was the truth, even though he knew otherwise, but still—he was shocked that Angela had chosen to go there. He couldn't help but wonder what else she might be lying about.

An hour later, Damion and Samantha returned to the gas station. The mechanic emerged from the garage, wiping his hands on his overalls. "Looks like you need a new water pump."

Damion wiped the sweat from his brow—it wasn't the answer he had been hoping for. "How much is that going to set me back?"

"Shouldn't be more than a couple hundred bucks, plus labor, but I don't have that part on hand. I have to order it from a shop in Bakersfield."

"How long is that going to take?"

"I should have you back on the road by noon tomorrow."

"Tomorrow?" Samantha asked. She looked around at the desolate surroundings. There wasn't another town or structure for miles. "What are we supposed to do until then?"

"I guess we're going to have to get a room." Damion cast a glance toward their lone lodging option, a seedy-looking

Motel 6. "You okay with that?"

"Well, it's not like we have much of a choice." Samantha fanned herself with a magazine. "Come on, let's go—I'm going to melt if I don't get out of this fucking heat."

Samantha sat cross-legged on the bed, snacking on one of the sandwiches Damion's mom had packed. The accommodations were hardly 4-star, but as long as the TV and air conditioning worked, Samantha couldn't complain. She had already decided that this tiny hotel room was her own personal purgatory, where she'd been exiled to repent for the long list of sins she'd racked up since Tony walked into her life. She'd gotten what she deserved though. She allowed herself to become the other woman, and karma had turned around and smacked her upside the head as payback. She'd lost the guy, her self-respect, and now had the long, hard road of single motherhood to look forward to. Yeah, karma was a bitch.

"Samantha," Damion said, interrupting her thoughts. "Are you even listening?"

"No, I'm sorry, I missed that last part." She set her sandwich aside. "I've got a lot on my mind."

"I can see that. I know I'm probably the last person you feel like confiding in, but if you want to talk, I'm here. If you need a hug, I'm here. Hell, if you feel like punching someone..."

He angled his chin toward her and pointed to his jaw. "Take your best shot."

Samantha considered Damion's offer. With her hormones raging, she had a ridiculous amount of anger built up courtesy of Tony and Angela. But as hurt and angry as she was, she just didn't have the heart to take it out on Damion. Truth be told, Damion had been a true friend the past few months, coming through in all the areas where Tony came up short. With the exception of his brief stint as Tony's puppet, Damion had been present, reliable, caring, and attentive. Samantha truly believed he was sorry for the part he had played in this mess. She figured it would be okay to let her guard down a little. "Now that you mention it," Samantha said softly, "a hug does sound good."

Wasting no time, Damion took her into his arms. Samantha relaxed against his shoulder as he rubbed her back. After everything she'd been through, she had to admit that it felt good to have someone to lean on.

Damion rested his chin on the top of her head. "It's going to be okay."

Samantha wiped a tear from the corner of her eye. "When you say it like that, I almost believe you." She longed to tell Damion about the baby, but knew it would put him in an impossible position. Damion would insist that Tony had a right to know, but Samantha didn't agree. Besides, co-parenting wasn't exactly an option since she had no desire to see Tony ever again.

Damion lifted her chin with his index finger until their eyes met. "Do you know how incredible you are? You deserve to be put on a pedestal and worshipped like a queen."

"Tony didn't seem to think so," she said, her tone laced with bitterness.

Damion wished he could tell Samantha that it was love, not the lack of it, that drove Tony to break her heart the way he did. Tony truly believed it would be easier for Samantha in the long run if she hated him, and after the hell they'd put her through, Damion wasn't about to spill the beans now. "Tony is a fool," he offered. "And you're a catch. Trust me, it won't be long before someone new comes along and makes you forget all about Tony. Shoot, under different circumstances..."

Samantha raised an eyebrow. "Under different circumstances, what?"

Damion brushed an errant curl out of her eyes, unable to keep his own feelings a secret any longer. "Oh, I don't know. Maybe I could have been that guy."

Damion's confession caught Samantha completely off guard. She had no idea Damion looked at her as anything other than a little sister. "Really?"

"Like I said—Tony's a fool."

Samantha couldn't help but wonder how different things

might have been if she'd met Damion first. Damion was such a good guy, with a fraction of the baggage Tony carried. Samantha had come to rely on him for support and counsel, and he'd proven time and time again that he was worthy of her trust. Had she picked the wrong guy?

They stared at each other, each contemplating a detour on the path they'd been set upon. Samantha wasn't sure who leaned in and initiated contact first, but she soon found herself swept away by the most unexpected kiss. Making no effort to resist or withdraw, she allowed herself to get lost in the moment. They lay back on the bed, his kisses slow and tentative at first, then increasing in urgency as Samantha yielded to his subtle advances.

Damion pulled away abruptly and caught his breath. "I'm sorry, I shouldn't have done that."

"We both did it," Samantha said, seeking out his lips once again. "It was nice."

Damion traced the outline of her supple lips with his thumb. "It *was* nice. But so wrong on so many levels."

"How do you figure? Tony cut me loose, remember? I'm free to kiss whoever the hell I want."

"I know, but he's still my best friend. It would kill him if the two of us hooked up."

Samantha shrugged, unconcerned. "Even better."

Damion collected himself. Was Samantha acting on a genuine attraction, or was this just an opportunity for her to stick it to Tony? "I know you want him to hurt, Sam, but you can't use me to do it."

Samantha, tired of feeling rejected and cast aside, drew back into her self-protective shell. "Suit yourself," she said, giving Damion her full back.

Damion stared at the back of her head for a long while before returning to his own bed and flipping on the TV.

⁂

It was close to midnight the next day when Samantha finally returned home. Faby had already gone to bed, but Gabe was still up playing video games when she walked in. "How'd it go?" he asked, as she sat down beside him on the couch.

"Tony kicked me to the curb, I got bitched out by Angela, and almost slept with Damion," Samantha reported.

"Jesus." He set the controller down. "Want me to fix you a drink?"

"I wish, but I can't drink."

"Why not?"

"Because I'm pregnant."

Gabe stared at her, stunned. "You're *what?* Are you sure?"

"Yup. A doctor confirmed it on Tuesday."

"Man. Shit." Gabe paused, at a complete loss for words. "Wait—how is Tony gonna do you like this when you're carrying his child?"

Samantha sighed. "I didn't tell him. He kinda has his hands full since Angela is pregnant, too."

"What? You're kidding, right?"

"Do you really think I would joke about something like this?"

Gabe shook his head—he thought things like this only happened on TV. "What are you going to do? Are you going to keep it?"

"I can't abort this baby, Gabe."

"Man. Wow. Shit." Gabe took a few moments to process, then offered up a little smile. "I'm going to be an uncle."

Samantha grinned back, her first genuine smile in days. "Yes, you are. And if you play your cards right, you may even capture the coveted role of Godfather."

"Oooooh, I like the sound of that. I've always wanted to be a Godfather." He grew serious again. "Who else knows?"

"You're the first person I've told, and I kinda want to keep it that way until I figure things out. I need to get used to the idea of being a mom before I can deal with everyone else's opinions about what I should do."

"No problem, your secret's safe with me. Now how did you end up in bed with Damion?"

"The car broke down on the way home and we had to stay overnight in a motel. We got to talking and he confessed that he has a little crush on me."

Gabe leaned back. "Well duh, even I knew that."

"Really? I didn't see that one coming at all."

"That's because you have Tony tunnel-vision."

"Had," Sam corrected. "Tony was the biggest mistake of my life."

Gabe couldn't believe his ears—Samantha had done a complete 180 in regards to Tony. "What about all that soulmate stuff?"

"I was wrong. My soulmate could never hurt me like this. If Tony ever really loved me, he couldn't have done this."

Gabe squeezed her hand. He was relieved to see that Samantha wasn't holding out hope for a reconciliation. Like Carlos, Tony had finally shown his true colors, and it was time for her to kick his ass to the curb. For good. "You know I got your back, right?"

Samantha smiled. "Yes, I do, and I love you for it."

"I love you, too." Gabe put an arm around her shoulder and drew her close. "And for what it's worth, I think you're going to be a great mom."

Samantha blinked back tears. Gabe always managed to say exactly the right thing when it really mattered. She was so glad she decided to tell Gabe about the pregnancy; it made a world of difference to know she wasn't in this alone. Yes, it would be hard, but she would get through it. Somehow, someway...

Chapter Forty

*D*amion carried the last box out to his car as he prepared to say goodbye to Santa Cruz, his home for the past three years. He'd lived in a lot of different places in his life, but Santa Cruz would always hold a special place in his heart. His feelings about the move were mixed. While he was excited to be reunited with his friends and family in Los Angeles, he would miss the peace and serenity of the sleepy coastal town, with its ocean breezes and majestic redwood forests. But more than anything, he would miss the woman who quite unexpectedly had managed to get under his skin and turn his world upside down. He could already feel a nasty case of Samantha withdrawal settling in.

Damion hadn't seen Samantha since their almost-tryst in the motel room, but she had been on his mind constantly, their forbidden kiss playing on an endless loop. The timing may be all wrong, but Damion couldn't deny that he wanted an encore, an opportunity to give Samantha all the things Tony couldn't. Maybe after some time passed and her wounds healed, they could have a chance, a real chance, at love and happiness.

Damion approached her front door with trepidation, unsure of how he'd be received. She probably wasn't ready to see him yet, and he could understand why, but Damion couldn't afford to give her any more space. He wouldn't leave town without saying goodbye.

When Samantha answered the door, Damion was taken aback by how great she looked. She didn't look tired or hungover, as he was used to finding her in the mornings; there was no puffiness or red in her eyes. In fact, even without a hint of make-up, Samantha had the most radiant, natural glow to her skin. He wondered why he hadn't noticed that before.

Samantha greeted him with a smile. "Hey stranger." She noticed the boxes and bags in the backseat of his car. "Are you taking off?"

"Yeah," he replied. "It's about that time. I just wanted to stop by on my way out of town and say goodbye. See how you were doing."

"I'm glad you stopped by." She motioned for him to enter. "Are you hungry? Faby made French toast for breakfast and there's a few slices left over."

"I actually ate already," Damion said. "But I'd love a cup of coffee."

"There's a fresh pot in the kitchen. Help yourself and I'll be right back."

Samantha disappeared into her bedroom while Damion

took in the new and improved surroundings. Gone was the clutter and mess. The floor was clear and vacuumed, magazines stacked neatly on the glass coffee table. Even the cords of the Playstation were coiled and secured with a twist tie. "What happened here?" Damion asked when Samantha returned, a familiar wooden box tucked under her arm. "Looks like Mary Poppins paid ya'll a visit."

Samantha laughed. "Not quite. When Faby's upset, she cooks. Me—when I'm not drinking—I clean."

"Well damn, I wish I'd known this months ago. I could have put your trauma to good use."

Damion's attempt at humor fell flat. Samantha didn't even crack a smile.

"My bad. That wasn't funny."

"No," she said. "It wasn't."

Damion poured himself a cup of coffee and took a seat, pondering how to remove his foot from his mouth. He'd made it past the front door, and wasn't ready to get thrown out just yet. "I'm sorry, just ignore me. Obviously I'm in need of some sensitivity training."

That one got a smile out of her. She set the box down in front of him. "Can you give this to Tony?"

"Is that his treasure box?"

"Yup. I've decided to take the high road and not pitch the contents into the fireplace."

Damion laughed. "I'm sure he'll appreciate that. Anything else I can do?"

"Nope, that's it." Samantha was glad to finally be rid of that box, the container of broken dreams and empty promises. She felt better already. "Were you able to fit everything into your car?"

"Yup. I gave most of my stuff away, so there wasn't much left to pack. Whenever I go through a major life transition, I tend to liquidate all my assets."

"Why's that?"

"I'm big on clean slates. A material purge is my way of signifying a fresh start."

Samantha liked the idea of a fresh start. Ever since she found out about the baby, she'd been reworking her five-year plan, thinking through the various adjustments that would need to be made. She didn't want to abandon the pursuit of her degree, but with the baby due the following spring, she would have to take a leave of absence for at least one quarter, possibly more. It made the most sense to transfer to a school closer to her family, but she loved Santa Cruz and didn't want to leave if she didn't have to. Life as a single mother would be hard, but she knew she could do it. Her mother had raised four kids on her own and they had all turned out fine... unplanned pregnancies aside.

"A fresh start sounds like a great idea," she said. "I may

have to try that one myself."

Damion squeezed her hand. "You gonna be okay?"

Samantha nodded. "I'll be fine."

"Alright, well, don't be a stranger. Remember what my mom said—you have an open invitation at Casa Waters."

"Your mom is awesome. I can see where you get your kind and nurturing spirit." She smiled. "I'll never forget how supportive you have been through this whole ordeal."

Damion tried to ignore how final that last bit sounded. There was still so much he wanted to say, but this was hardly the time for an outpouring of sentiment. Any attempt to take things to the next level would have to wait for another time, another place.

"Well," Damion said, stretching his arms wide for a parting hug. "Until we meet again."

As Samantha stepped into his embrace, Damion wondered how on earth he was ever going to let her go.

Chapter Forty-One

Damion banged on the door to Tony's apartment. This would be his first time seeing Tony since he broke the cardinal rule of friendship and made a move on his best friend's girl. Damion should have been wracked with guilt over his actions, but he was too busy obsessing over Samantha to be bothered by regret. He hoped Tony didn't catch wind of his betrayal.

Tony answered the door and greeted his boy with a pound. "Good to see you, man," he said, as they broke from their man-hug.

"Good to be seen," Damion replied, stepping inside. He surveyed the empty living room. "Where's the wifey?"

"Shopping with her mom."

"Nice." Following Tony into the kitchen, Damion searched for a neutral topic of conversation. "What's been going on? How's Ashley? She mentioned in her last email something about a new boyfriend. Have you met this guy yet?"

Tony grabbed two beers out of the fridge and handed

one to Damion. "Not yet. She's doing her best to keep him away from me. Something about not wanting me to scare him away."

"Well that's not going to work. No one should be spending any amount of time with Ash without our express seal of approval." When they were younger, whenever Tony got overwhelmed trying to care for his mother, Damion would help out by giving Ashley a little extra attention. From helping her study for the SATs to post break-up counseling, Damion was always looking out for his little sis. That protective instinct only grew stronger as the years wore on. "We need to pay homeboy a little visit."

Tony nodded in agreement. "You're right. I've been so preoccupied with my own drama that I've been slipping on my brotherly duties. Good looking out."

"Hey, that's what friends are for," Damion said.

The men took their ice-cold Coronas and settled on the patio, relaxing in the warm Southern California sunshine. "So how does it feel to be back?" Tony asked. "Is your mom happy to have her baby boy home?"

"Yeah, she's loving it. And I'm definitely lovin' the home-cooked meals she be servin' up three times a day. Nothing beats being well-fed."

Tony licked his lips. "True dat. Now that you're back, don't be surprised if I become a permanent fixture at your dinner table. I've been dreaming about Mama's gumbo."

"Come through whenever—you know how much Ma loves a full house. Bring Ashley too, and this boyfriend of hers." Damion intentionally neglected to extend the invitation to Angela, and Tony didn't seem the least bit offended.

Reunited with his wingman, Tony felt a surge of energy for the first time in weeks. "Man, we need to celebrate your homecoming. You down to hit the clubs tonight, or what?"

"Hell yeah. As much as I loved Santa Cruz, the nightlife was sorely lacking. I'm ready for a packed dance floor, nonstop hip hop, and beautiful brown people as far as the eye can see."

"You and me both. I've been scoping out the scene—a lot has changed since we left. Most of our old haunts are still poppin', but there's also a new reggae joint in Venice I keep hearing about, and a bar in WeHo that has live jazz on Tuesdays. We gotta hit them all up."

"That sounds great, but what about the Angela factor? You know damn well she's gonna have something to say about you clubbin' it up every night."

"Angela can complain all she wants—she got what she wanted. But if she thinks I'm going to remain on house arrest for the duration of this relationship, she's sadly mistaken. I've got to get out of this house man, before *I* become fucking suicidal."

Despite his blossoming feelings for Samantha, Damion

was still sympathetic to his buddy's plight. "I take it things haven't gotten any easier?"

"Easier? How can things get easier when I'm living a lie?" Tony lit a cigarette, his kneejerk reaction whenever he was forced to think about his doomed future with Angela. "Not only am I in love with someone else, but I can't even honestly say that I love Angela anymore. All this drama with the pills —it pretty much killed every tender feeling I had. I used to at least feel pity, but not anymore. She trapped me into this life, and I hate her for it. I don't think that's ever going to change." Tony finished off his beer. "I made a huge mistake, Dame."

Damion leaned back in his chair, the muscles in his jaw starting to twitch. He knew what was coming next. "Let me guess—you want Samantha back."

"Yeah, I do."

Damion shook his head, disapproval clearly registering on his face. "That ship has sailed, homie."

"But we're meant to be together. You said it yourself — she's the One. Every day that passes only clarifies that fundamental truth."

Damion tried to keep his eyeballs from rolling up into the back of his head. "You should have thought of that before you broke her heart into a million pieces."

"She would give me another chance—I know she would," Tony rambled on. "If I explained that I only pushed her away to protect her, I know she'd forgive me."

"Are you listening to yourself?" Damion asked, anger and frustration hijacking their male bonding session. "You have put that girl through enough with your indecisive, wishy-washy, push-me-pull-me routine. What makes you think that trying to leave Angela this time is going to yield a different outcome? We've all been here before, and this yo-yo thing has got to stop. If you really love Samantha, you will just let her go already, for everyone's sake."

Tony was taken aback by Damion's emotional outburst. "I didn't realize you felt so strongly about the issue." He eyed his friend suspiciously. "You got a crush on my girl?"

Damion stood with such force that he sent the plastic patio chair flying backwards. "Fuck you, Tony. You weren't there. You didn't have the balls to look that girl in the eye and break her heart; you sent *me* to do it. *I* was the one who had to deal with the damage and destruction you caused. I hate to break it to you, but any love Samantha felt—you killed it."

Tony was on his feet now, toe to toe with Damion. "You don't know what you're talking about."

"No, you're the one who doesn't know what he's talking about. I'm sorry if you're having second thoughts, but to try and get her back now, after everything you've put her through —that's just selfish. And if you insist on walking down that road again, you're going to have to do it without my help."

"Nobody's asking for your help," Tony snapped. "Or your permission."

Damion fought the urge to reach out and literally slap some sense into his friend. He needed to leave before things escalated. "Fine, have it your way." He turned to go, then remembered Samantha's last request of him. Pulling Tony's treasure box out of his knapsack, he laid it on the table. "She asked me to give this back to you," Damion said, as Tony stared at the box, speechless. "She's done with you, Tony. Do us all a favor and let her be."

And with that, Damion stormed out of the house, leaving Tony alone with his guilt, regret, and the consequences of his actions...

Chapter Forty-Two

Samantha was trapped in a terrible nightmare. She was back at the cliff, but instead of sitting on the edge enjoying the sunset, she was dangling over the side. Clinging tight to Tony's hand, she could feel the spray from the waves on her heels, the salty mist stinging her eyes as she struggled to hold on.

Flailing beside her was Angela, holding tight to Tony's other hand. Angela thrashed about, kicking her legs and begging for Tony to pull her up. But he couldn't. There was no way for him to save one woman without dropping the other into the turbulent surf below.

"Tony!" Angela screamed. "Help me!"

Tony glanced from one to the other, agonizing over the impossible decision that lay before him. Tears rolled down his cheeks as he locked eyes with Samantha, silently pleading for her forgiveness and understanding. "I'm sorry, Sam," he whispered, as his grip started to slip. "I have to let you go."

And then he did.

Samantha bolted upright in bed, gasping for air. Beads of sweat rolled down the sides of her face, and her T-shirt was soaked through, clinging to her back. She doubled over in pain as a spasm caused her abdomen to contract. Was that normal?

Clutching her stomach, Samantha made her way down the hall to Gabe's room. She flipped on the light, surprising both Gabe and his guest who were tangled up beneath the covers.

"Oh, I'm sorry," Samantha said, embarrassed. Until she recognized Gabe's guest. "What the… Faby, is that you?"

Faby emerged from under the blanket, her cheeks bright red. "Sheesh, didn't your mama teach you to knock?"

Samantha was so stunned to find her two best friends in bed together that she almost forgot why she had barged into the room to begin with. Several questions begged to be asked, and answered, but an official interrogation would have to wait. "Gabe, I… I think something's wrong with the baby."

Now it was Faby's turn to be shocked. "Wait, back up, what did you say? What baby?" She glanced back and forth between Samantha and Gabe, waiting for someone to fill her in.

Gabe was already out of bed and pulling on his pants. "What happened? Why do you think something is wrong with the baby?"

Samantha was trying her hardest not to panic, but with each contraction, her fear multiplied. She leaned against the doorframe for support as another pain sliced through her abdomen. "I woke up about half an hour ago with pretty bad cramps," she explained. "I didn't think anything of it, but now I'm bleeding."

Faby was up now, too, pulling one of Gabe's sweatshirts over her head. She seemed to have fully absorbed the baby news, and was transitioning into crisis management mode. "Everything's going to be fine," Faby said calmly, slipping on her shoes. "We just need to get you to the hospital."

Gabe slipped an arm around Samantha's waist. "Can you walk?"

"Yeah."

"Okay," Gabe said, shooting Faby a worried look over Samantha's shoulder. "Just try to relax. Like Faby said, I'm sure everything is going to be just fine…"

Chapter Forty-Three

Samantha stood on the balcony of her sister's apartment, watching the sun set into the water beyond Venice Beach. It was Finals week back in Santa Cruz, and Samantha wondered how her roommates were making it through. Faby was probably pulling all-nighters trying to get her papers done, while Gabe procrastinated by playing Playstation. She would rejoin them in a few weeks, after Christmas break, and start winter quarter with the rest of her classmates. She'd only taken a quarter off, and shouldn't be that far behind—nothing a few courses during summer session couldn't fix. Besides, after three months at home with her family, Samantha was starting to feel claustrophobic. She was ready to get back to school, and her life. It was time.

Samantha still couldn't believe she lost the baby. The doctor had to repeat the news three times before it registered, and even then it felt like he was talking to someone else. What a cruel twist of Fate—just when she'd gotten used to the idea of being a mom, it had all been taken away from her. Friends and family tried to spin it, saying it was probably for the best and everything happens for a reason and blah, blah, blah... But Samantha couldn't feel any relief over such a loss. All she knew was that a child, her child, was gone, and she would punch the next person who tried to tell her it was a blessing in disguise.

A cool breeze blew in off the coast and Samantha fought back a chill. The baby had been her last connection to Tony, and the pain and sadness was so familiar, like she was losing him all over again. Even though he had cast her aside, the love she felt for him endured, much to her distress and frustration. Samantha had resigned herself to the fact that there would always be a hole in her soul where Tony used to be.

A noise startled Samantha. Her sister had stepped onto the patio. "Hey, I didn't hear you come in."

"I know, you looked like you were a million miles away." Megan joined her at the railing. "Thinking about the baby again?"

When was she not thinking about the baby? "No," Samantha lied. "Just wondering how Gabe and Faby are making it through Finals."

Megan frowned. "You know, that's really not necessary."

"What?"

"The brave front. If anyone can understand what you're

going through, it's me. I wish you would let me help you."

Samantha focused on a ship in the distance. What she wouldn't give to hop aboard a boat and sail off to parts unknown, far away from the tragic circumstances of her life and the people determined to make her talk about it. "I'm fine."

"You lost a child, Sam—that's not something you just get over. You have to let yourself grieve."

"I'm grieving in my own way."

"Are you? Cause to me it looks like you're shutting down."

Samantha stared across the sea, mute. Why couldn't Megan just leave it alone?

"I know you think you have it under control, but emotions like this won't stay buried forever. One day it's going to hit you, and when it does…" Megan paused, as if distracted by an unwelcome flashback. "I don't want you to go through this alone like I did."

Samantha studied her sister's profile. Megan had gotten pregnant and had an abortion when she was fifteen, but didn't tell anyone about it until years later. Fear and shame drove her to deal with her pain in isolation, which only compounded the trauma. Obviously, Megan was trying to stop her from making the same mistake.

"Does it ever get any easier?" Samantha asked.

Megan closed her eyes, the memories like pin pricks on her most sensitive areas. "Easier, no," she confessed. "But you do get used to it."

Samantha didn't think she'd ever be free of the guilt. "It's my fault, you know."

Megan took her sister's hand. "Twenty percent of all pregnancies end in miscarriage. This was nobody's fault."

Samantha pulled away, refusing to be absolved. "No, sis, you didn't see me. After Tony left, I was a mess. I was drinking, chain-smoking, stoned every day. All that stuff had to have affected the baby."

"You didn't know."

"And why didn't I know? Because I was too drunk and out of it to notice I'd missed two periods. I killed my baby, Meg."

"No, you didn't. There's only one baby killer on this balcony, and that's me."

Samantha immediately regretted her thoughtless choice of words. "Oh God, I'm sorry. I didn't mean—"

Megan held up her hand. "It's okay, I've made peace with my demons. This is about helping you come to terms with yours. You can't go back and change the past, Sam."

"Trust me, of that I am painfully aware."

"Good. So now we take steps toward healing, and that starts with forgiving yourself for whatever it is you think you did wrong."

"You realize that's easier said than done."

"Of course I do. But eventually you're going to have to

let go of the pain and move on."

"I'm all too familiar with the five stages of grief," Samantha said with a sigh. "But I'm not there yet. I need a little more time, and space, to process things in my own way."

Megan could see she was wasting her breath. If Samantha was determined to be miserable, there wasn't much anyone could do to change that until she was ready. "Alright," Megan said. "I'll back off. For now." She raised her arms in mock surrender. "This is me stepping down off the soapbox."

"Thanks," Samantha replied. "I appreciate it."

"So are you ready to go? Mom will pitch a fit if we're late for Sunday dinner."

"Yeah, just let me throw on a sweater real quick. I thought Chris was coming?"

"He's meeting us there."

"Oh, okay." Samantha looked at her reflection in the sliding glass door and practiced her happy face. No doubt she'd have to fend off more poking, prodding, and psychoanalysis from the rest of the family, and pretending she was fine was the only thing that kept folks from hovering.

"Alright," Samantha said, her fake smile firmly in place. "Let's do this."

Chapter Forty-Four

*I*t was the weekend before Christmas, and Samantha and Faby had embarked on a shopping expedition of epic proportions. They weren't alone. Navigating the dense crowds, they made their way in and out of almost every store on 3rd Street Promenade. The lines were long, and the inventories picked over, but their spirits remained high as retail therapy worked its magic on their moods. Every so often they'd give their credit cards a break, pausing to check out one of the lively street entertainers, a trademark fixture on 3rd Street. The performers, undeterred by the faint drizzle, pulled out all the stops to bring holiday magic and revelry to the numerous patrons on the boulevard. Samantha was never big on Christmas cheer, preferring the role of Grinch, but it was hard not to smile at the mimes in Santa suits preparing balloon reindeer for giggling children, or the troupe of breakdancers rockin' out to Run DMC's "Christmas in Hollis." Yes, there was something about the Christmas spirit that was downright contagious, and despite her usual disdain for the holidays, Samantha found herself caught up.

They stopped in Express, where Samantha hoped to find something for her sister. In minutes, they both had an armful of garments for potential purchase.

Faby held a baby blue cashmere sweater up to her chest. "What do you think?" she asked as she pivoted in front of the mirror. "I've always loved this color on me."

"We're supposed to be buying gifts for other people," Samantha scolded, thumbing through the items on the sale rack, "and so far I've watched you buy yourself three tops, a pair of capris, a cocktail dress, and not one thing for any of the people on your list."

"That's not true," Faby said. "I bought something for my Aunt Silvia at that antique store."

"Oh, excuse me—I stand corrected," Samantha said with a laugh.

Faby held up a garnet silk blouse. "This would look great on you."

Samantha took a look at the price tag and wrinkled her nose. "*That* is definitely not in the budget," she said. "Besides, I have nowhere to wear something that fancy."

"What about your birthday dinner?"

"Why do I need a brand new blouse when I have you and Meg's closets to raid?"

Faby caught a glimpse of something over Samantha's

shoulder that made her blood run cold. "Just humor me and try it on," Faby insisted, pushing the blouse into Samantha's arms. "It's your 21st birthday—you deserve better than someone else's hand-me-downs."

Samantha fingered the delicate silk—Faby had excellent taste. "I suppose it wouldn't hurt to try it on."

"I saw a black skirt near the front that would go great with that top," Faby said. "I'll grab it and meet you in there."

"Okay. Size 6."

"I know." As soon as Samantha disappeared into the dressing room, Faby dropped the clothes she was holding on the nearest table and marched toward the store entrance. In moments she was standing face to face with Tony.

"What are you doing here?" she demanded.

"Nice to see you too, Fab," he said, scanning the inside of the store for another glimpse of Samantha.

Faby did her best to obstruct his view. "You didn't answer my question—are you stalking us or something?"

Tony turned his attention to the hostile Latina in front of him, hands planted firmly on her hips. "There's no stalking going on—like everyone else, I'm doing some last minute Christmas shopping. Running into you guys was pure coincidence." *Or Fate,* he thought.

Faby positioned herself between Tony and the door. "You need to leave before she comes out here and sees you."

Tony folded his arms across his chest—he never cared for Faby's overbearing bossiness. She was always telling everyone around her where to go and what to do. "I'm not going anywhere until I speak to Samantha."

"Over my dead body. You have caused enough disruption and heartache in that girl's life, and if you think I'm going to let you anywhere near her, you've got another thing coming. Samantha is not interested in anything you have to say."

"If she truly feels that way, she can tell me herself."

Faby waved a finger in his face. "What exactly do you expect to accomplish, Tony? Huh? A walk down memory lane so Samantha can re-live the most painful time in her life? You want to fill her in on how great things are going with Angela? Or do you just want to ruin the only semblance of peace she has now that she's finally, *finally*, gotten over you?"

Tony was caught off guard by the force and hostility of Faby's verbal assault. "I just wanted to say hello," he stammered.

"Save it—no one here is interested. Samantha has moved on. She's found someone who loves and adores her, who makes her a priority, something you could never do. After months of nursing a broken heart, she's finally happy again. Do us all a favor and go home to your pregnant girlfriend and pretend you never saw us here, okay?"

Tony felt terrible that he'd let Samantha believe Angela was pregnant this whole time. He needed to set the record straight. "Faby, I really need to—"

"I'm not playing around, Tony. Samantha's brothers are watching the game down the street. All I have to do is shoot them a text and let them know you're out here lurking. I'm sure they'd be more than happy to forcibly remove your sorry ass."

"Alright, fine. But will you just tell her—"

"No," Faby snapped.

Tony could see that he was wasting his breath trying to appeal to Faby's soft side, if she even had one. After casting one last glance at the store, he quietly retreated.

Satisfied that Tony had been effectively cockblocked, Faby headed back into the store. She found Samantha standing in the dressing room doorway, looking gorgeous in the garnet blouse. It's a good thing Tony hadn't caught a glimpse of her in that number, or no amount of threats would have been able to keep him away.

"That looks great on you," Faby exclaimed, nodding in approval.

"Thanks. Where have you been?"

"I saw an old friend from high school outside. I just wanted to say hi real quick." Faby took another look at the price tag hanging off the sleeve. "You know, it's really not that expensive—you should get this."

"Absolutely not," Samantha said. "I am not spending what little money I have on myself. Now if we're done playing dress up, I've got a whole list of family members I need to shop for."

"Alright, you win," Faby said, praying the coast was clear. "Let's stop in Spencer's next—I want to get Gabe one of those blow-up dolls for Christmas."

Samantha laughed. "And why does he need a blow-up doll when he's got you to keep him warm at night?"

"Please," Faby said dismissively, "that was just a one time thing."

"Sure it was."

"Come on, you remember my state of mind after Carlos and I broke up. I was depressed… and hard up… and that night, really, *really*, drunk. Clearly not in my right mind. Gabe caught me in a weak moment, that's all."

Samantha was unconvinced. "Uh huh. Anyone ever tell you 'thou doth protest too much'?"

"Oh shut up," Faby said, cheeks flushed red with embarrassment.

Samantha leaned in close and nudged Faby with her shoulder. "So you never did tell me," she prodded. "How was it that *one time*?"

"We are *so* not having this conversation," Faby said, taking off down the street.

Samantha caught up to her, amused that the notoriously unshakable Faby had been so easily flustered. "I'm not going to let up until you spill the beans, so you might as well tell me."

Faby stopped and turned to face her. "Fine, it was great. Are you happy now?"

"Great?" Samantha asked, surprised. Gabe was such a lazy goof, she couldn't imagine him being able to lay it down in the bedroom. "How great are we talking about here?"

"Best I ever had," Faby confessed, ignoring the shocked look on Samantha's face. "And if you tell him I said that, I will never, ever, speak to you again."

Samantha could hardly believe her ears. "You're being serious?"

"Unfortunately, yes." Faby gave a wistful sigh. "You know, for a white boy, Gabe is really packin'. Dude is hung like a horse."

"Whoa, whoa," Samantha screamed, covering her ears. "Too much freaking information!"

"Well you asked!" Faby shouted back. The two women looked at each other in mock horror before collapsing into a fit of giggles.

∽◦◦◦◦∾

Tony watched Samantha and Faby work their way down 3rd Street, laughing and joking as they weaved in and out of every store on the block. Both women carried several shopping bags, and they seemed to be enjoying themselves, despite the crowds and the lines. Tony couldn't help but follow them from a safe distance, his eyes drinking in Samantha's image as if she were an oasis in the middle of the dusty Sahara.

She looked amazing, even better than he remembered. Seeing her again in the flesh, after having to rely solely on the fading images in his memory, was a shock to his system. It had been much easier to push her out of his mind when there had been hundreds of miles between them. But in moments, every repressed feeling he had rushed to the surface. He was still in love with her.

Tony bristled as he turned Faby's words over in his head. *Samantha has moved on…* He balled his fists at his sides, incensed at the thought of another man's hands on his woman. He had told himself that it was best for Samantha to move on and forget about him, but the reality of it was much harder to swallow. Teetering on the brink of a jealous rage, he felt himself starting to lose control. This was so wrong. Samantha was not supposed to be finding love with another man, any more than he was supposed to be held prisoner in a loveless relationship. There had to be a way to alter the path their lives had taken, to set things back on their proper course. There had to be a way for them to find their happy ending.

Tony marched toward Old Navy, tired of lurking in the shadows like some criminal. He didn't give a damn about Faby's threats or warnings—he was going to speak to Samantha. There was so much between them that still needed to be said.

He reached the store entrance as Samantha and Faby were coming out. They headed north, away from him, toward the parking structure. He was almost within shouting distance when Samantha's twin brothers came around the corner. Since they had never met, the twins paid him no mind as he ducked into a nearby Starbucks. Faby's warning echoed in his head, *I'm sure they would be more than happy to forcibly remove your sorry ass...* He was desperate to speak to Samantha, but wasn't interested in an audience or causing a scene. Samantha was obviously home for the holidays—it shouldn't be that hard to track her down and arrange a meeting.

Chapter Forty-Five

Samantha returned from birthday lunch with the family stuffed and ready for a nap. There was nothing like Claim Jumper's monster portions to induce a bonafide food coma. Crawling into bed with her laptop, she logged into Hotmail. She was pleasantly surprised to find a message from Damion.

Happy Birthday!!!

> *Long time no talk… I hope all is well on your end, and that you're still lighting up the world with that beautiful smile of yours. Not sure if you're home for the holidays, but if so, I'd love to take you out for a birthday lunch/dinner/drink. Let me know…*

D

Samantha read the email several times before responding. She'd thought about Damion a lot the past couple of months, often wondering how different things might have turned out if she'd met him first. Would she be living out a blissful happily ever after instead of the nightmare she was trapped in? The kiss the two of them shared, though ill-timed, had opened her eyes to a realm of possibility she hadn't known existed. The possibility of a simple, uncomplicated existence with a man who truly adored her.

She hit the reply button. *Lunch would be great,* she typed. She added the phone number at her sister's house and hit the send button before she had time to change her mind.

Samantha lay back and closed her eyes, only to have her attempt at sleep interrupted by a shrill ring. *Damn, that was fast.* Samantha grabbed the phone off the nightstand. "Hello?"

"Happy Birthday!" Faby sang into the phone. "How was lunch?"

Samantha breathed a sigh of relief. As much as she looked forward to reconnecting with Damion, she could only handle so much stimulation in one day. "It was great. I wish you could have made it."

"Me too. But guess what? My cousin Veronica is going to let me borrow her ID so I can go clubbing with you guys tonight." Faby, the baby of the group, didn't turn twenty-one until September.

"Really?"

"Really! What time does the party train depart?"

"We're meeting Rob and DC for dinner around seven."

"Then I'll be at Meg's by six. See you soon, birthday girl!"

Samantha hung up, wondering where she was going to

find the energy to get through the evening's festivities. She was not a big fan of birthdays. With hers falling three days after Christmas, she was used to having her birthday thunder stolen by the larger holidays, and had learned long ago to keep her expectations low. Part of her just wanted to stay in with a pint of ice cream and a movie.

Megan knocked on the bedroom door. "Hey, these just came for you." She placed a large bouquet of roses on the dresser and handed her a gift-wrapped box.

Samantha examined the mysterious package. "No card?"

"Nope. Nothing on the flowers either." Megan sat down on the edge of the bed. "Looks like you have a secret admirer."

Samantha unwrapped the gift and found the garnet silk blouse she'd tried on at Express the other day. A bright smile spread across her face. "It's from Faby."

Megan lifted the blouse from the box and a small envelope fell into Samantha's lap. "Oh, here's the card."

Samantha's heart stopped when she saw the familiar handwriting, the color draining from her face.

"What's the matter?" Megan asked.

Samantha pushed the box away. "I was wrong—it's not from Faby."

"Well, who is it from? You look like you've just seen a ghost."

"Yeah, I guess you could say that." Samantha handed the

card to Megan. "It's from Tony."

"I saw you trying this on the other day," Megan read. "You've never looked more beautiful. If you're still in town, I'd love to see you. I need to see you." Megan shook her head. "Wow, he's got some nerve."

Samantha stared at the silk blouse in shock. He'd been there on the Promenade that day? Why hadn't he said something? *He was probably with Angela*, she thought, bile rising in her throat.

"What are you going to do?" Megan asked.

Samantha ran a hand through her hair. She'd fantasized many times about Tony coming back and telling her that things were over with Angela, that they could finally be together. As much as he'd hurt her, she still loved him, and longed for the life they'd planned. But she couldn't travel down that road again, only to encounter the same disastrous result. The thought of opening old wounds that had just started to heal was almost too much to bear.

"I don't have anything to say to him," Samantha said, her voice devoid of emotion.

"Are you sure?"

Samantha tore the card in half. "Yes, I'm sure."

Megan had assembled a collection of Samantha's favorite people to come out and celebrate her 21st birthday. In addition to her boyfriend Chris, and Faby, Megan had invited Samantha's two closest friends, Rob and DC, to join the party. The trio had been best friends since childhood, and Rob and DC were pretty much the only people from high school that Samantha kept in touch with. Rob was the quintessential nice guy—a bit on the nerdy side, but definitely the "bring home to mama" type. DC, on the other hand, was a true playa, always juggling women and chasing tail, but for some reason Samantha had a soft spot for him. When DC wasn't offending the female population en masse with his over-the-top male chauvinism, he was pretty good for comic relief. Megan was counting on him to keep the mood light and get Samantha's mind off her problems, if only for one night.

Rob and DC were at the bar when Chris and the girls arrived. When they informed the hostess that their party was complete, they were promptly seated. Everyone commented on how stunning Samantha looked in her new silk blouse, while Faby bit her tongue and tried to hide her fury at Tony's gall.

After dinner, the group moved on to Zanzibar in Santa Monica, where DC was able to get them in VIP style—right to the front of the line with no cover. They were shown to a private booth where a bottle of Ketel One waited on ice, complete with an assortment of juices and tonic water. The booth was decorated with balloons and a sparkly "Happy Birthday" banner that brought tears to Samantha's eyes. Her friends had gone all out to make this night special, and she was touched. "Thanks, you guys," she said, as everyone settled in. "This spread is incredible."

"Only the best for my Sammy," DC said, fixing the birthday girl a drink. He continued to play bartender until everyone had a glass in hand. "To Samantha, the downest chick I know," he said, raising his glass. "Thanks for teaching me everything I needed to know about women."

Faby leaned in close to Samantha. "So *you're* responsible for this monster?"

"Hey," Samantha said, jumping to defend her buddy's honor. "Underneath all that macho posturing is a heart of gold."

Faby rolled her eyes. "Uh huh, I'll have to take your word for it." She cringed as DC looked her up and down, licked his lips, and capped off his not-so-subtle appraisal with a salacious wink.

"Just ignore him," Rob said, placing a protective arm around Faby's shoulder. "When he sees a pretty lady, he sometimes forgets his manners."

Faby beamed up at Rob, quite taken by the tall, handsome gentleman. "Would you mind accompanying me onto the dance floor Roberto?" she cooed. "In case I get accosted by any more horny perverts."

"It would be my pleasure," Rob replied, flashing a million-watt grin as he led her onto the dance floor.

Samantha couldn't help but smile as Rob and Faby walked off, hand in hand. Those two were a match made in heaven; she had no idea why it never occurred to her to set them up before.

"Will you quit babysitting that drink," DC scolded, interrupting her matchmaking fantasies. "We've got that whole bottle to finish."

Samantha set her drink down. "I appreciate all the trouble you went through to set this up," she started, "but I'm gonna take it easy on the drank."

"What? That's nonsense." DC pressed the drink into her hand. "This is your 21st birthday. Your ass is legal now! You're supposed to be living it up!"

"I know, I just… I haven't really felt like drinking since… well, you know." Samantha lowered her eyes, trying to hide the tears that had started to form.

DC turned to Megan for back-up, but Meg just shook her head. "Just leave her alone, DC," she whispered, before heading toward the dance floor with Chris. "She has her reasons."

DC finished his vodka and tonic. "Okay, so you don't drink anymore," he conceded, as he mixed himself another cocktail. "What about dancing? Do you still dance?"

"Yes, I still dance," Samantha assured him.

"Alright then, what are we waiting for? It's time for you to get out on that dance floor and shake what yo mama gave ya!"

They stayed until the club closed down, dancing the night away, and even though Samantha remained sober throughout, it was the most fun she'd had in a very long time. Rob and Faby, having hit it off so well, wanted to continue the party back at his place, so Samantha offered to drive DC's drunk ass home. After an extended round of sloppy, drunken goodbyes, everyone went their separate ways.

Samantha drove in silence as DC flipped impatiently through the radio presets, searching for hip-hop, but finding only techno and slow jams on all his favorite stations. He clicked the radio off in annoyance. "I freakin' hate slow jams."

"You and me both," Samantha said with a chuckle.

DC patted her leg. "So, did you have fun tonight, Sammy?"

"As a matter of fact, I did."

"Good," DC said, staring out the window. "I don't like seeing you sad. It makes me want to kick someone's ass."

"Well aren't you just the sweetest," Samantha said with a smile. "But you don't have to go around defending my honor anymore."

"Maybe not, but I am sick and tired of fools not treating you right. I mean, Eric was my boy and all, but I wanted to rearrange his face when I heard he'd stepped out on you."

Samantha flinched at the reminder of her first love's betrayal. "You don't know how much I appreciate that you broke your man-code to tell me about Eric's cheating. If you hadn't told me the truth, I might never have found out."

"Please," DC said. "You and I go back to the second fucking grade. You really think I'd sit back and let some fool do you like that? Like I said, he's lucky I didn't beat his ass." His fist violently connected with his palm. "Don't get me started on what I'll do if I ever cross paths with this Tony character."

For Tony's sake, Samantha hoped he managed to steer clear of her faithful friend. DC had been a scrawny kid growing up, the target of much playground abuse at the hands of bigger, meaner kids. As a result, he spent much of his adulthood channeling his inner thug, always quick to assert himself physically when he felt slighted or disrespected. It was one bad habit Samantha couldn't wait for him to grow out of.

Samantha pulled up in front of DC's apartment building. "Well, I guess I'll bring your car back in the morning," she said, unbuckling her seatbelt to give DC a goodbye hug. "Thanks again for the best birthday ever."

"Girl, you know I got you. But what's this 'bring the car back in the morning' nonsense. You should just crash here tonight."

"Yeah, I guess that does make the most sense."

"Come on then," he said, hopping out of the car. "I'm ready for another drink."

As they settled on DC's plush leather couch, Samantha

allowed herself to relax in his arms, familiarity giving way to a genuine comfort and ease. It felt good to be held, to feel safe and protected once again. Along with Rob and Gabe, DC was the only other man she allowed herself to trust.

DC brought his lips down to meet hers. On more than one occasion, DC and Samantha had invoked the classic "friends with benefits" arrangement, and found comfort in each other's arms. Because of the mutual respect they had for each other, they always managed to keep things refreshingly uncomplicated. And she had to admit, sex with DC was pretty damn good. She kissed him back for a few minutes before pulling away. "What do you think you're doing?"

A naughty smile lit up his hazel eyes. DC was a fine brotha, and there was a reason he was such a hit with the ladies. "I'm giving you your present," he whispered, covering her neck with soft kisses. "Everyone deserves to get laid on their birthday."

Samantha laughed and nuzzled her head into his chest. "How about we just cuddle instead?"

"You sure? You know I give the best orgasms in the 310."

Samantha considered his offer for a minute. "It's tempting, but not tonight."

DC stood up and extended his hand. "Alright then, birthday girl—your wish is my command. Let's get our snuggle on…"

Chapter Forty-Six

Samantha entered the crowded restaurant and immediately spotted Damion at a corner table. He was wearing jeans and one of his signature political statement T-shirts, this one urging folks to "Save Darfur." His dreads were a little longer, and his goatee a little thicker, but other than that, he was exactly as she remembered—a tall, handsome, Nubian god.

Damion rose to greet her, producing a bouquet of aromatic lilies from under the table. "Happy Birthday," he said, giving her a kiss on the cheek.

Samantha blushed as she took the flowers. There was no mistaking the desire in his eyes. "Thank you," she said. "They're beautiful."

Damion pulled her chair out as she took a seat. "Thanks for agreeing to meet me," he said, catching a whiff of her coconut perfume. "I've missed you."

"Me, too," Samantha confessed. "It's funny how you get used to having someone around. How do you like being back home?"

"It's great. I'm living like a king at my mom's house. She cooks, does my laundry, picks up after me. I'm spoiled rotten —one of the perks of being her only son."

"Yeah, you really lucked out in the mom department." Samantha was having the opposite experience with her own mother, who was doting and attentive, but in a suffocating, overbearing sort of way. She had only lasted three nights under her mother's roof before relocating to her sister's place.

"What about your writing?" she asked. "Are you any closer to finishing your dissertation?"

"I wish. That's the downside to being back in L.A.—too many distractions. I landed an internship at this Indie record label in West Hollywood, and they have me coordinating the Venice/Santa Monica street teams. I'm out on the town almost every night, hitting up clubs, bars, and shows to promote our events and artists. Granted, I'm making a ton of industry connections, but my writing is definitely suffering."

"I'm sorry to hear that. I know how anxious you are to finish so people can start calling you 'Dr. Waters.' "

"Ha, ha. I've actually been thinking about moving back to Santa Cruz for a few months after this internship ends. Things move too damn fast here. Maybe with some fresh air and access to my advisors, I can crank out these final chapters and be done with it."

Samantha's heart skipped upon hearing about Damion's

possible return to the Cruz. "I hope it all works out. It would be nice to have someone around to go to breakfast with."

Damion rubbed his stomach. "Girl, you have no idea how much I crave breakfast in Santa Cruz. Zachary's, Linda's, Café Brasil—you just can't beat the food at any of those joints."

"I found another restaurant to add to the list," Samantha shared. "Tiny place out by the drive-in called the Silver Spur. Their cinnamon rolls are to die for."

"Oh yeah? I'll have to check it out when I get back." Damion had been on the fence about another stint in Santa Cruz, but Samantha's enthusiasm at the prospect of his return was all the incentive he needed. "How about you, Sam? What's been going on in your life? How'd your quarter go?"

Samantha flipped through her menu. Damion didn't know about the miscarriage, and she had gone back and forth about whether or not to tell him. "I... uh..." She scrutinized the menu, avoiding his eyes. "I took last quarter off."

"You did?" Damion couldn't hide his surprise and confusion. "What'd you do?"

"I moved back home."

"What? You've been in L.A. this whole time?" Samantha nodded. "What happened?"

"It's kind of a long story..."

Damion leaned forward, and Samantha could see wrinkles of concern etched into his forehead. "I've got plenty of time."

The waitress interrupted them to take their drink orders. Samantha ordered a lemonade; Damion opted for a Heineken.

"I'm waiting," he said, as the waitress moved on to the next table.

Samantha closed the menu and took a deep breath. What was that people said about the truth setting you free? "A couple of days before Tony dumped me," she started. "I found out I was pregnant." Damion's mouth fell open. "And then after you left town, I lost the baby." Samantha paused, taking a moment to collect herself. No matter how many times she told the story, it never got any easier. "The whole thing messed me up pretty bad, so I took some time off to come home and heal."

Damion sat back in his chair. "You were pregnant with Tony's baby?"

"Yes."

"Why didn't you tell him?"

"He kinda had his hands full with Angela's pregnancy — the last thing I wanted to do was stress him out." Samantha's voice dripped sarcasm. "Besides, Tony made it very clear that he didn't give a damn about what happened to me."

Damion shook his head. "Sam, Angela was never pregnant."

"What?"

"She made the whole thing up to get you to stay away. There was never a baby."

Samantha couldn't believe it. And this was the woman Tony had chosen over her? "You've got to be fucking kidding me."

"What can I say—Angela is not the person we grew up with. Jesus, you should have said something. It might have made a difference."

"It wouldn't have made a difference, Dame. All it would have made is a mess. Trust me on that one."

The waitress returned with their drinks and Damion took the opportunity to absorb Samantha's shocking revelation, viewing the disastrous sequence of events in a new light. He couldn't believe it—while he and Tony had retired to their respective corners to pout and lick their wounds, this girl had been going through hell. By herself. Painfully aware of the part he played in the tragedy, Damion was beside himself with guilt. He'd abandoned Samantha when she needed him most.

"I am so sorry," Damion said, after the waitress took their orders.

Samantha raised a hand to stop him. "No need to apologize—none of this is your fault. You've been nothing but supportive and kind, and I'm glad I finally have a chance to thank you for everything you've done for me."

How could she be so gracious after the horrible way she'd been treated? Having totally lost his appetite, Damion pushed his bread to the side. "Are you okay?"

"For the most part, yeah. It was rough for a minute, but

I'm slowly making peace with things. My friends and family have been great, especially my sister, Meg. They've provided a really safe space for me to rest and recover."

"I wish I could have been there for you, too."

"You're here now," Samantha said, taking a sip of water. "Besides, I'm done living in the past. I go back to school next week, and plan to pick up where I left off. It's time to focus on the future again, instead of mourning what might have been."

Damion was in awe of her strength. It made him love her even more. "To the future," he said, raising his glass.

"To the future."

The waitress brought their meals, and they moved on to lighter topics. Damion was happy to see that Samantha appeared to be doing well, all things considered. Her eyes lit up when she talked about the birthday celebration her friends put together.

"I go to Zanzibar quite a bit," Damion said. "I'm surprised we didn't run into each other."

Samantha munched on a French fry. "It's probably better that we didn't—Faby was with us, and she has declared war on all things Tony."

Damion frowned. He was sick and tired of existing in the shadow of all the shitty things Tony had done. "Is that how you see me, as a constant reminder of Tony?"

"Come on, he's your *best* friend. The only reason you started hanging out with me in the first place is because he asked you to."

"That may be true," Damion argued. "But over time we developed a bond of our own. Something that has nothing to do with Tony. Something that exists in spite of Tony." He took her hand. "My feelings for you are real, and as strong today as the night we kissed."

They held each other's gaze, each taking a moment to replay the forbidden kiss in their minds. Damion wondered if Samantha was as anxious for an encore as he was.

"It could never be," Samantha said, answering his unspoken question.

Her words crushed him. "Why not?"

"Because I still love Tony, and probably always will." Damion released her hand. "I know that's not what you want to hear. Trust me, I'm not too happy about it either. But it's how I feel. You deserve someone who can love you with their whole heart, Damion, not just part of it."

"So do you."

Samantha smiled. "And hopefully, someday, I'll find that person. But there's too much history here. I don't ever want to put you in a position where you have to choose between Tony and myself."

Deep down, Damion knew she was right. Tony was still

carrying a blazing torch for Samantha, and he would never be okay with the idea of his best friend settling down with the love of his life. To move forward with Samantha would mean ending a lifelong friendship, what amounted to an impossible choice. "This blows," Damion muttered, as he grudgingly accepted his Fate.

"Hey," she offered. "There's nothing that says we can't be great friends. And I would like that, very much."

"Just try and get rid of me," Damion said with a smile. He dropped several twenties on top of the bill the waitress had brought. "You feel like walking off this meal?"

Samantha gathered her purse and flowers. "Sure."

They strolled the streets of Venice Beach, eventually making their way to the Boardwalk. It was a gorgeous afternoon, the temperature hovering just above eighty degrees. They laughed and joked, browsing the merchandise on display by the numerous street vendors. Damion insisted on buying Samantha a moonstone bracelet he saw her admiring, which made her day. After stopping for ice cream, they found a spot on the sandy strip of beach to enjoy the sunset.

"What do you think are the odds of seeing the green flame today?" he asked.

"You know, ever since you described the phenomenon to me, I've looked for this 'green flame' at every sunset. But so far, nothing." She turned to him, eyebrow raised. "I'm starting to think you made the whole thing up."

"I did not! Google it!"

"I may just do that." Samantha stared across the water, her heart pulled toward another string of memories. "Tony was always chasing sunsets," she reminisced. "Every day we spent together, no matter where we were, he always made sure we stopped whatever we were doing to watch the sunset."

Damion ignored the jealous flare that ignited at the mention of Tony's name, and put his friend cap back on. "You miss him, don't you?"

"On occasion. I try not to think about him, but a stray memory sneaks in every now and then." She finally summoned the courage to ask the question that had been on her mind all day. "How is he doing?"

Damion shrugged. "It's not the life he wanted, but it's the life he chose."

Samantha had always admired Damion's attempts at diplomacy, but his answer was so vague it prompted a follow-up question. "Is he happy?"

Damion hesitated. He didn't want to open a can of worms, but after witnessing the destruction that well-meaning misinformation could cause, he refused to lie to Samantha again. From here on out, it would be the truth and nothing but the truth. "He's pretty miserable, Sam. Just trying to make the best of a bad situation."

"Did you know that he sent me a birthday present?" she asked. "He knows I'm in town and wants to see me."

This was news to Damion—he thought he had steered Tony away from that course of action. "No, he didn't mention it. Are you going to see him?"

"I don't know." Samantha lifted her eyes to meet his. "What do you think I should do?"

"Come on, Sam. I'm not exactly an objective third party."

"True. But you've been there every step of the dysfunctional way. You have a direct line into the psyches of both parties. I'm asking for your two cents—do you think anything good can come from seeing Tony again?"

Damion thought a long while before answering. "I guess that depends on what your motivation is. I'm all for closure, but if you see Tony, you risk stirring up all those old feelings again, right? Problem is, Tony's situation with Angela hasn't changed. It might be different if he'd taken strides toward extricating himself from his relationship *before* contacting you, but the fact is, he's still with her. If all you want is a chance to tell him off and say goodbye, that's one thing. But if any part of you is hoping for something more, you're just setting yourself up for a fall."

Samantha nodded. "Yeah, that's what I figured. Thank you."

"For what?"

"For being my friend and having my back. I really

appreciate everything you've done for me. Your friendship has helped so much, Damion. More than you know."

"If you ever need anything, all you have to do is ask."

"I know." They made their way back to their cars in silence, hearts heavy over a story that would never be told.

"Thanks again for the lovely afternoon," she said, lingering in their parting embrace.

"It was my pleasure," he whispered, choking back a surge of emotion. "I'll be sure to give you a call when I get back to the Cruz."

"I look forward to it," Samantha said with a smile. She started her car and blew him a kiss before pulling out of the parking lot.

Damion could do nothing but watch and wave as the girl of his dreams drove down the street, and out of his life.

Chapter Forty-Seven

*T*ony looked up the street for Damion's car. It wasn't like Damion to be late, and Tony was in desperate need of a break from Angela's incessant nagging. Her list of demands was endless, and he had grown weary of jumping through hoop after hoop with no tangible result. She'd begged him to stay, and he had. She'd complained about the lack of sex, so despite his complete lack of desire, he managed to service her twice a week. He'd even severed all ties to Samantha, the woman he truly wanted to be with. Tony had done everything Angela asked, but it still wasn't good enough. He was beginning to wonder why he bothered with any of it.

Tony was still holding out hope that Samantha would call. He refused to believe that she would just blow him off, even though he had more than earned her cold shoulder. Maybe she hadn't received his gift. Her sister could have intercepted the package, the way Faby had blocked him at the mall. If he didn't hear from her by the end of the week, he was going to take a trip to Santa Cruz. He was finally ready to admit he'd made a horrendous mistake, and try to make things right. All he needed was another chance.

Damion's car turned the corner and stopped in front of his building. Tony hopped into the passenger seat. "You're late."

"Sorry. My lunch date ran over."

"Oh yeah? Anyone I know?"

Damion stared straight ahead, ignoring Tony's question.

Tony studied Damion's profile and noticed the muscles in his jaw twitching. He was obviously upset about something. "What's the matter with you?"

"Nothing," Damion said.

"Come on, I've known you long enough to know better. What happened? Did you end up on hell date or something?"

"It wasn't that kind of date. Just lunch with an old friend."

Tony couldn't understand why Damion was being so vague. In the lifetime that they'd known each other, there had never been a secret between them. "What's up with all the mystery?" he pressed. "Who were you with?"

"I was with Samantha."

Tony whipped his head to the left and glared at his friend. "*My* Samantha?"

"Yeah, it was her birthday last wee—."

"I know when her birthday is," Tony snapped. He just didn't realize Damion was keeping track of such things. "I sent her a gift, but she must not have gotten it."

"She got it," Damion said, the tick in his jaw picking up speed.

"Excuse me?"

"The blouse? She got it."

"Oh." Tony didn't know what bothered him more—that Samantha had rejected his attempt at reconciliation, or that his best friend had been sneaking around and seeing her behind his back. Jumping to all the wrong conclusions, Tony's confusion morphed into rage. He clenched and unclenched his fists as the anger begged for release.

"It was just lunch," Damion explained, pulling into a parking spot near the basketball court. "We got pretty tight up in Santa Cruz."

"So I see. Why didn't you tell me you were going to see her?"

"Because it was none of your business." Damion grabbed the basketball and headed toward the court.

Tony followed, close on his heels. "Did you sleep with her?"

Damion took a shot from just behind the three-point line. "Your ass is trippin'."

The fact that Damion didn't deny an affair confirmed Tony's suspicions. He scooped up the rebound and held the ball. "I asked you a question."

"I'm not doing this with you right now—I came here to play basketball. I'm going to see if these guys wanna get in on a game."

Tony didn't take kindly to being dismissed. He also couldn't stand the thought of Damion living happily ever after with Samantha while he was stuck with crazy Angela. Suddenly, all the things wrong with Tony's life converged at the breaking point, pushing him over the edge. Enraged, he threw the ball hard at Damion's back.

Damion whirled around. "What the fuck is your problem?"

"How long have you been scheming to steal my girl?" Tony advanced and shoved Damion hard, causing him to stumble backward.

The two men glared at each other. The future of their friendship hung in the balance as a territorial standoff over a woman eclipsed twenty years of brotherly love.

"First of all," Damion said. "She is not your girl. Second of all, let's not rewrite history here. It was your actions and cowardice that drove her away. I had nothing to do with it."

"But you sure didn't waste any time rushing in to comfort her."

"You *asked* me to look after her!"

"And you went above and beyond the call of duty, didn't you playboy?" Tony shoved Damion again. "Did it take long to get into her pants, or did she open right up?"

Damion shoved him back. "I'm not gonna sit here and let you disrespect Samantha like that. Shut your mouth or I'll shut it for you."

"Oooh, look at Prince Damion, all ready to throw down to defend fair Samantha's honor. How sweet."

"You're not the only one who loves her, man."

Tony momentarily halted his assault. "I knew it."

"Well, what's not to love? She's an amazing woman. You were a fool to let her go."

That was the last straw for Tony. He took a swing at his best friend, aiming to knock the pretty boy smirk right off his face.

He missed. Damion then connected with a blow of his own that sent Tony to the ground in a heap. He remained doubled over for several minutes, unable to retaliate.

"Look," Damion said, standing over him. "I understand your anger. But it isn't right to lay it at my feet. I didn't steal your girl. The only reason you're not with Samantha right now is because of the choices *you* made. You broke her heart. You hurt her in ways she may never recover from. If she chose not to contact you after all this time, it was probably a matter of self-preservation. Stop trying to paint yourself as some kind of a victim here."

Tony struggled to get to his feet. Blinded by rage, he was incapable of listening to reason. All he could do was lash out. "She'll never love you the way she loves me," Tony taunted. "All you are is a consolation prize."

"And all you are is some guy she used to know."

"Yeah, whatever. Enjoy my sloppy seconds."

"I will."

Damion hopped in his car and sped off, and Tony, having lost everything that mattered to him, started the long, lonely walk back to Angela.

Epilogue

Samantha wiped at the sweat trickling down the side of her face. Along with the other members of her graduating class, she was trying not to melt as the afternoon sun beat down on her black cap and gown. In a few moments, she would become the proud recipient of a Bachelor of Arts in Sociology, and while she had no idea what she was going to do with her fancy degree, the sense of accomplishment she felt was very real. She couldn't believe she'd actually made it.

When the Provost called her name, a large cheer rose from the audience. Glancing toward the source of the whoops and hollering, she found her parents, siblings, and a host of aunts, uncles, cousins, and friends on their feet, clapping and waving. She shook the Provost's hand and accepted her faux diploma, then proceeded offstage to where Faby waited. The two women embraced, then turned to watch Gabe receive his diploma. He pumped his fist triumphantly in the air as his family exploded in applause. When he joined Samantha and Faby, the trio linked arms and walked back to their seats together.

"We did it," Gabe said, drawing the girls close.

"We sure did," Faby said, overcome by emotion. "I love you guys."

"I love you, too," Samantha said, fighting back tears of her own.

The rest of the ceremony was a blur as Samantha let her mind wander, college's most memorable moments playing like a slideshow in her mind. She allowed herself to linger on thoughts of Tony. Over time, her anger had faded, forgiveness working to erode the hatred in her heart until only the root emotion, love, remained. For better or worse, the mark Tony had made on her life was lasting, and the day felt incomplete without him there.

"Ladies and Gentlemen—I present to you, the Class of 2004!"

The graduates stood and switched their tassels over, to the sound of deafening applause. As the group began their recessional, Samantha stared across the sea of friends and family members crowded onto the Oakes lawn, the collective pride apparent on each and every face that beamed back at her. She almost lost her footing when she spotted a lone figure on the perimeter, hands in his pockets, eyes hidden behind dark shades. Tony.

She lost sight of him as the crowd closed around her, and in minutes she was surrounded by loved ones, everyone serving up a healthy supply of hugs and congratulations.

"We are so proud of you," her mother gushed, tears of joy sparkling in her eyes. "And graduating with Honors to boot!"

"I guess Meg isn't the only smarty-pants in the family," her brother Derrick added. "Congratulations, sis."

"Thank you for coming," Samantha said, overwhelmed by the showering of love. "It means so much to me that you're all here."

"Where else would I be on my best girl's big day?" DC asked, pulling Samantha into one of his signature bear hugs. "Besides, I never realized there were so many breezies in Santa Cruz. I'm like a pimp in a candy store up in here."

Rob laughed. "I swear, we can't take you anywhere, man." He smiled brightly as Faby caught his eye and waved. "Though I have to admit, the women out here *are* beautiful."

Samantha scanned the crowd, but the Tony figure had disappeared. She must have imagined him. There was no way he'd come all this way to see her after all this time.

The graduates and their respective families returned to Sam, Gabe, and Faby's house to celebrate, and spirits were high as everyone dug into the feast Faby's mom and aunts had prepared. Samantha had never seen so much food in her life, and while there were almost fifty people scattered throughout the house waiting for their turn at the buffet, Samantha had no doubt they'd still have days worth of leftovers. Gabe was going to be in heaven.

"Samantha, phone!" someone called from the kitchen.

Samantha took the phone from one of Faby's aunts. "Hello?"

"Happy graduation."

It had been years since she'd heard his voice, but she'd know that silky baritone anywhere. Her heartbeat picked up a pace. "Tony."

"The one and only."

Samantha stepped outside and sat down on the front steps, her knees weak. "So it was you. I thought I was hallucinating."

"I wanted to be there when you walked the stage," Tony said. "I tried to find you after the ceremony, but you guys took off so quick."

"Yeah, folks were anxious to get back to the food. Where are you now?"

"At the Sunset Inn on Mission. Is it alright if I come over? I'd really like to congratulate you in person."

Samantha glanced down the road. Her brothers, Rob, and DC had challenged Gabe and his three brothers to a basketball game at a nearby park. She could just see all eight of them rushing to the rescue if Tony came within a hundred yards of the premises. "I don't think it's a good idea for you to come here."

"Then can we meet somewhere?"

Samantha considered her options. "I should be able to sneak away for a little bit. How about we meet on West Cliff in half an hour?"

"I'll be there."

⌘

Samantha made her way to the clifftop ledge where it had all began over two years ago. There was a certain symmetry about reuniting here, as if everything was coming full circle. Tony was sitting in his spot when she arrived, exactly as he had been that fateful morning, his gaze fixed on the horizon. Samantha had underestimated how unsettling it would be to see him again after all these years. Desire, anger, and disappointment simultaneously bubbled to the surface and jockeyed for position, each emotion triggering a different instinctual response. What should she do? Run to him? Run away? Push him over the side of the cliff? She took a moment to collect herself, and then started toward the edge.

Tony rose to greet her. "Hey." His smile failed to hide his nervousness.

Samantha stopped, leaving several feet between them. "Hey."

Tony reacquainted himself with her image, the face he had fallen in love with, that he only got to see in memories. "Thanks for agreeing to meet me." He took a tentative step forward. "You look great."

Samantha took a seat on a large, flat boulder. "Thanks."

Tony sat down beside her. An awkward silence filled the air as they watched the surf pound against the shore. He cast his eyes across the picturesque landscape, marveling at the unspoiled beauty of the area. This town evoked feelings of home for him more than any place he'd ever been. Nothing in L.A. came close to the magic of Santa Cruz, just like no other woman could compare to Samantha in sight or spirit. "I've missed this place so much," he said, drawing in a deep breath. "I can't believe it's taken me so long to come back."

His words were like salt in her freshly opened wounds. "Me either," Samantha said, memories of his abandonment lodged in the forefront of her mind. "I thought this was your happy place."

"It was... It is. I guess I haven't had much time for happiness since I left."

Samantha drew her knees to her chest. "So what brings you back now?"

"I had to see you."

"Well, here I am."

"Yes, and all grown up. When I left, you were a girl, trying to find her place in the world. But you're all woman now." He smiled, almost like a proud parent. "You wear it well."

Samantha blushed. There was something about being the subject of his gaze that made her feel like a young girl again, desperate for her lover's approval. "I'm still figuring things out," she admitted. "But these have definitely been transformational times."

"I'm sorry I wasn't there," he said, taking her hand. "I'm sorry for a lot of things."

His touch triggered a geyser of emotion. "Like choosing to stay with a lying, manipulative witch over the woman you once referred to as the missing piece to your soul?" Samantha snatched her hand from his grasp. "How could you throw me away like that, Tony? You were beyond cruel."

"I know. I wanted you to hate me. I thought that if I obliterated any shred of hope that we could ever be together, somehow it would be easier for you to move on. But it was all an act. I never stopped loving you."

"You have the funniest way of showing it."

"I didn't have a choice, Sam. I tried to leave Angela once, and she tried to kill herself again. Right in front of me. I didn't know what to do. I figured at least one of us should be free…"

Samantha noticed the glint of a gold band on his left ring finger. Her heart sank. "You married her?"

Tony turned the ring around on his finger. "This," he said, holding up his hand, "is just another in the long line of mistakes I've made since I left you."

Samantha couldn't conceal her shock and surprise. "Damion never said anything about you and Angela getting married."

Tony tensed at the mention of Damion's name. "That's

because he doesn't know. Damion and I haven't spoken in years."

Once again, Samantha had to retrieve her jaw from the ground. She shook her head in disbelief. "I had no idea."

"You guys still keep in touch?"

"We check in over email from time to time. He got this amazing opportunity to teach at Goldsmiths University in London. He's been in England for the past year."

"Any plans to join him over there?"

Tony's question caught Samantha off guard. "What? No. Damion and I are just friends."

"Uh huh."

"Wait a minute—don't tell me *I'm* the reason you guys are no longer speaking."

"Between friends, there are lines you don't cross," Tony explained. "Damion crossed that line."

"Nothing happened between me and Damion," Samantha insisted, mortified. "Please tell me you didn't throw away a lifelong friendship over some misunderstanding."

"He never hit on you?"

Samantha chose her words carefully. "There was a hint of an attraction at one point, but we decided not to pursue it. Damion knew I wasn't over you."

That seemed to calm Tony down a bit. "How about now? Are you over me yet?"

"What does it matter, Tony? You're *married*."

"Like I said, marrying Angela was a huge mistake. The only reason I proposed is because Angela got pregnant. I was trying to do the right thing."

"Was it a real baby or a fake baby this time?"

"Who knows. She had a miscarriage at the end of her first trimester. So she says. My sister is convinced she made the whole thing up to trap me."

Samantha's stomach turned as memories of her own painful miscarriage resurfaced. What kind of woman could lie about something like that? "Sounds like you picked a real winner."

"Tell me about it. Anyway, whether there really was a baby or not, it's probably best that things ended the way they did. It could be considered child abuse to bring a kid into our train wreck of a relationship."

Samantha wondered if he'd feel the same way about the child she lost. Would he also think it was a blessing in disguise? She decided right then and there never to tell him about the baby. She wasn't going to give him a chance to break her heart all over again.

"What about you?" he asked. "Have you found someone to make you happy?"

"No," Samantha said, gazing across the sea. "I'm focusing on making myself happy these days."

Tony nodded in approval. "All grown up." A familiar desire burned in his eyes. "It's a beautiful thing."

They stared at each other for a long while. It was all coming back to her, the love, the soul connect, the way he made her feel like she could do anything, be anything. He had seen the best in her, and taught her how to dream bigger. He taught her to embrace the road less traveled, even though he had set her up to walk it alone. But as easy as it was for old feelings to be reignited, she was also watching every "could've been" and "should've been" crystallize into "will never be," right before her eyes. They may have had a perfect love once, but they had messed it up. It was clear now that they'd come too far down the road to ever go back.

Tony leaned forward to cup her face, and then slowly brought his lips to meet hers. It was every bit as magical as their first kiss, but both knew this was goodbye. Samantha pulled away first, not wanting to get lost in the moment, or worse, sent spiraling out of control.

"I should go," she said. "Before they send out a search party."

"Right." Tony rose to his feet and helped her up. "Thanks again for meeting me, for giving me a chance to make amends. I know it came two years too late but—"

"No, I'm glad you called," she assured him. "We were long overdue for some type of closure."

The word closure was like a knife through Tony's heart. While he was trying to accept that they would never be together, he wasn't ready to let her go. "Just so you know," he said, "it was never about not loving you." He stared deep into her eyes. "I have always loved you, with every breath in my body, and probably always will. But sometimes, love just isn't enough."

Samantha nodded, fighting back tears. She had needed so badly to hear him say those words, to know that the love between them had been real, that her heart hadn't lied to her. She collapsed into one last embrace, wishing she could press pause on this moment and stay with him, just like this, forever.

"I love you," he whispered.

She wanted to say it back, but couldn't. She was afraid that if the words passed over her lips, it would start all over again—the loving, the longing, the waiting. And she refused to go back to that dark, unfulfilling place, no matter how badly she still wanted a life with him. He was right, sometimes love wasn't enough.

"Goodbye, Tony," she said, planting one last kiss on his lips. Then she turned, and with her head held high, broke away from the past, and took the first step toward the rest of her life.

DISCUSSION QUESTIONS

1. From the moment they met, Tony and Samantha had a "connection." Can people really fall in love this fast? Is the idea of love at first sight a realistic concept, or does true love develop over time?

2. What is the definition of a soulmate? Can someone have more than one soulmate?

3. Was Samantha wrong to pursue a platonic relationship with Tony after she found out about his girlfriend? Can men and women who are attracted to each other be "just friends"?

4. Even though Tony and Samantha never slept together while he was with Angela, were they still cheating? Is emotional cheating worse than physical cheating?

5. Should Samantha have been more concerned by what Damion referred to as Tony's 'distressing pattern of conflict avoidance'? Why was it so easy for her to ignore such a blatant red flag? Does love make us blind to our partner's faults?

6. After Angela's "suicide attempt," did Tony do the right thing by staying with her? What would have been a better way to deal with the situation?

7. Angela went to great lengths to trap Tony into staying with her. What drives women to that level of desperation? What can society do to address the low self-esteem issues prevalent among young women?

8. Tony felt he had to 'break Samantha's heart to set her free'. Was this the right decision, or should he have been honest with her? Are there circumstances when lying is the more compassionate course of action than telling the truth?

9. If you were Samantha, would you have told Tony about the baby? Do you think it would have made a difference?

10. Damion represents the nice guy that always finishes last. Why do some women gravitate toward bad boys (or men who are bad for them), while ignoring the nice guy standing right in front of them?

11. Damion broke a cardinal rule of friendship by falling for his best friend's girl. Are our best friend's exes off limits? Was Tony out of line for reacting the way he did when he found out about Damion's relationship with Samantha?

12. Did the novel have a satisfying ending? If you could have written an ending for the four primary characters (Tony/Samantha/Damion/Angela), what would it have been?

*Read on for an excerpt from **The Space Between**,
the sequel to **When Love Isn't Enough.***

Prologue

From the terrace of my hotel suite, I stared down at the collection of people gathered to witness our nuptials. It was a small ceremony, nothing fancy, with only our nearest and dearest in attendance. In a few minutes, it would be time to head down to the beach, in my strapless white gown, to become Mrs. Damion Waters.

Panic gripped my rapidly beating heart. *I don't think I can go through with this.*

Not because I didn't love him—I loved Damion with all my heart. He was my *best* friend, a truly amazing man. I'd never had someone so devoted to my care and comfort. But that spark, that out of control, life-consuming fire—it just wasn't there. I'd tried to convince myself that a steady, solid, reliable love was more important than passion, but after the events of last month, I had come face to face with the fact that I was kidding myself. Settling. Maybe if I'd never known that kind of passion, I wouldn't miss it so much. But I knew what it felt like to love someone so much you could barely breathe, and no matter how hard I tried, I couldn't forget.

Damn you, Tony. Damn you, damn you, damn you.

My sister, Megan, came up behind me, resting her hand on the small of my back. "You about ready?" she asked.

I set my bouquet of calla lilies on the table. "Can you get Damion for me?"

"Isn't it bad luck for the groom to see the bride before the wedding?"

"Meg, I don't think there's going to be a wedding…"

Chapter One

Samantha

Three years earlier…

I've tried really hard to live my life with honor and integrity, especially when it comes to matters of the heart. After all, the heart is a fragile thing, the seat of human vulnerability, our Achilles heel. A major break can do irreparable damage, and I'm speaking from experience on this one, having lived through the after effects of an all-consuming, life-wrecking love affair.

When I was 19-years-old, I met the man who I believed to be my soulmate. We had that magical chemistry you see in movies; the moment we laid eyes on each other for the first time, we just *knew*. Up to that point, I was somewhat of a cynic—my first "love" had ended in heartbreak and completely damaged my ability to trust. But the connection I shared with Tony, said soulmate, was not something I could deny. And believe me, I tried. There are just some people who, once they get hooks into your heart, are impossible to shake.

Yes, it's always exciting to meet the man of your dreams, and discovering he returns your feelings is all kinds of euphoric. Fate at work. But the path to our happy ending wasn't exactly clear. Tony came with a rather significant complication—a girlfriend. A girlfriend who, for reasons I still struggle to understand, he found it difficult to sever ties with. Tony, bless his non-confrontational, peace-loving heart, couldn't stand the thought of hurting anyone. As Damion used to say, this was Tony's best and worst quality.

###

Damion—a tall, dark, dreadlocked Adonis—was Tony's best friend. When we met, Damion was in his fourth year as a graduate student in the History of Consciousness Ph.D. program at UC Santa Cruz, where we all went to school. Damion is one of those impossibly smart, activist-oriented, hip-hop intellectuals; his insightful critiques of the establishment were reminiscent of KRS-One and Public Enemy. Heavily influenced by the psychologist Frantz Fanon, he double-majored in History and Psychology at the University of Oregon and was now writing his dissertation on the psychology of the oppressed and the absence of contemporary social movements in the United States.

Damion's greatest passion was the empowerment of underrepresented minorities in underserved communities, and he was committed to using his voice to speak out against all forms of injustice. An accomplished orator and professional keynote/emcee, he could frequently be found onstage at some event, mic in hand, trying to incite the next revolution. He never passed up an opportunity to drop knowledge and wisdom on impressionable, young minds. Possessing hypnotic charisma, Damion would open his mouth and audiences would fall in rapture. To this day, I've never met someone with greater powers of persuasion.

Damion also gave awesome hugs, which I took advantage of on many occasions while I waited for Tony to figure things out. When Tony finally managed to free himself from his relationship with Angela, we embarked on what was supposed to be a long and passionate journey together. But Angela had other plans. A series of tragic events drove a wedge between Tony and me, turning us into star-crossed lovers. Convinced that we were destined to be together, I put my life on hold and waited for him… refusing to give up on the future we had planned.

During our estrangement, Tony and I did most of our communicating through Damion, and Damion provided a strong, supportive shoulder for me to cry on during those long, hard months. Honestly, I don't know if I would have made it through that phase of my life without Damion. During the lowest of the lows, he was a true friend, and over time, I came to rely on him.

Tony never made it back to me, and I was left devastated and heartbroken. I truly believed he was *The One*; it never occurred to me that there were forces in this world strong enough to keep soulmates apart. That maybe true love *couldn't* conquer all. I don't know what was more tragic—losing Tony, or losing the part of me that still believed in true love and the possibility of happily ever after.

In the wake of Tony's abandonment, Damion and I built upon our budding friendship. My wounds were still pretty raw, deep lacerations that refused to scab over. To guard against infection, I decided to keep people, men especially, at a distance. I was determined to protect myself by any means necessary. But for some reason, my defense mechanisms never kicked in when Damion was around. I've always felt completely safe with him, and his tender, loving care played a huge part in my healing.

Damion was also a fantastic influence on me scholastically. While I worked toward my BA in Sociology, Damion was finishing up his dissertation and trying to line up a job in preparation for his inevitable entry into the real world. He was so focused and driven, quite the contrast to my peers who were more interested in partying than planning for the future. I found myself emulating his work ethic and attitude towards academics, and earned straight-A's my junior and senior years.

We never spoke about Tony. Of course I was curious, but I knew better than to open that door again. Tony had made his choice (if you could even call it a choice), and I had vowed not to waste another moment with my life on hold. There had been enough of that nonsense.

Somewhere along the way, Damion developed a crush on me, which we came very close to acting on while I was rebounding from Tony. But deep down, I knew it was wrong. Not only were Tony and Damion like brothers, but I was in no position to return Damion's feelings. Damion had been such a good friend to me; it wasn't right to use him as a distraction. Which is all he could have been because I was still very much in love with his best friend.

Damion was the perfect gentleman and never pressed the issue, appearing content with the platonic bond we'd forged. I'd see him once or twice a week and we'd go hiking, to the movies, or catch a show downtown at the Catalyst. I actually credit him with bringing the fun back into my world after a long bout of depression and hibernation.

"Come on," he said, dragging me towards the Rock-O-Plane, one of his favorite rides at the Santa Cruz Beach Boardwalk. "We have time for one more ride before the show starts."

Steel cages dangled from the limbs of the Ferris wheel towering above us. "I don't know, Dame. That might be a little too much spinning for my current state of intoxication."

"Oh, you'll be fine," he said.

He was always saying that, "you'll be fine." Right before he nudged (or shoved) me outside of my comfort zone.

"Alright, but if I puke all over your Jordan's, it's on you. Literally."

I managed to keep the contents of my stomach where they belonged, and after a laughter-filled spin on the Rock-O-Plane, we headed down to the beach for the show. Every Friday night the Boardwalk hosted a free concert on the beach, and the line-up was great for the nostalgia factor. So far we'd seen Eddie Money, the Family Stone (minus Sly), and the Gin Blossoms. Tonight's entertainment would be provided by 90's pop queen, Tiffany.

We had a blast drinking beer and singing along to her cheesy (but classic) tunes like "I Think We're Alone Now." I hadn't heard that song in years, yet still knew *every word*. To my amusement, I discovered Damion knew every word as well. That was one of the lovely paradoxes about Damion— while he was smart, studious, and articulate enough to hold his own in a debate with Cornel West, he was still able to access his inner 10-year-old with ease. The man could put in work, but also knew how to play, as accomplished in the art of silliness as any other subject.

As my Junior year drew to a close, Damion successfully defended his dissertation and was preparing to head to London. He'd been offered a postdoctoral fellowship at Goldsmiths University, where he planned to conduct research for a comparative study on U.S. and UK youth uprisings. This was an amazing opportunity for him, and I shared his excitement. But as his departure date drew near, the magnitude of what this meant for our friendship began to sink in. Damion, my faithful companion and BFF, was moving to *London.*

A week before his departure, we took one final trek into the Pogonip, a heavily forested state park adjacent to the UCSC campus. Our ritual was to hike deep into the woods and pause for a smoke break underneath our favorite tree, Papa Wood. In the book, *The Celestine Prophecy,* James Redfield claimed that old-growth redwoods were a critical source of energy that people could tap into to increase their own personal reserves. Papa Wood, whose trunk was easily twelve feet in diameter, definitely fell into the "old-growth" category and we'd spent many afternoons with our backs against his sturdy trunk, meditating on the mysteries of life.

Damion took a seat and passed me his palm-sized glass pipe, the bowl packed with Santa Cruz's finest tasty greens. I took a hit and passed the pipe back to him, a stream of smoke passing over my lips as I exhaled.

"I can't believe this is our last session under this tree," Damion said.

"Don't remind me." I was enjoying my bubble of denial about Damion's departure, not yet ready for the inevitable burst.

"I don't think they have redwood forests in England," he mused. "I wonder what I'll do when I need to replenish my energy. I've been spoiled living in Santa Cruz so long. Folks are of a very high spiritual caliber here."

"If there are spiritual folks to be found, I have no doubt you will draw them to you. You're a magnet when it comes to that stuff." And it was the truth. Damion was a living, breathing poster child for the Law of Attraction—he put peaceful, positive vibes out into the Universe on a regular basis and was continuously blessed with opportunity and good fortune. I truly believed my life had been improved by sheer proximity, and was worried that his departure would trigger a depressive doom spiral.

"Won't be the same without my wing woman," he said with a wink.

"Maybe now you'll be able to find yourself a lady friend who can offer more perks than companionship," I teased.

Damion's smile faded, his brows bending toward the center of his face. "Still won't be the same."

I'd tried many times to encourage Damion to take a dip in the dating pool, but he always had an excuse handy:

"These days, dating and drama go hand in hand. Who's got time for that?"

"A girlfriend will just distract me from the work I need to do on my dissertation."

"It doesn't make sense to start a relationship right now—I'm getting ready to leave the country."

And so on. While those were all valid points, I always suspected there was more to it, like he was still carrying a torch for me. Which is why I frequently tried to direct his affection elsewhere. But now that his attention was about to be permanently reassigned as he was physically removed from my sphere, separation anxiety was setting in. The more I contemplated "Life without Damion," the more I realized how attached I'd become over the past year. Without any drama or complications, we'd been fulfilling each other's need for companionship and emotional connection. His absence was going to create a huge void in my life, and I was starting to freak out. Isn't that the way it always is though? You never realize how much something means to you until you're on the verge of losing it…

Chapter Two

Samantha

Damion's last night in Santa Cruz was very emotional. I dread goodbyes—they always bring me back to the day Tony left. But this one was particularly hard because the person I usually turned to for comfort and support was the one leaving.

Damion was a beloved member of the UCSC community, and his going-away party was festive and well-attended by students and faculty alike. His mother even flew in from Los Angeles, and it was wonderful to see her again. I had met Damion's mother for the first time when Damion had taken me down to LA for my final showdown with Tony. It was during this trip that I realized a future with Tony was no longer a possibility, and Mama Waters (as she is affectionately known) was a great comfort to me, even though Tony is like a son to her.

As I sat on the porch that July night, almost a year ago, Mama Waters sat down beside me with a pot of chamomile tea. I clutched the warm mug between my palms, holding on for dear life. My tears hadn't stopped flowing since Tony drove away; I was inconsolable.

Damion had been a wonderful support, driving me down to LA for the confrontation, against his better judgment, but I'll never forget how comforting it was to have the company and counsel of another woman at that moment of intense fragility. You see, Tony hadn't just left me, he had left me with child… I didn't share the details of my plight with her, but for some reason I sensed that Mama Waters understood the depth of my agony, the severity of my wound. She didn't press, preach, or judge. In fact, she barely spoke at all, except to impart these timeless words of wisdom:

"Things don't always turn out like we planned, and that's okay. You have to trust that there's a bigger plan at work. We are always being prepared for something better, or protected from something worse." She patted my hand. "We may not see it at the time, but I promise you, it's true."

Those words served as my mantra during my darkest days.

Her outlook on life was remarkable considering all she'd been through. Mama Waters was the epitome of grace under pressure. A single mother, she had raised Damion and his brother in one of the roughest neighborhoods in South Central Los Angeles, where the life expectancy of black males was painfully short. She experienced this firsthand when her firstborn son, Khalil, was gunned down in a gang-related shooting a few months before his 16th birthday. Determined to save Damion from a similar fate, she worked two jobs to earn enough money to move them to a safer neighborhood in a better school district. Damion was all she had left and she would not let him become a statistic.

Mama Waters hadn't walked the easiest of roads, but the years of struggle made moments like this all the more poignant. Damion, her baby boy, had beat the odds. He was now the recipient of a Ph.D., *Doctor* Damion Waters. Not bad for a boy from the hood. But what was truly impressive is that he was just getting started. Damion's idealism and activist bent were the real deal—he was determined to make a difference in this world. He wasn't content to settle on a career, he wanted to build a *legacy*.

Every guest at Damion's going away party that offered a toast (and there were many) spoke of how Damion had changed their life. Helped them see something in a different light. Damion, having inherited his mother's positive outlook, had a calming effect on people. The ability to bring peace to others with his mere presence was Damion's special gift, one that was much appreciated since there was no shortage of people out there doing thoughtless, fucked up shit to each other. But not Damion. He made everything better, and asked for very little in return. Which only made him more beloved.

Mama Waters stood proudly in the corner as love and appreciation was showered upon her son. The speeches went on and on until Damion refocused the love in his mother's direction, giving credit where credit was due. We were all holding back tears as he expressed his love and admiration for his mother, clearly the driving force behind every ounce of greatness he aspired to.

"This woman," Damion proclaimed as his mom tried to shake the blush from her cheeks. "She sacrificed so much, every step of the way, so that I could have access to opportunities for a better life. The greatest gift you can give your kids is the chance to chase their dreams. I'm a project kid; I'm not supposed to be here, with fancy letters after my name, poised to wield actual power against the establishment. And I wouldn't be here without the love, support, and guidance of this incredible woman, my mother, Mrs. Corrine Waters.

"Ma, thank you for all you sacrificed to get me here. For putting a roof over my head and putting me through school. For always putting me first. For teaching me that there is nobility in selflessness. I do this all for, and because of, you."

The room erupted in applause. Raising a man of that caliber is no small feat, and we all owed Mrs. Waters a tremendous debt of gratitude.

###

Damion stopped by my house before he hit the road, his last stop before bidding farewell to the Cruz. I admit, I was tempted not to answer the door, hoping Damion would refuse to leave town if I denied him the opportunity to say a proper goodbye. I'd never experienced such severe separation anxiety, not even with Tony. It could be years before we saw each other again, and the reality of what that meant was finally starting to hit me.

I know, codependent, much?

"London's just so *far*, you know?" I pouted.

"It is," he said. "But think of it this way—now you have somewhere to stay if you ever decide to visit Europe."

"I may just take you up on that. A flight to London sounds like a great graduation present." I forced a smile. Having something to look forward to, no matter how impractical, made parting a bit easier.

As he pulled me into an embrace, I tried not to think about how this was our *last* hug. But my emotions eventually got the best of me as tears escaped my eyes and hurried down my cheeks to soak the sleeve of his shirt.

"I'm going to miss you so much," I whispered. "You're one of the best friends I've ever had."

Damion stepped back and wiped the tears away with his thumb. "No matter where I am in this world, I will *always* have your back. But you're going to be fine." He planted a kiss on my cheek. "You're a lot stronger than you think."

I wasn't feeling particularly strong at the moment, but I *wanted* to be the brave woman Damion saw when he looked at me. Was I really ready to stand on my own two feet, with no crutches or shoulders to lean on?

I was about to find out.

Chapter Three

Damion

Samantha will never know how close I came to *not* boarding that flight to London.

When I felt the first trace of moisture on her cheek, I was done. What was I doing? Was I really trying to be an ocean away from the woman I loved? It didn't make any damn sense.

Not that she knew I loved her. No, that just would have made things awkward as she mourned the loss of the love of her life, my best friend, Tony Carteris.

Fucking Tony. He had really messed this one up—for all of us. If he had done right by Samantha the first time around, I never would have been put in this position. Tony saw her first, and loved her first, and would have had my full support in riding off into the proverbial sunset with this amazing girl. But for some reason, he had the hardest time manning up and handling his business, i.e., Angela.

Ugh, *that* girl. The anti-Samantha. Selfish, conniving, a professional victim. Angela had Tony twisted up in knots of guilt and obligation and it just wasn't right. The two of them were trapped in a toxic, dysfunctional relationship, the most miserable existence. I'll never understand why Tony chose to forgo light and true love for something dark and seeped in despair.

After Tony broke up with Samantha (in the coldest, cruelest way possible), he asked me to look after her. Make sure she was all right. In Tony's defense, he did truly believe that pushing Samantha away so she could move on and find happiness was in her best interests. But deep down, he knew he'd done a fucked up thing and caused Samantha unnecessary pain. I guess Tony figured anointing her personal protector would ease some of his guilt. How was he, or I, supposed to know I'd end up falling for her, too?

Samantha is an easy person to love. Smart and beautiful, compassionate and kind, she possessed the emotional fortitude of someone twice her age. My attraction to her was instantaneous, and while I tried and tried to fight it, the feelings only grew as time wore on.

As you can imagine, Tony was *not* happy when he learned about my little crush. Yes, I violated guy code by falling for my best friend's girl, but it's not like I acted on it. Even if I wanted to, there was no room for me in Samantha's heart—she was in love with my best friend.

She's *still* in love with my best friend.

I'm not big on unrequited love, so fleeing to Europe seemed like a great way to keep the situation from escalating.

I had received fellowship offers from both Cornell University and UCLA, but Goldsmiths in London was the one that served dual purposes. Not only would I be able to conduct ethnographic research in a country with a long history of civil unrest, but 5500 miles was exactly the kind of distance I needed to get control of my feelings and try, as futile as those attempts may be, to get over Samantha.

Also Available from TPC Books

SELLOUT
by James W. Lewis

SELLOUT follows these three individuals and the consequences of dating outside their race. In the quest to find what they think is missing in their lives, they encounter guilt, fear and mess they never anticipated... including murder.

A Hard Man Is Good to Find
by James W. Lewis

An erotic romance about a woman who meets the man of her dreams with the exception of one major issue - his refusal to have sex with her!

One Blood
by Qwantu Amaru

A supernatural curse terrorizes a group of people unaware of their hidden connections.

For ordering information visit:
www.pantheoncollective.com